KILL SIX BILLION DEMONS was originally a webcomic.
can be found online at http://killsixbilliondemons.com

CREATED BY:
Tom Parkinson-Morgan

YISUN said: Let there be no genesis,
for beginnings are false, and I am a consummate liar.

-Psalms

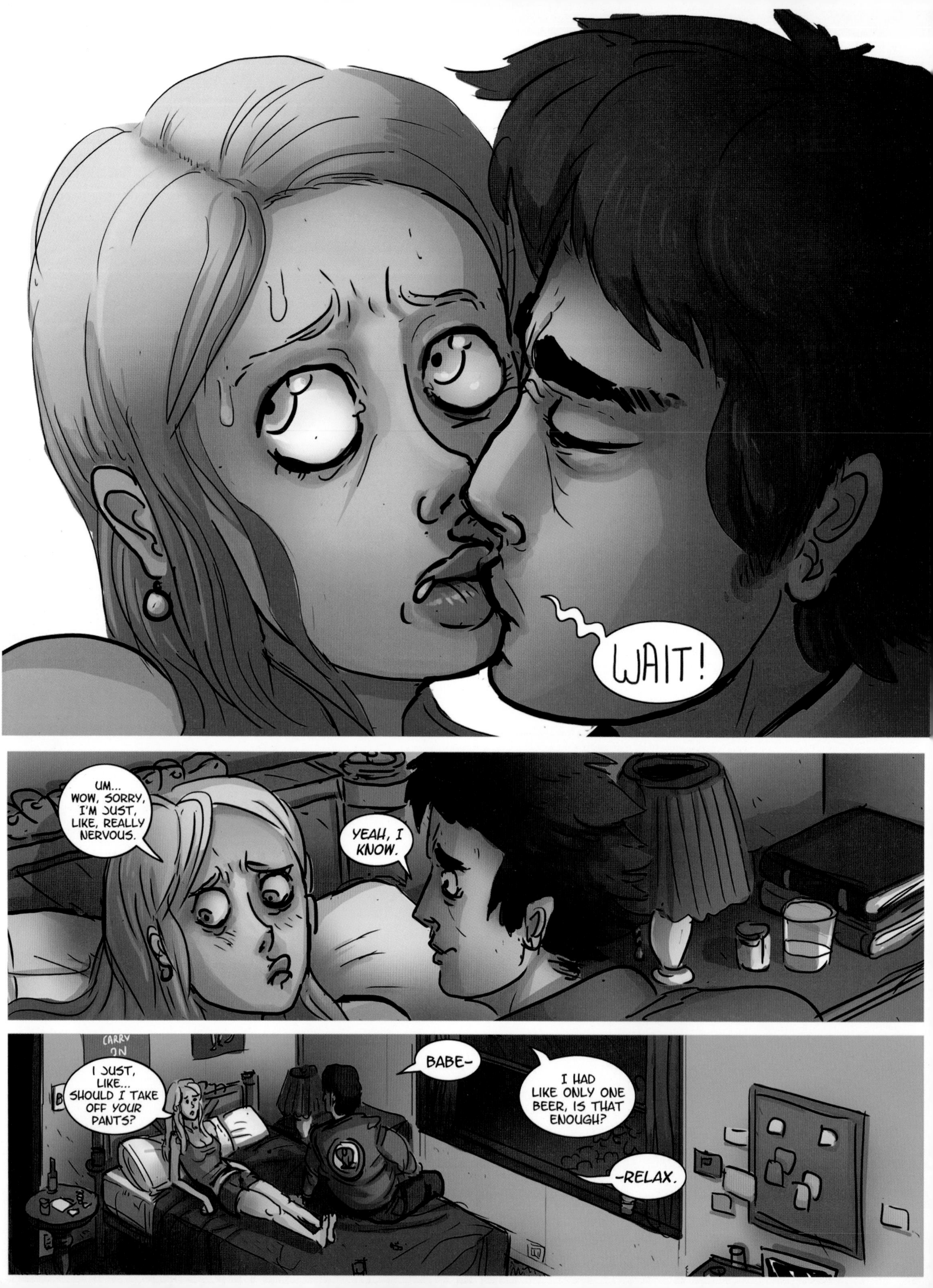
WAIT!
UM... WOW, SORRY, I'M JUST, LIKE, REALLY NERVOUS.
YEAH, I KNOW.
CARRY ON
I JUST, LIKE... SHOULD I TAKE OFF YOUR PANTS?
BABE-
I HAD LIKE ONLY ONE BEER, IS THAT ENOUGH?
-RELAX.

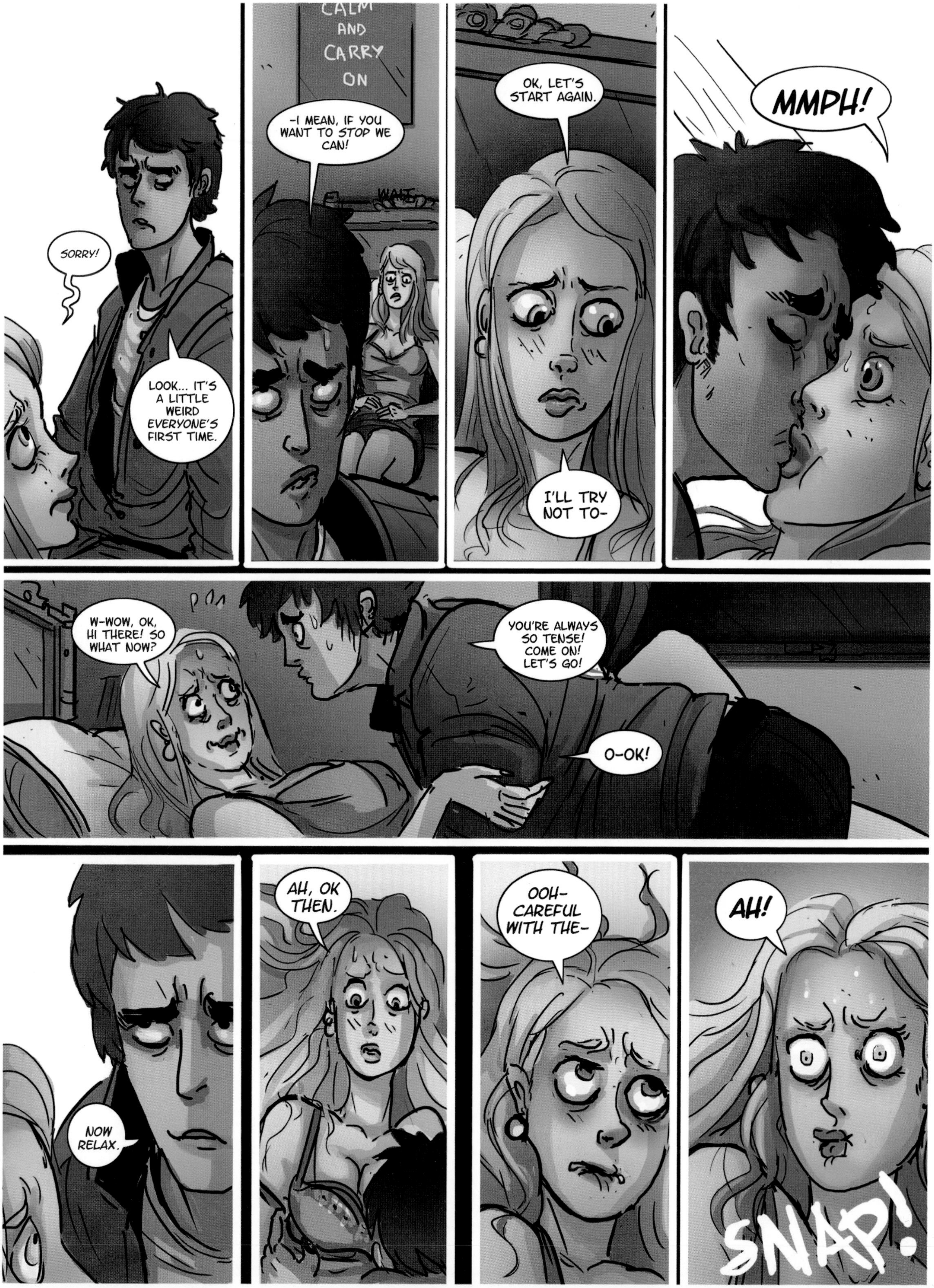
SORRY!
LOOK... IT'S A LITTLE WEIRD EVERYONE'S FIRST TIME.
CALM AND CARRY ON
-I MEAN, IF YOU WANT TO STOP WE CAN!
OK, LET'S START AGAIN.
I'LL TRY NOT TO-
MMPH!
W-WOW, OK, HI THERE! SO WHAT NOW?
YOU'RE ALWAYS SO TENSE! COME ON! LET'S GO!
O-OK!
NOW RELAX.
AH, OK THEN.
OOH- CAREFUL WITH THE-
AH!
SNAP!

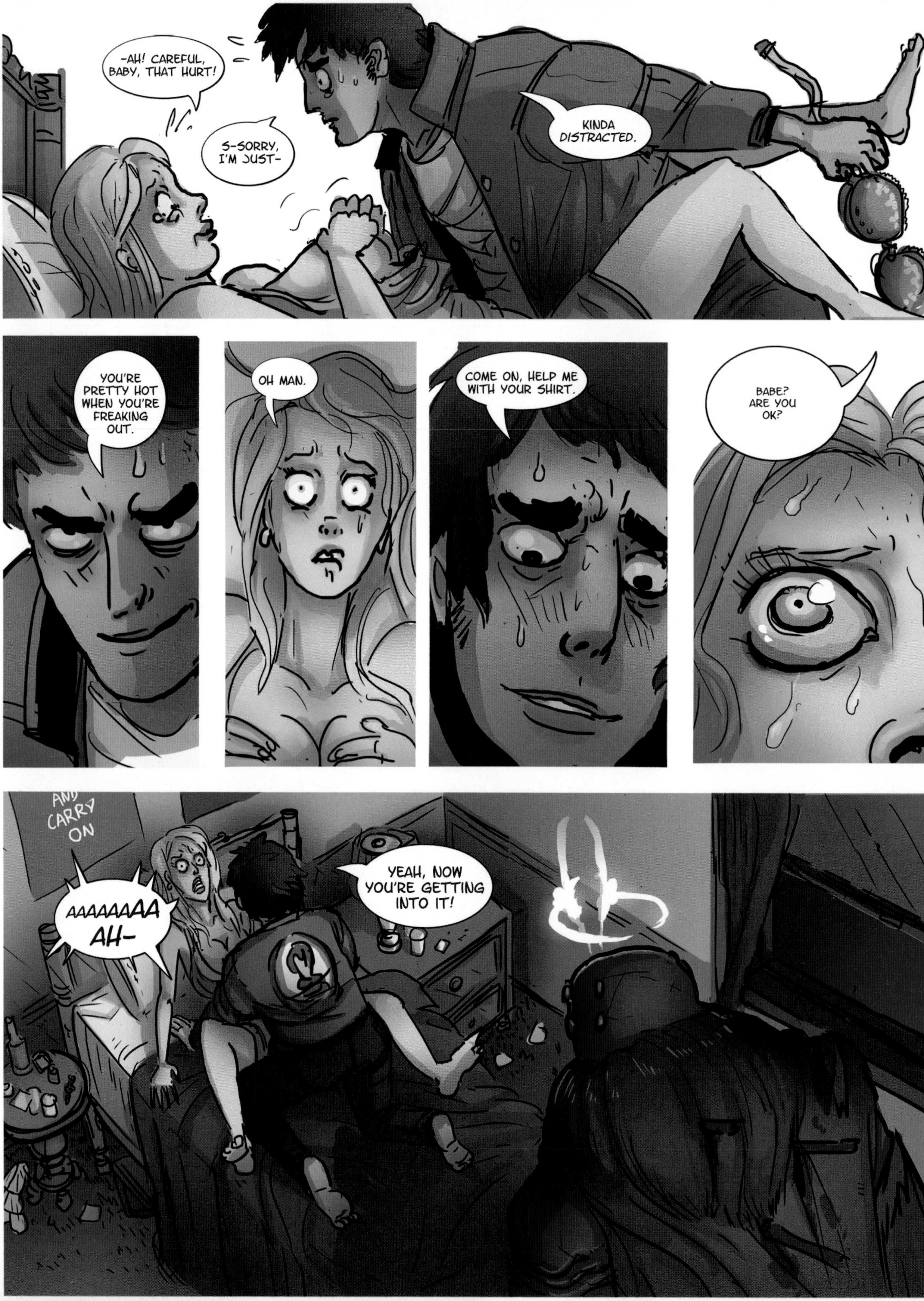
-AH! CAREFUL, BABY, THAT HURT!
S-SORRY, I'M JUST-
KINDA DISTRACTED.
YOU'RE PRETTY HOT WHEN YOU'RE FREAKING OUT.
OH MAN.
COME ON, HELP ME WITH YOUR SHIRT.
BABE? ARE YOU OK?
AND CARRY ON
AAAAAAAA AH-
YEAH, NOW YOU'RE GETTING INTO IT!

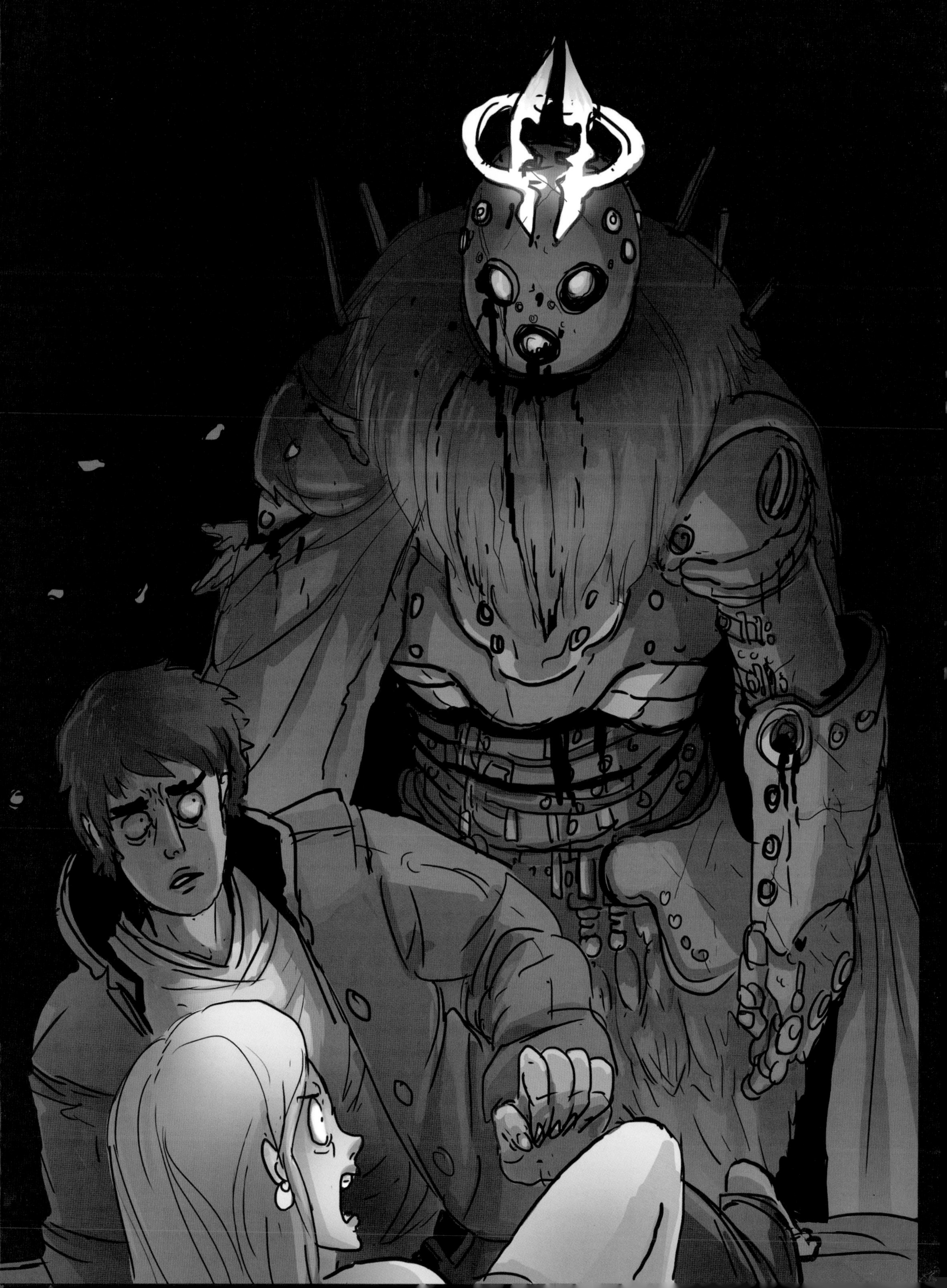

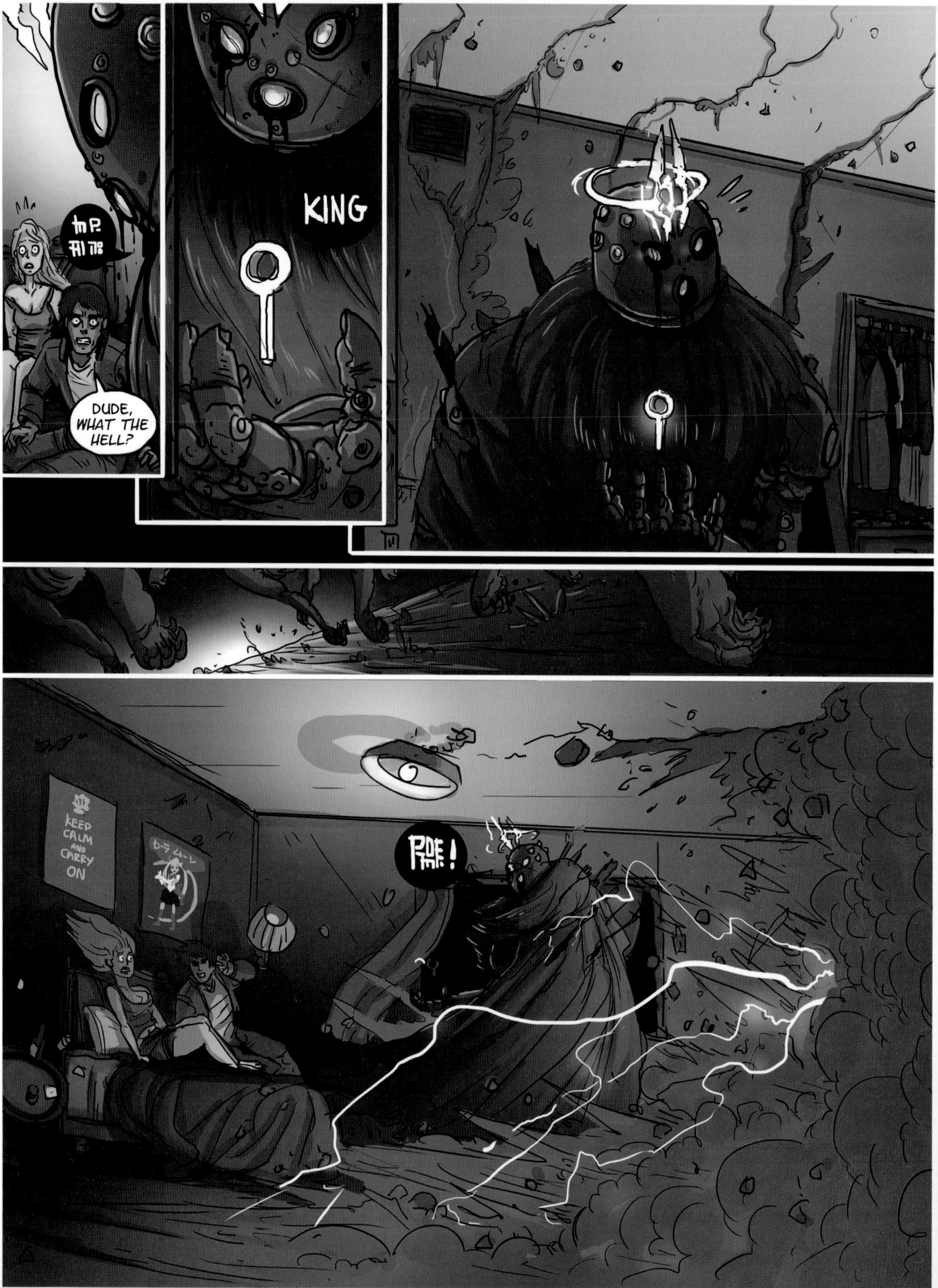
DUDE, WHAT THE HELL?
KING
KEEP CALM AND CARRY ON

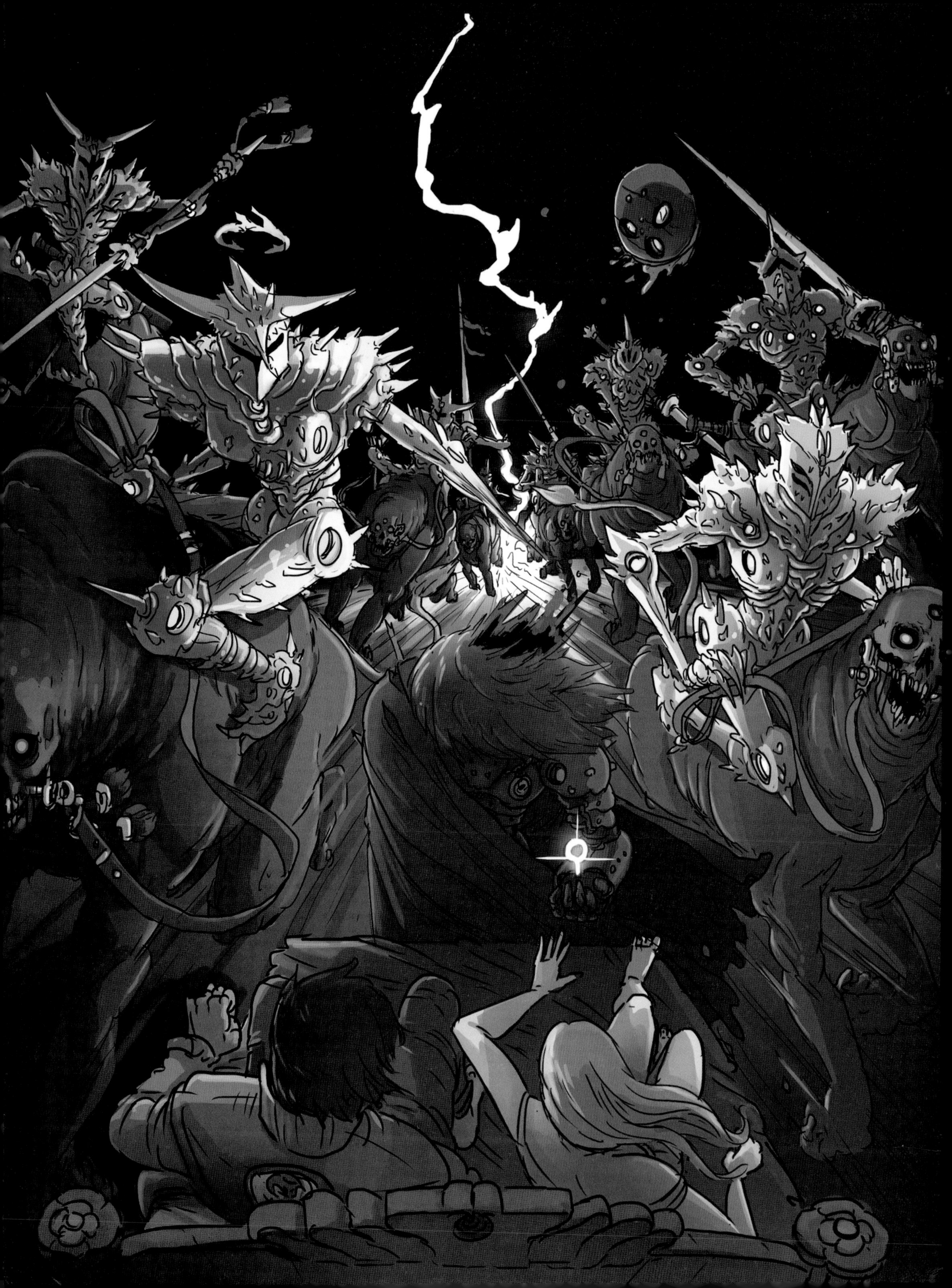

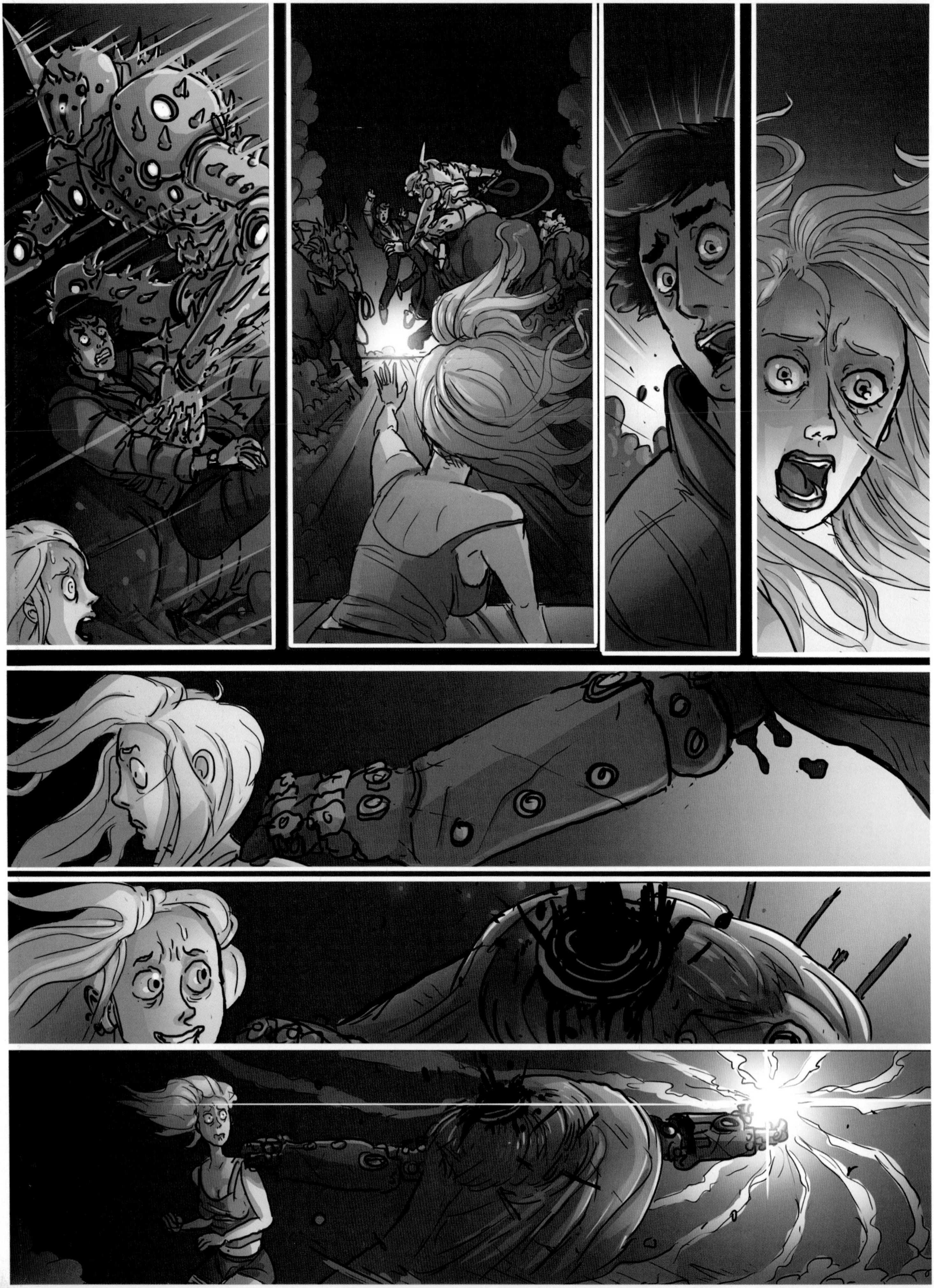

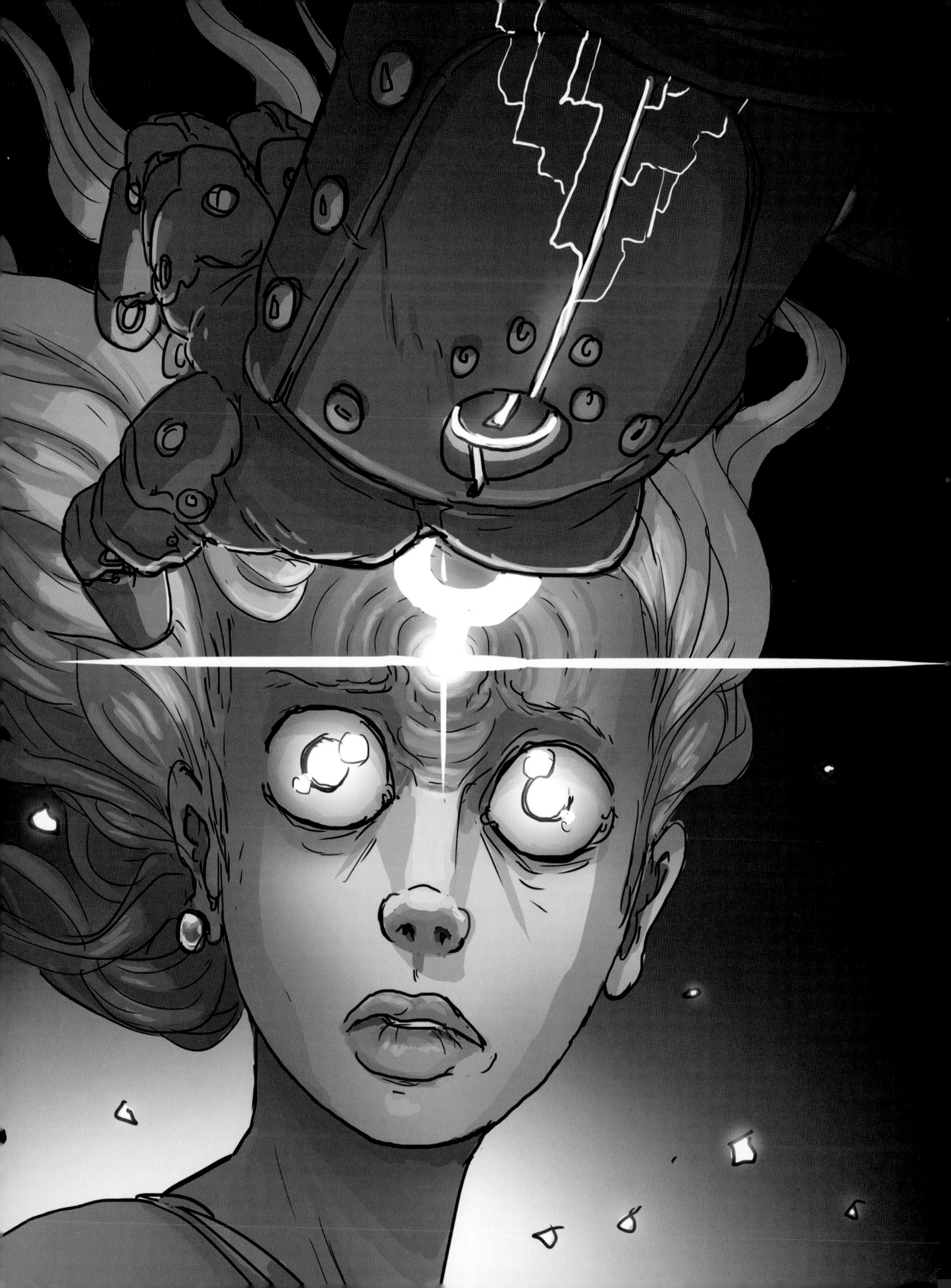

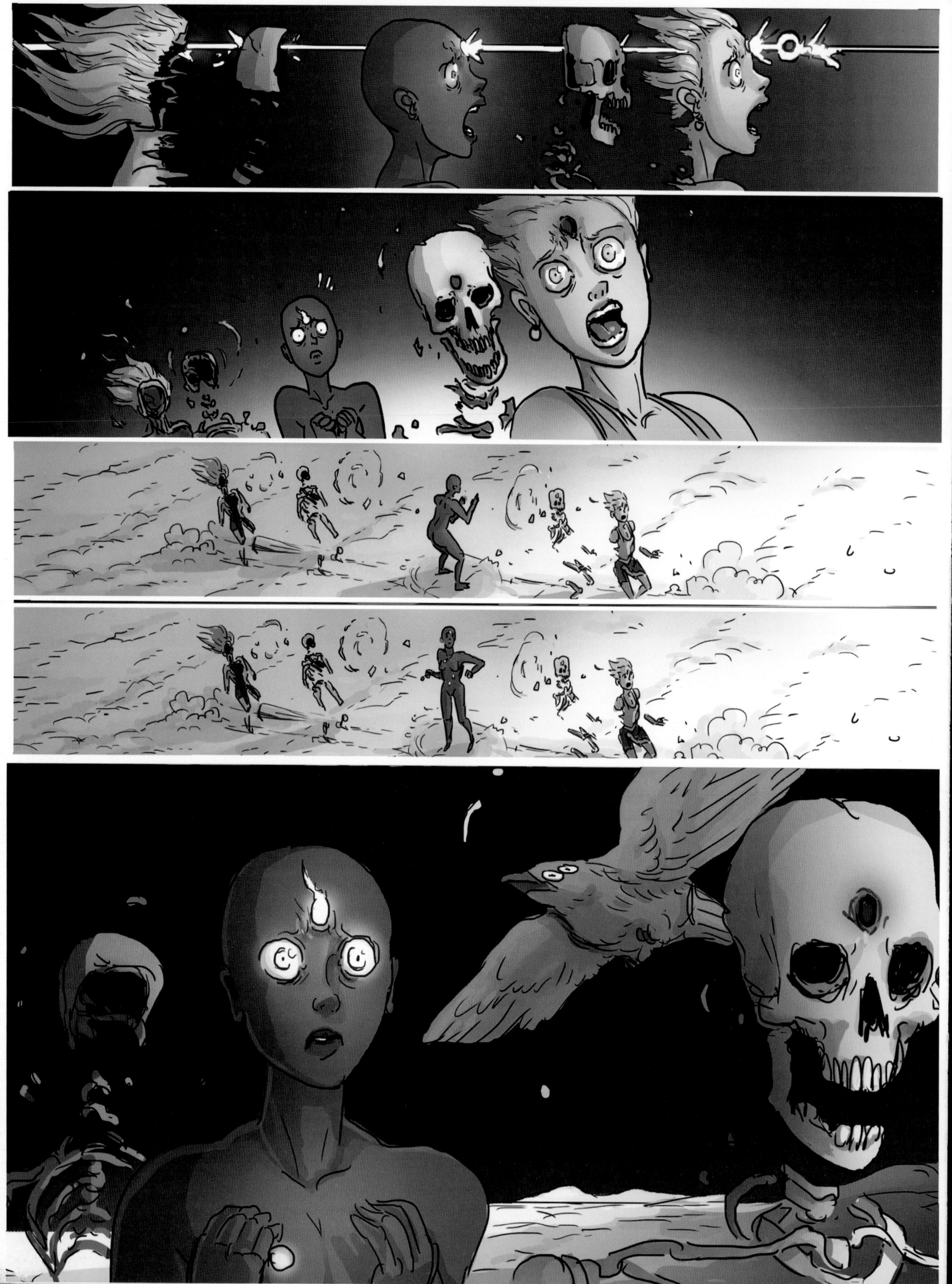

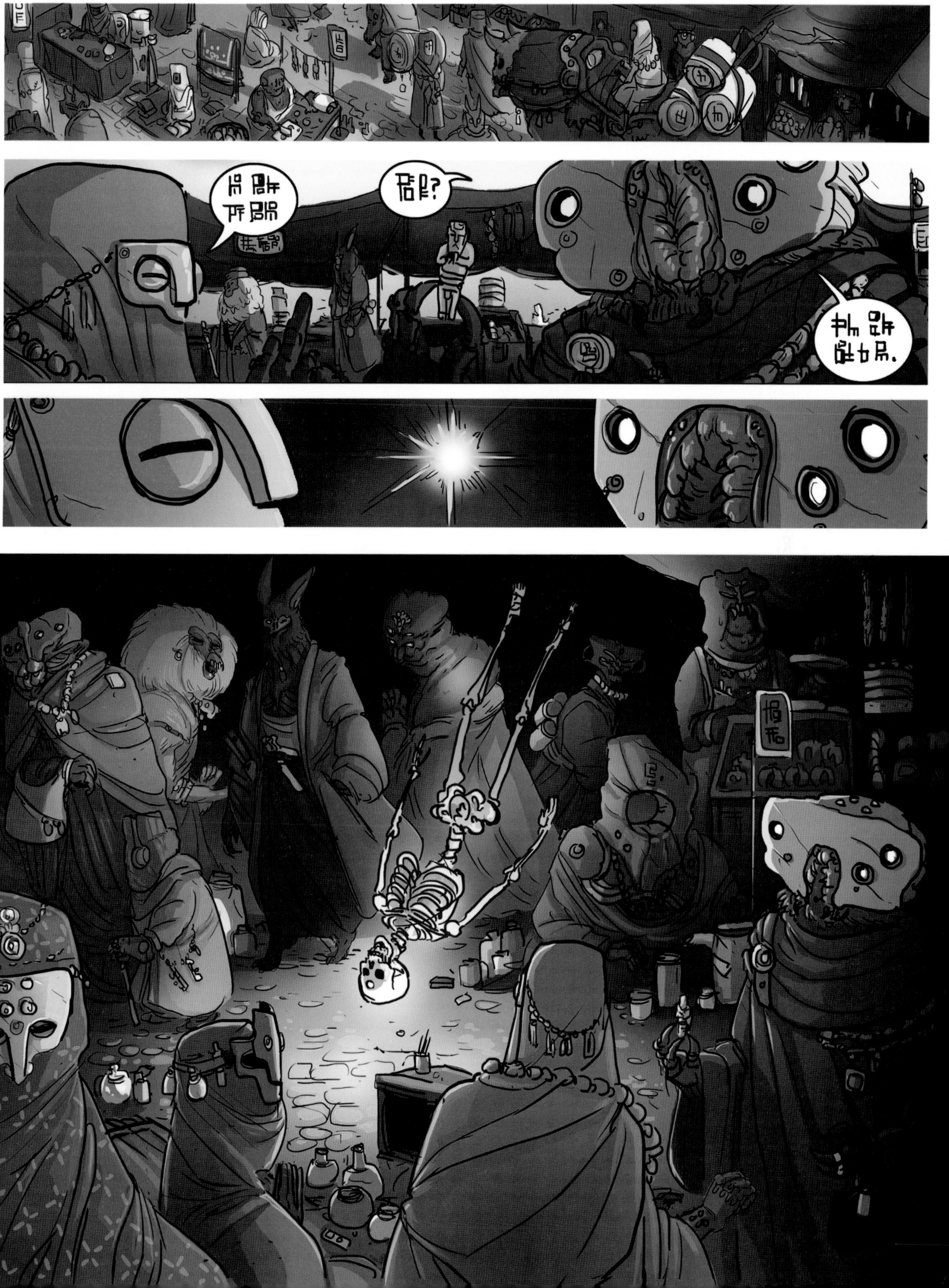

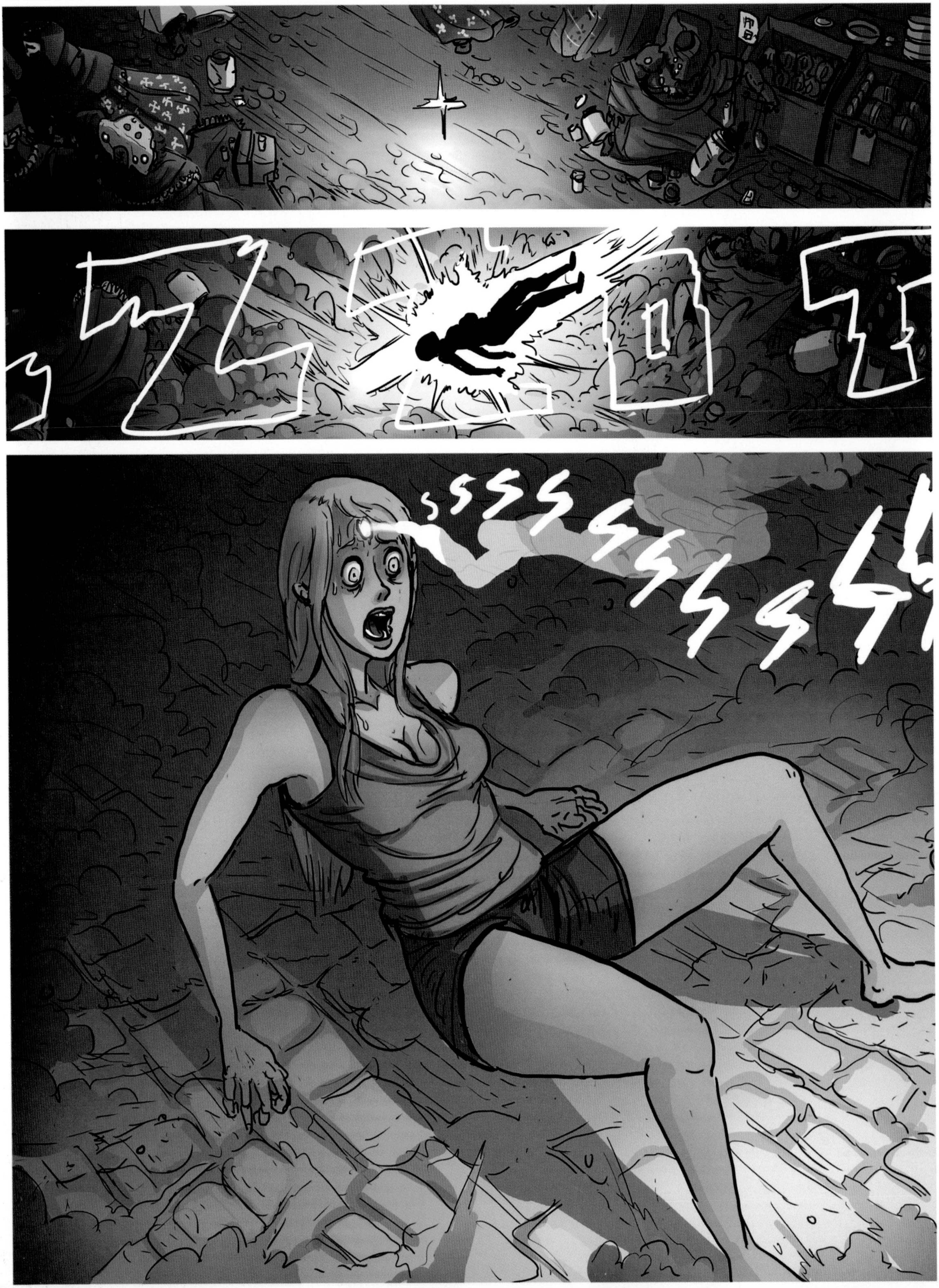
sSSSSSSSS

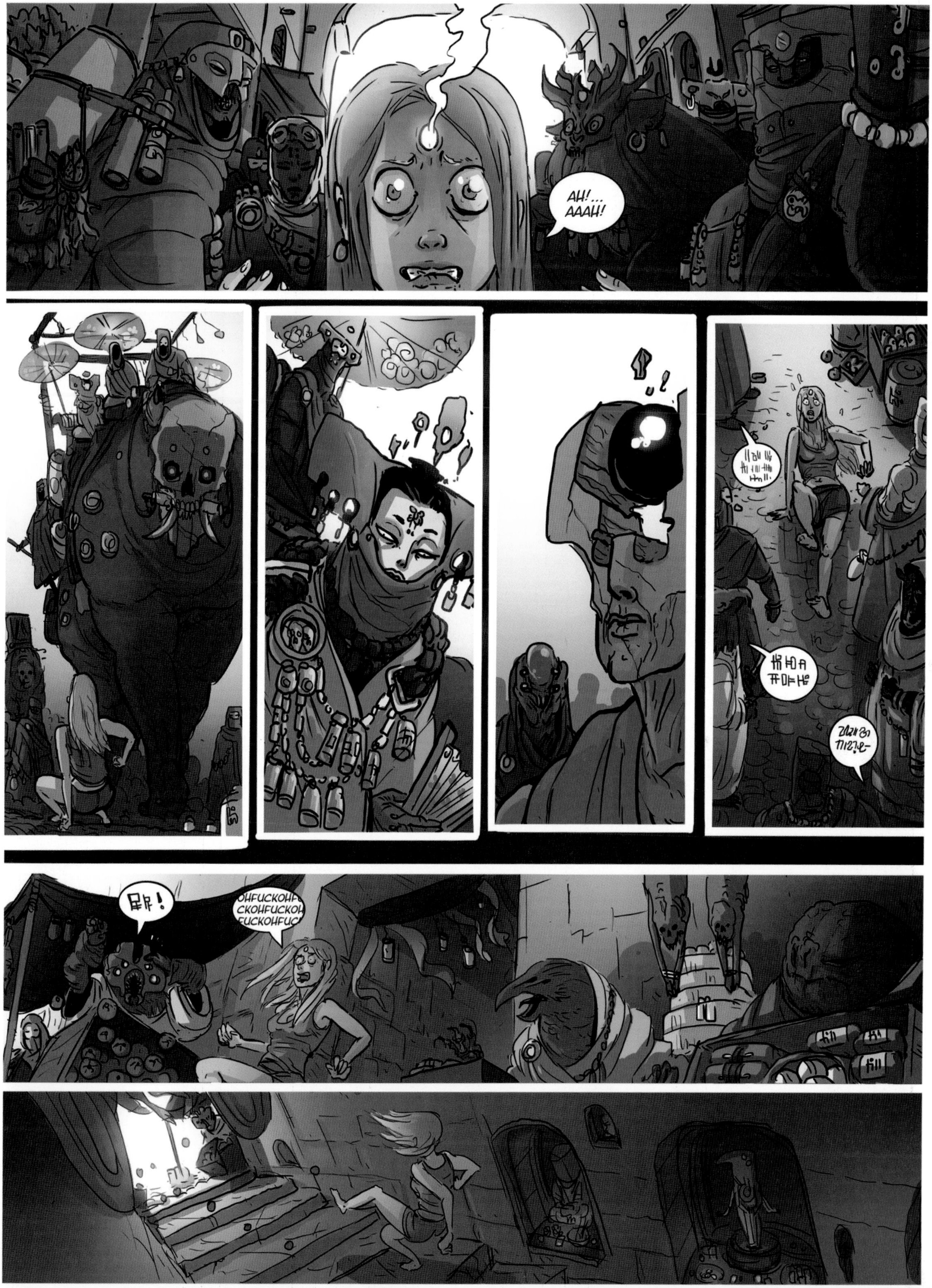
AH!... AAAH!
OHFUCKOHFU
CKOHFUCKOH
FUCKOHFUCK

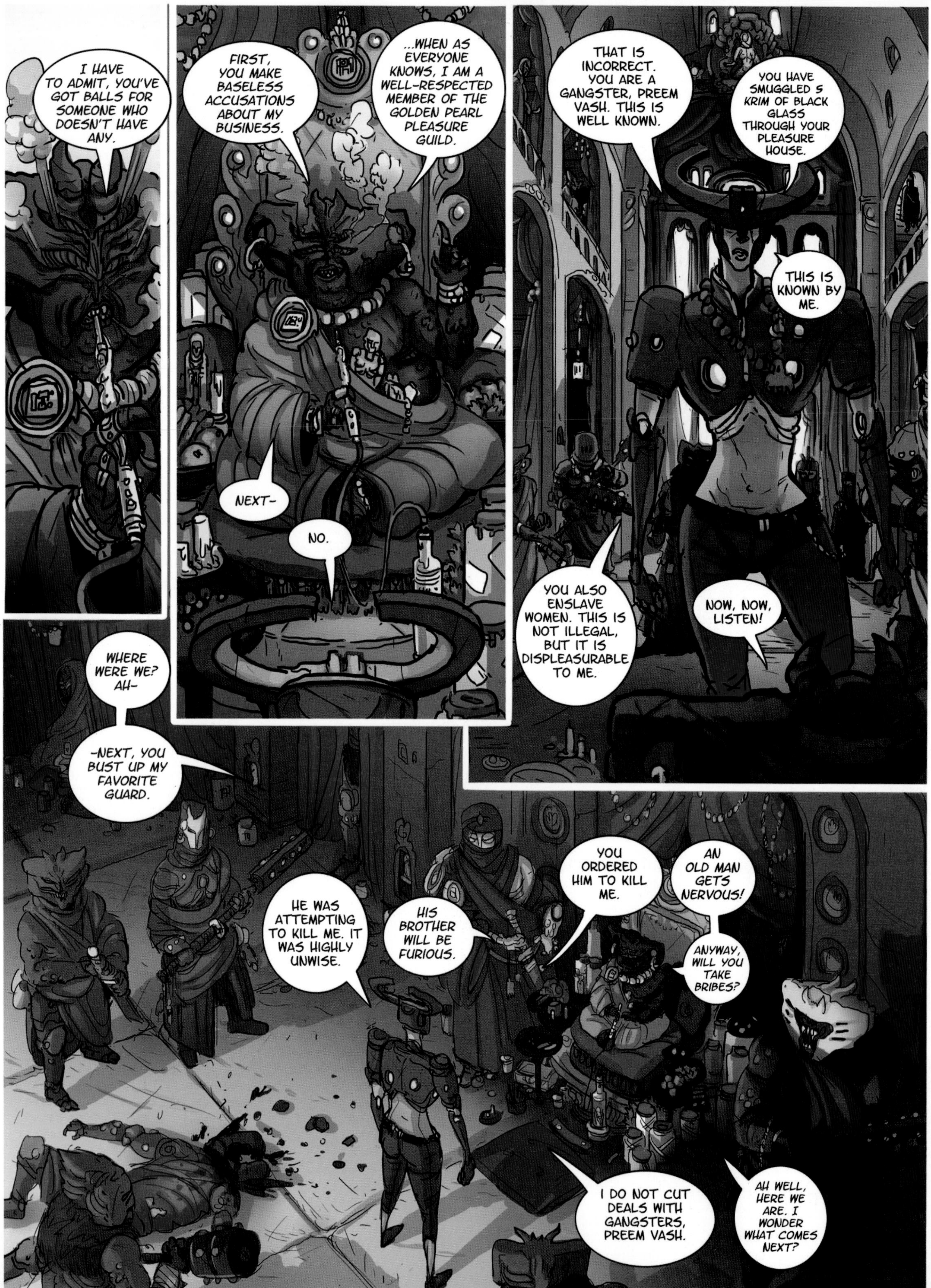
I HAVE TO ADMIT, YOU'VE GOT BALLS FOR SOMEONE WHO DOESN'T HAVE ANY.
FIRST, YOU MAKE BASELESS ACCUSATIONS ABOUT MY BUSINESS.
...WHEN AS EVERYONE KNOWS, I AM A WELL-RESPECTED MEMBER OF THE GOLDEN PEARL PLEASURE GUILD.
NEXT-
NO.
THAT IS INCORRECT. YOU ARE A GANGSTER, PREEM VASH. THIS IS WELL KNOWN.
YOU HAVE SMUGGLED 5 KRIM OF BLACK GLASS THROUGH YOUR PLEASURE HOUSE.
THIS IS KNOWN BY ME.
YOU ALSO ENSLAVE WOMEN. THIS IS NOT ILLEGAL, BUT IT IS DISPLEASURABLE TO ME.
NOW, NOW, LISTEN!
WHERE WERE WE? AH-
-NEXT, YOU BUST UP MY FAVORITE GUARD.
HE WAS ATTEMPTING TO KILL ME. IT WAS HIGHLY UNWISE.
HIS BROTHER WILL BE FURIOUS.
YOU ORDERED HIM TO KILL ME.
AN OLD MAN GETS NERVOUS!
ANYWAY, WILL YOU TAKE BRIBES?
I DO NOT CUT DEALS WITH GANGSTERS, PREEM VASH.
AH WELL, HERE WE ARE. I WONDER WHAT COMES NEXT?

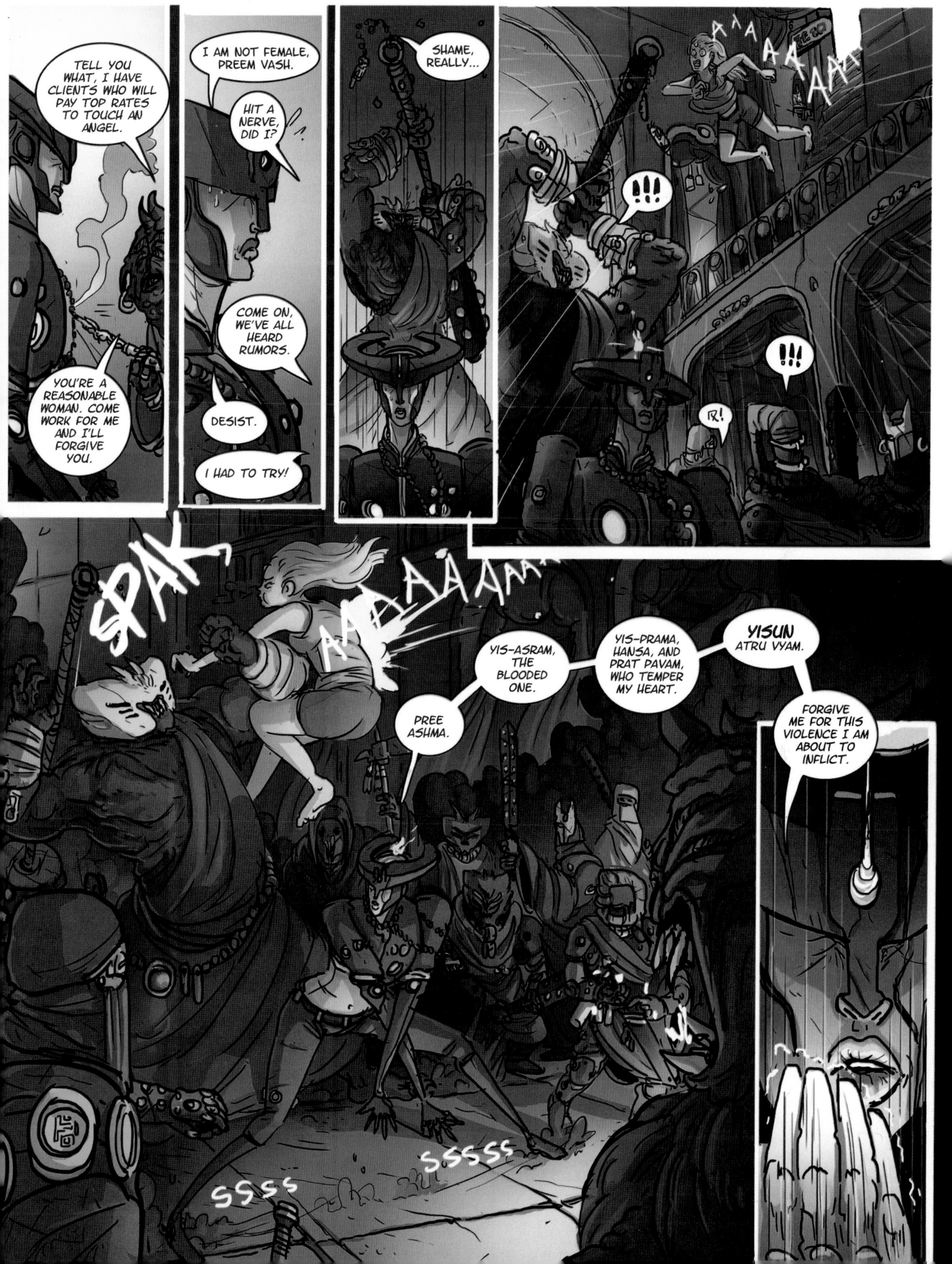

TELL YOU WHAT, I HAVE CLIENTS WHO WILL PAY TOP RATES TO TOUCH AN ANGEL.
YOU'RE A REASONABLE WOMAN. COME WORK FOR ME AND I'LL FORGIVE YOU.
I AM NOT FEMALE, PREEM VASH.
HIT A NERVE, DID I?
COME ON, WE'VE ALL HEARD RUMORS.
DESIST.
I HAD TO TRY!
SHAME, REALLY...
AAAAAAA
!!!
!!!
SPAK
AAAAAAAA
PREE ASHMA.
YIS-ASRAM, THE BLOODED ONE.
YIS-PRAMA, HANSA, AND PRAT PAVAM, WHO TEMPER MY HEART.
YISUN ATRU VYAM.
FORGIVE ME FOR THIS VIOLENCE I AM ABOUT TO INFLICT.
SSSSS
SSSS

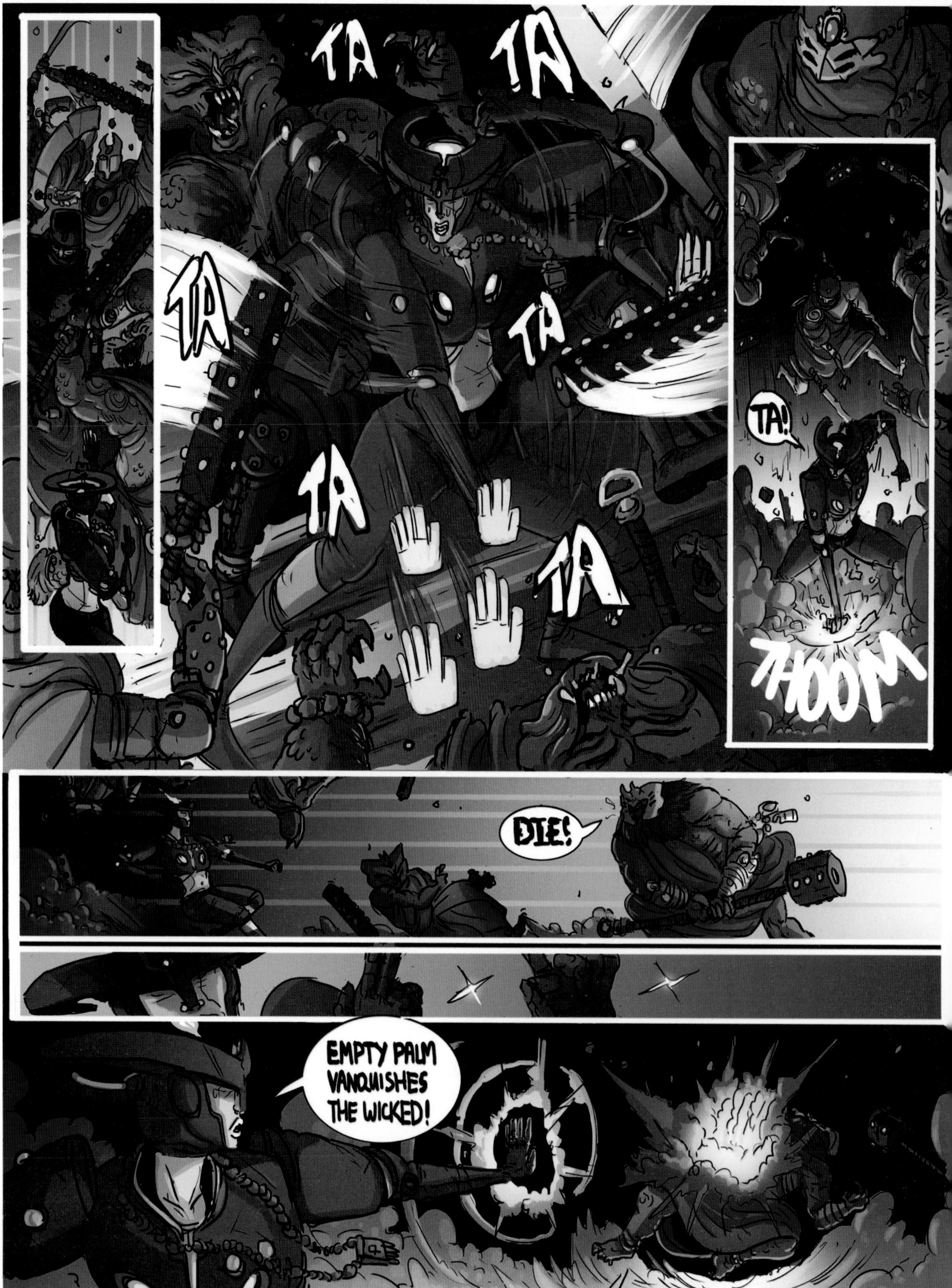

TA
TA
TA
TA
TA
TA
TA!
THOOM
DIE!
EMPTY PALM VANQUISHES THE WICKED!

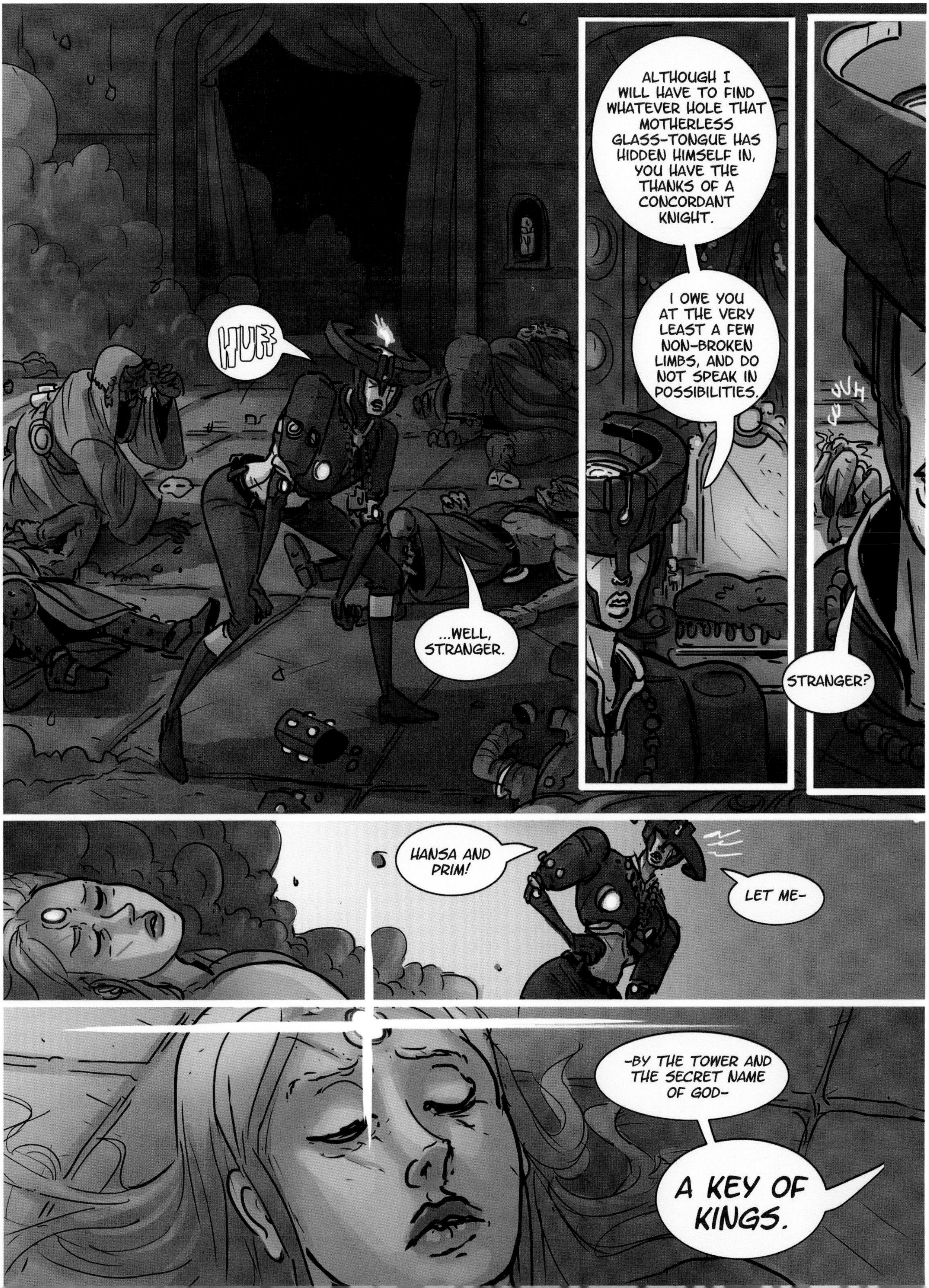
HUFF
...WELL, STRANGER.
ALTHOUGH I WILL HAVE TO FIND WHATEVER HOLE THAT MOTHERLESS GLASS-TONGUE HAS HIDDEN HIMSELF IN, YOU HAVE THE THANKS OF A CONCORDANT KNIGHT.
I OWE YOU AT THE VERY LEAST A FEW NON-BROKEN LIMBS, AND DO NOT SPEAK IN POSSIBILITIES.
STRANGER?
HANSA AND PRIM!
LET ME-
-BY THE TOWER AND THE SECRET NAME OF GOD-
A KEY OF KINGS.

THE GRAND ENEMY CALLED I

i. The Lie of the Giant and the Ant.

YISUN sat once with their disciple Hansa in YISUN's second clockwise glass palace. Hansa was one of their most ardent students and a grand questioner and unbeliever. Unlike YISUN's other disciple, Pree Ashma, he had no hunger in his heart for dominion of the universe, but a miserly scrutiny and a heart of iron nails. He was not an aspirant for royalty, and thereby attained it through little effort.

Hansa's questions were thus:

"Lord, how must I question space?"

'With an age, an ant may encircle a giant five million times,' spoke YISUN.

"Lord, how then may I question time?"

"A giant's stride takes an ant a week to surpass," YISUN spoke and smiled in the fourth way.

Hansa was discontent with this answer and rubbed the stem of his long and worn pipe which he always kept with him and would eventually lead to his annihilation. Since he was royalty, he knew this, and kept it close to him as a reminder of his circular death.

"Lord, then which should I be, the giant or the ant?"

"Both," spoke YISUN, "or either, when it suits you. Destroy the grand enemy called 'I'."

Hansa contemplated this in silence. Later he would recount this proverb to his daughter.

-Psalms

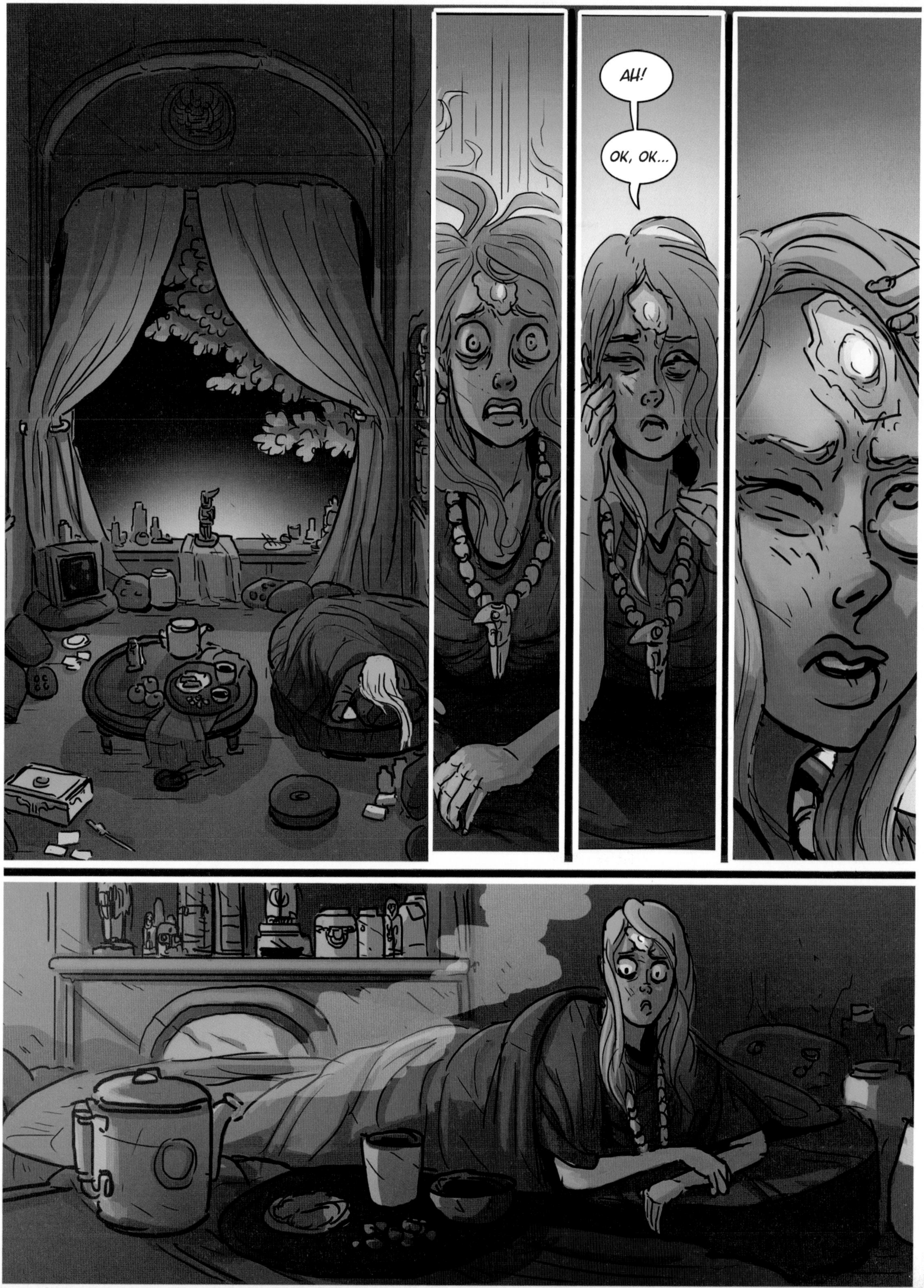
AH!
OK, OK...

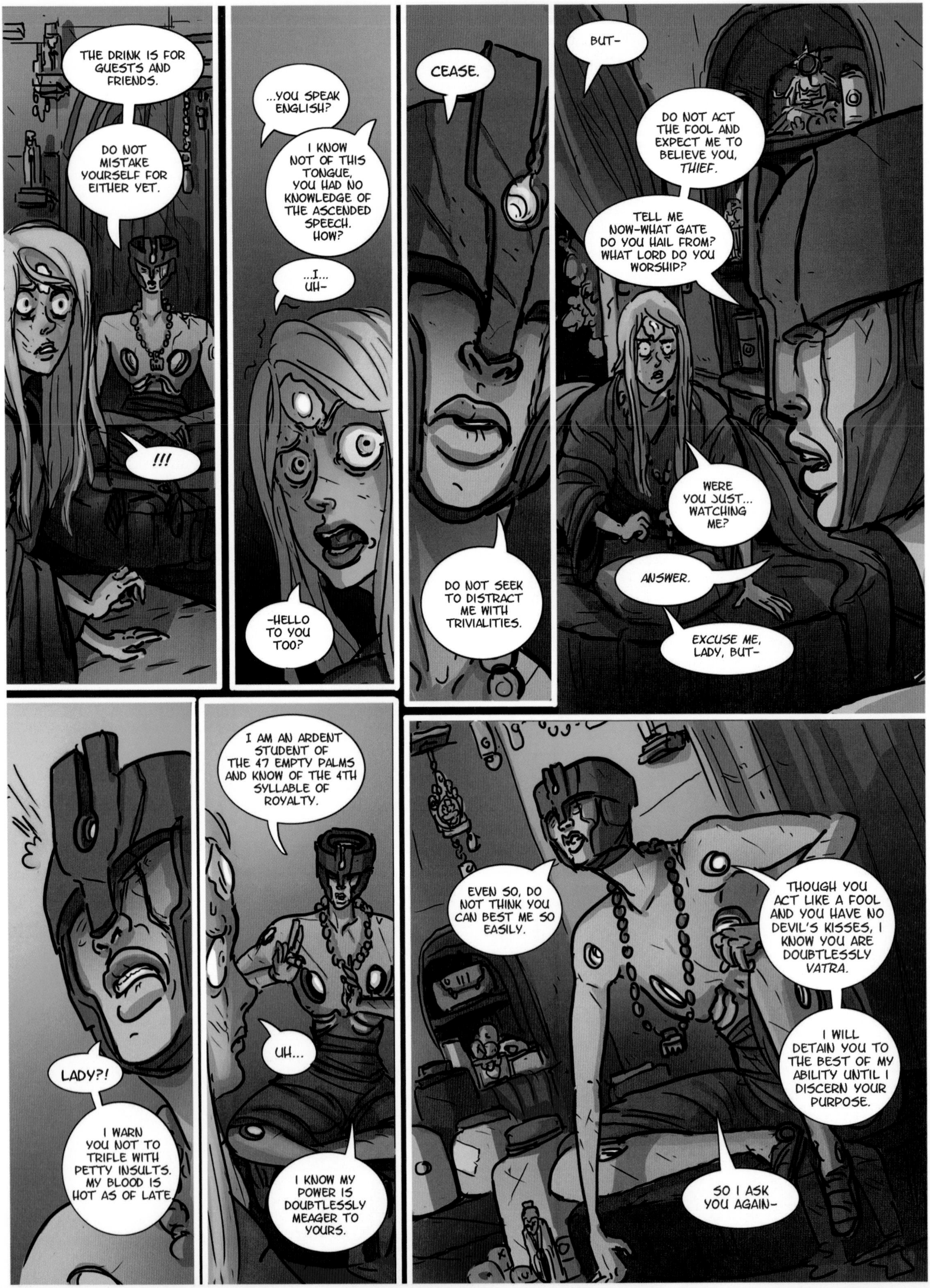
THE DRINK IS FOR GUESTS AND FRIENDS.
DO NOT MISTAKE YOURSELF FOR EITHER YET.
!!!
...YOU SPEAK ENGLISH?
I KNOW NOT OF THIS TONGUE, YOU HAD NO KNOWLEDGE OF THE ASCENDED SPEECH. HOW?
...I... UH-
-HELLO TO YOU TOO?
CEASE.
DO NOT SEEK TO DISTRACT ME WITH TRIVIALITIES.
BUT-
DO NOT ACT THE FOOL AND EXPECT ME TO BELIEVE YOU, THIEF.
TELL ME NOW-WHAT GATE DO YOU HAIL FROM? WHAT LORD DO YOU WORSHIP?
WERE YOU JUST... WATCHING ME?
ANSWER.
EXCUSE ME, LADY, BUT-
LADY?!
I WARN YOU NOT TO TRIFLE WITH PETTY INSULTS. MY BLOOD IS HOT AS OF LATE.
I AM AN ARDENT STUDENT OF THE 47 EMPTY PALMS AND KNOW OF THE 4TH SYLLABLE OF ROYALTY.
UH...
I KNOW MY POWER IS DOUBTLESSLY MEAGER TO YOURS.
EVEN SO, DO NOT THINK YOU CAN BEST ME SO EASILY.
THOUGH YOU ACT LIKE A FOOL AND YOU HAVE NO DEVIL'S KISSES, I KNOW YOU ARE DOUBTLESSLY VATRA.
I WILL DETAIN YOU TO THE BEST OF MY ABILITY UNTIL I DISCERN YOUR PURPOSE.
SO I ASK YOU AGAIN-

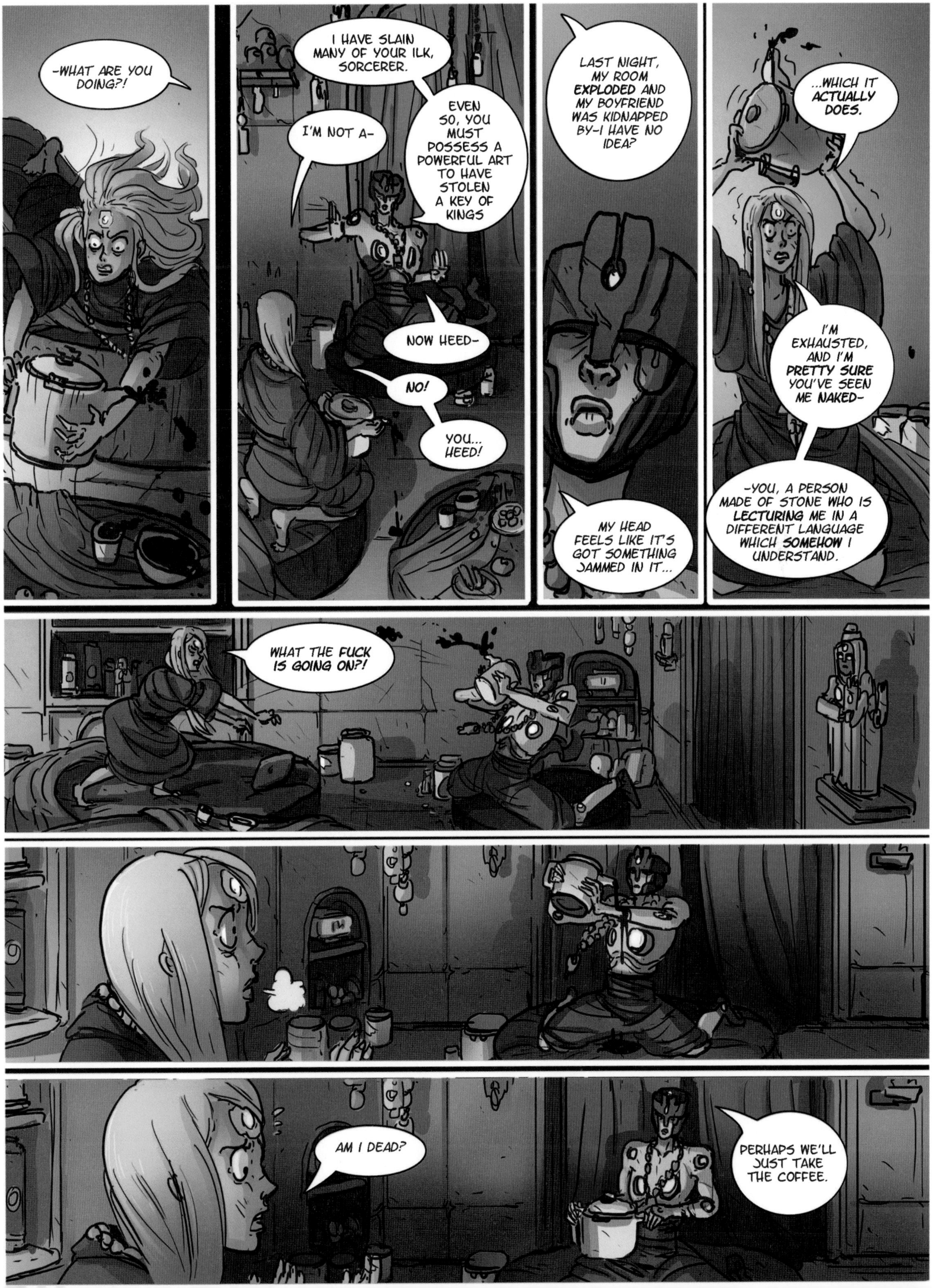
-WHAT ARE YOU DOING?!
I HAVE SLAIN MANY OF YOUR ILK, SORCERER.
I'M NOT A-
EVEN SO, YOU MUST POSSESS A POWERFUL ART TO HAVE STOLEN A KEY OF KINGS
NOW HEED-
NO!
YOU... HEED!
LAST NIGHT, MY ROOM EXPLODED AND MY BOYFRIEND WAS KIDNAPPED BY-I HAVE NO IDEA?
MY HEAD FEELS LIKE IT'S GOT SOMETHING JAMMED IN IT...
...WHICH IT ACTUALLY DOES.
I'M EXHAUSTED, AND I'M PRETTY SURE YOU'VE SEEN ME NAKED-
-YOU, A PERSON MADE OF STONE WHO IS LECTURING ME IN A DIFFERENT LANGUAGE WHICH SOMEHOW I UNDERSTAND.
WHAT THE FUCK IS GOING ON?!
AM I DEAD?
PERHAPS WE'LL JUST TAKE THE COFFEE.

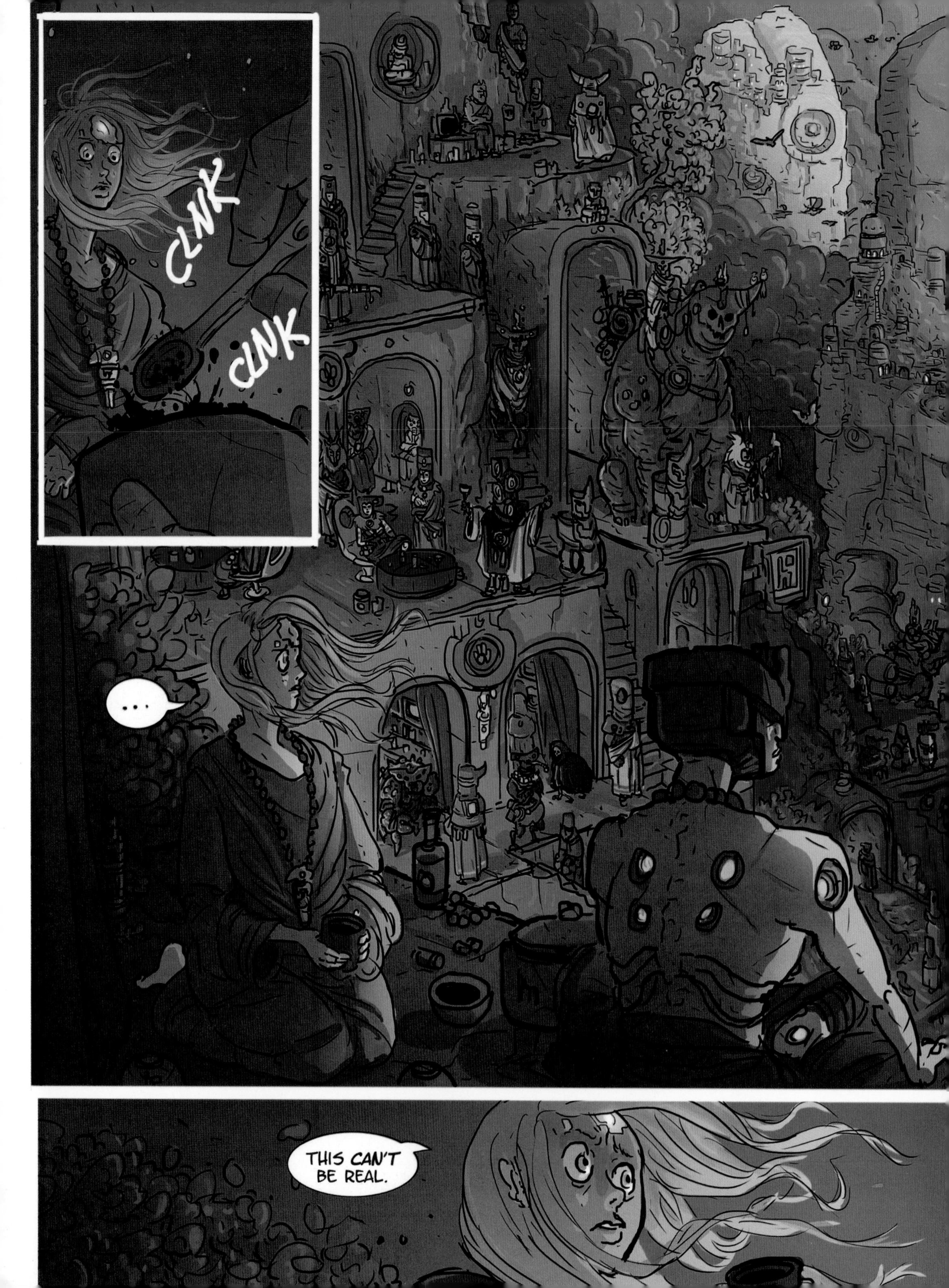
CLNK
CLNK
...
THIS CAN'T BE REAL.

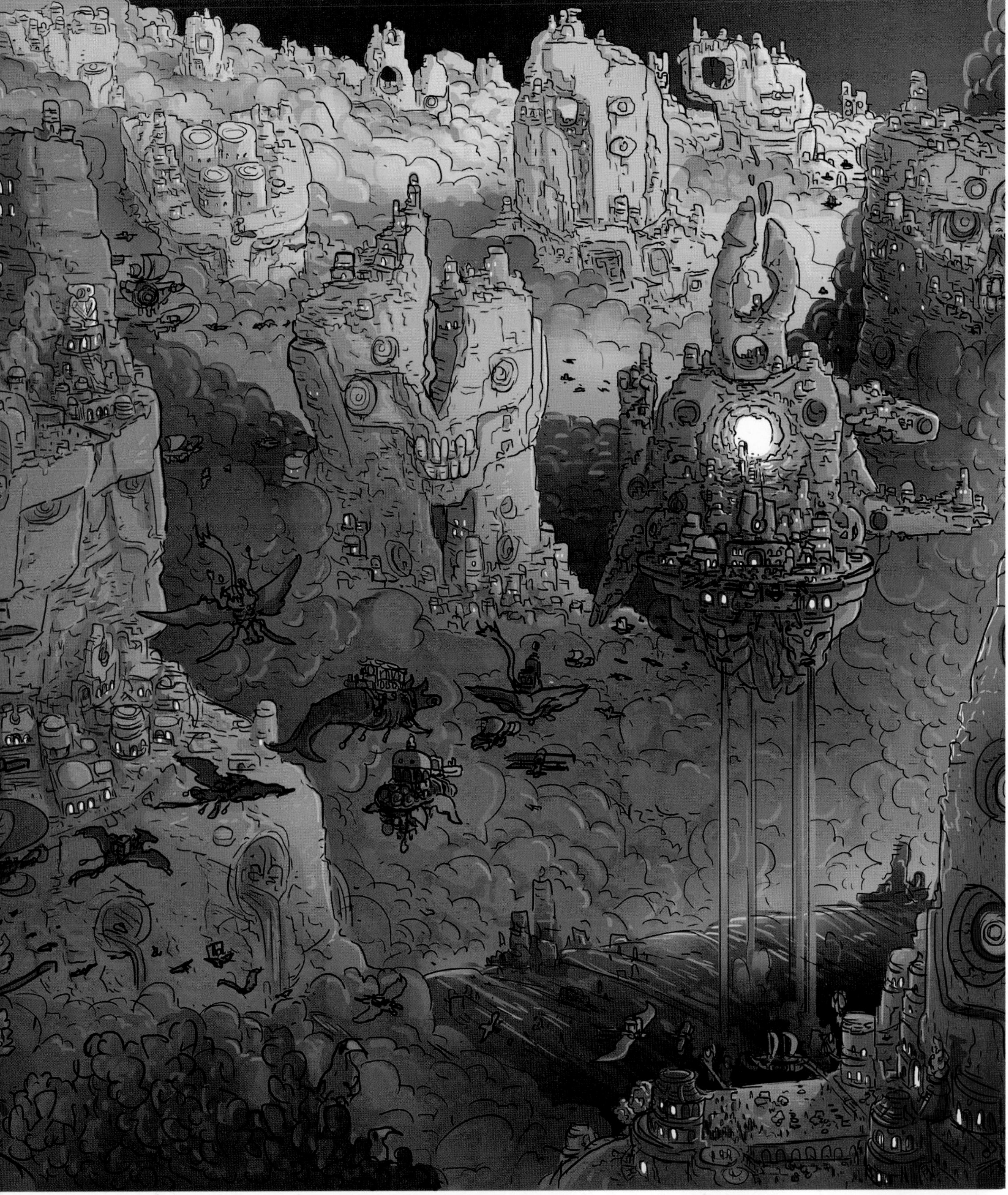

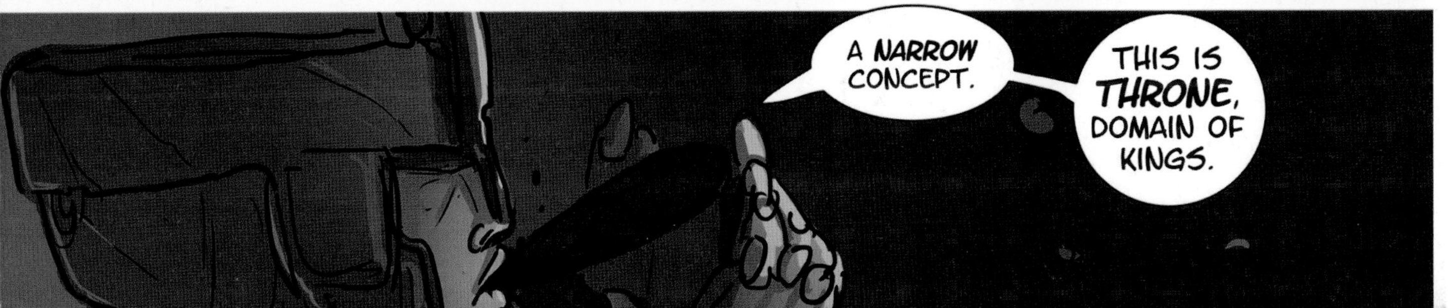
A NARROW CONCEPT.
THIS IS THRONE, DOMAIN OF KINGS.

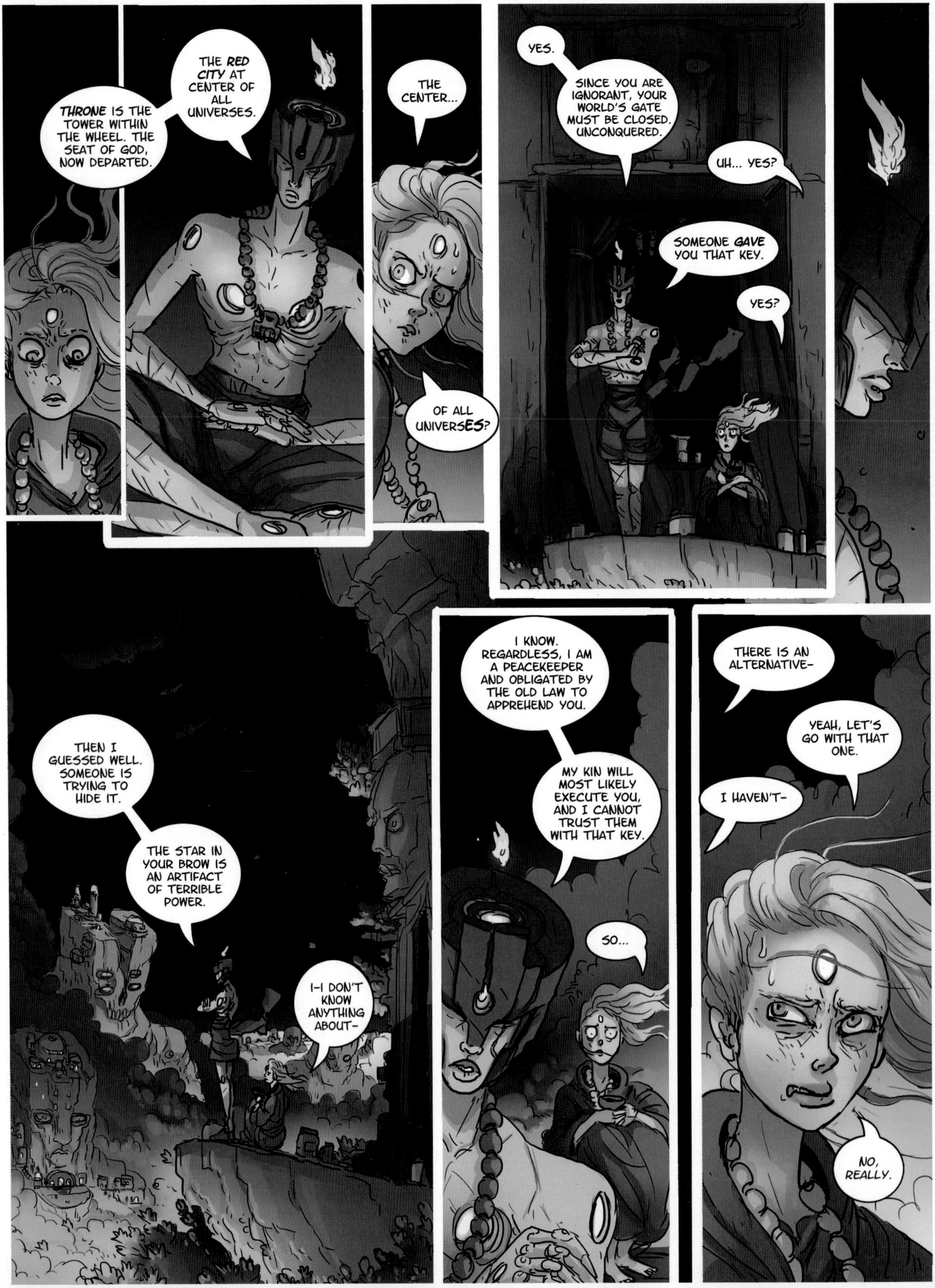
THRONE IS THE TOWER WITHIN THE WHEEL. THE SEAT OF GOD, NOW DEPARTED.
THE RED CITY AT CENTER OF ALL UNIVERSES.
THE CENTER...
OF ALL UNIVERSES?
YES.
SINCE YOU ARE IGNORANT, YOUR WORLD'S GATE MUST BE CLOSED. UNCONQUERED.
UH... YES?
SOMEONE GAVE YOU THAT KEY.
YES?
THEN I GUESSED WELL. SOMEONE IS TRYING TO HIDE IT.
THE STAR IN YOUR BROW IS AN ARTIFACT OF TERRIBLE POWER.
I-I DON'T KNOW ANYTHING ABOUT-
I KNOW. REGARDLESS, I AM A PEACEKEEPER AND OBLIGATED BY THE OLD LAW TO APPREHEND YOU.
MY KIN WILL MOST LIKELY EXECUTE YOU, AND I CANNOT TRUST THEM WITH THAT KEY.
SO...
THERE IS AN ALTERNATIVE-
YEAH, LET'S GO WITH THAT ONE.
I HAVEN'T-
NO, REALLY.

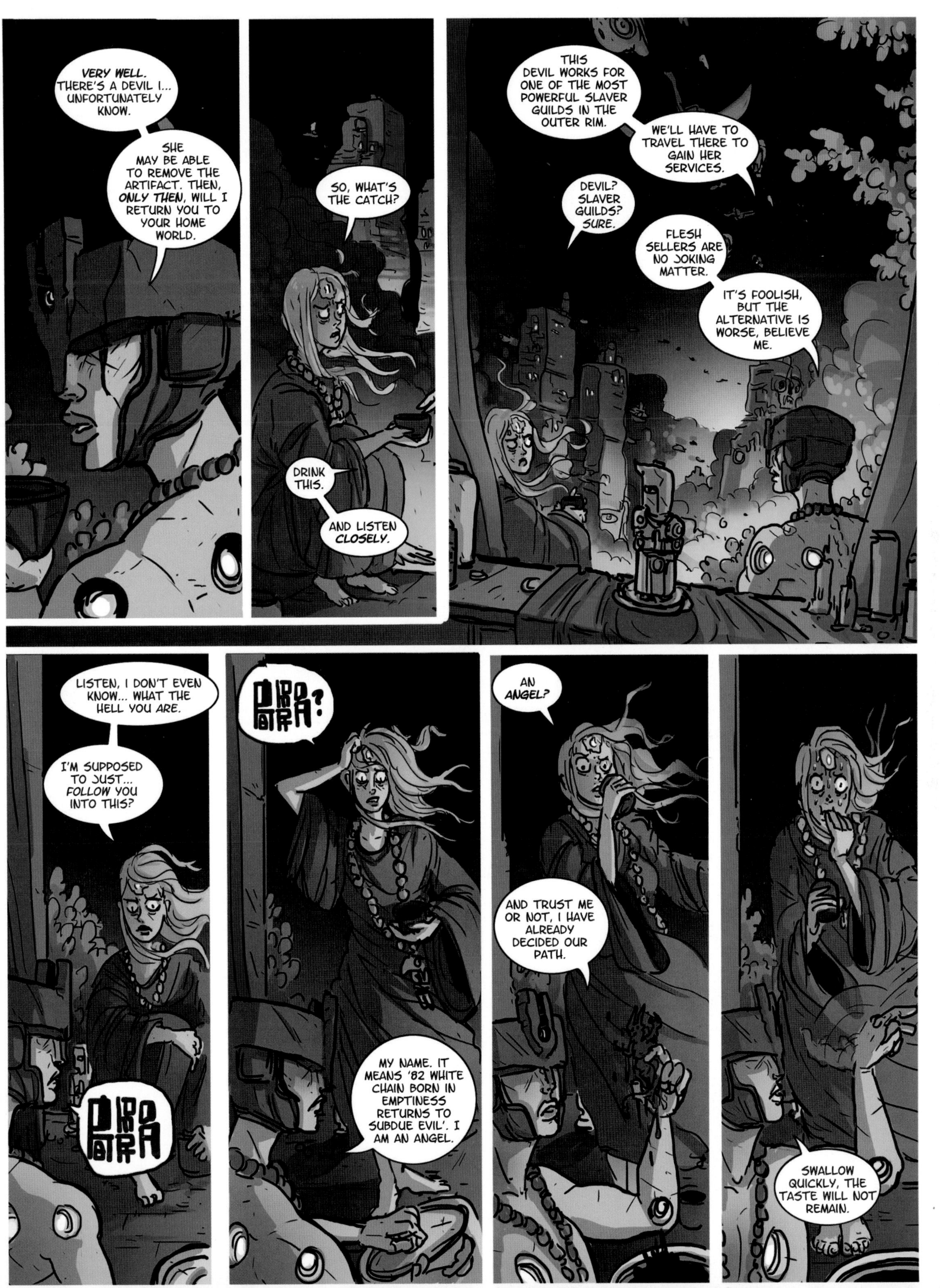
VERY WELL. THERE'S A DEVIL I... UNFORTUNATELY KNOW.
SHE MAY BE ABLE TO REMOVE THE ARTIFACT. THEN, ONLY THEN, WILL I RETURN YOU TO YOUR HOME WORLD.
SO, WHAT'S THE CATCH?
DRINK THIS.
AND LISTEN CLOSELY.
THIS DEVIL WORKS FOR ONE OF THE MOST POWERFUL SLAVER GUILDS IN THE OUTER RIM.
WE'LL HAVE TO TRAVEL THERE TO GAIN HER SERVICES.
DEVIL? SLAVER GUILDS? SURE.
FLESH SELLERS ARE NO JOKING MATTER.
IT'S FOOLISH, BUT THE ALTERNATIVE IS WORSE, BELIEVE ME.
LISTEN, I DON'T EVEN KNOW... WHAT THE HELL YOU ARE.
I'M SUPPOSED TO JUST... FOLLOW YOU INTO THIS?
MY NAME. IT MEANS '82 WHITE CHAIN BORN IN EMPTINESS RETURNS TO SUBDUE EVIL'. I AM AN ANGEL.
AN ANGEL?
AND TRUST ME OR NOT, I HAVE ALREADY DECIDED OUR PATH.
SWALLOW QUICKLY, THE TASTE WILL NOT REMAIN.

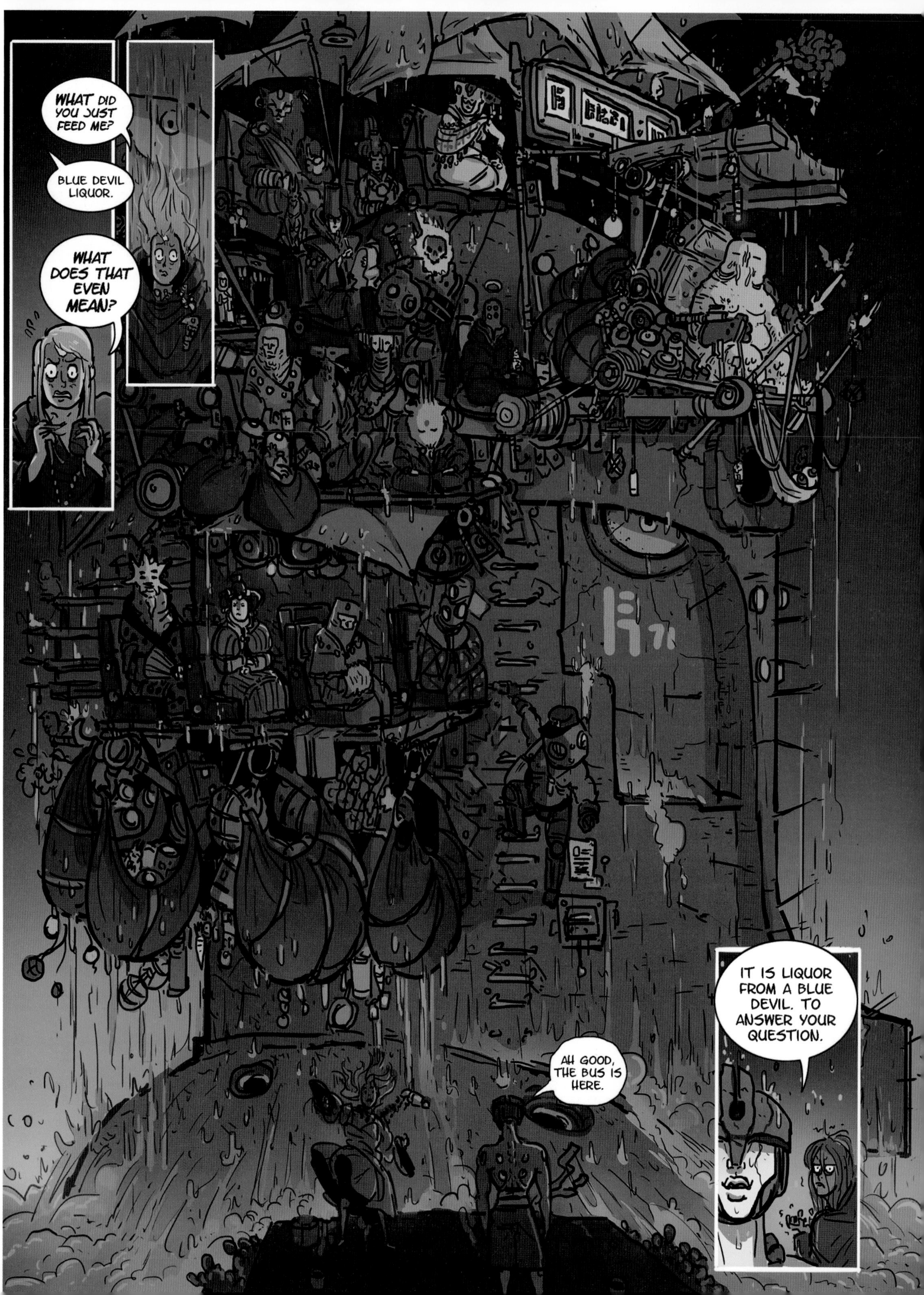
WHAT DID YOU JUST FEED ME?
BLUE DEVIL LIQUOR.
WHAT DOES THAT EVEN MEAN?
AH GOOD, THE BUS IS HERE.
IT IS LIQUOR FROM A BLUE DEVIL. TO ANSWER YOUR QUESTION.

THIS IS INSANE.

I AGREE. BUT NECESSARY.

HOW CAN I BE SURE THIS ISN'T ALL A DREAM, HUH?

NO TRUE SON OR DAUGHTER OF THE FLAME CAN.

WELL, WHAT IF I DON'T WANT TO COME!

STAY IF YOU WISH.

WELL, I WILL THEN! I'LL JUST SIT RIGHT HERE UNTIL I WAKE—

—UP!

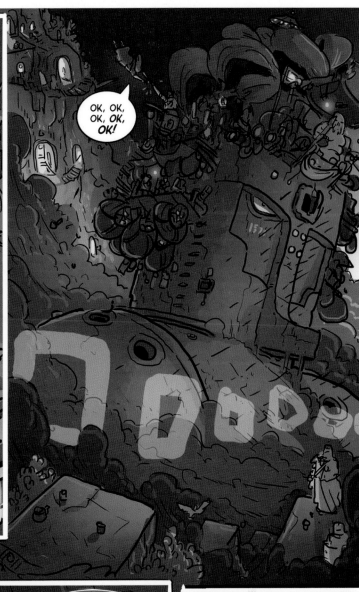

OK, OK, OK, OK, OK!

CALM YOURSELF. I HAVE BUSINESS TO ATTEND TO HERE.

I'VE BEEN FEEDING YOU A LITTLE LIQUOR FOR THREE TURNS, SO PLEASE DO NOT MIND THE HORNS, THEY WILL FALL OFF IN TIME.

I WILL TAKE BUT A MOMENT.

...HORNS?

FODDER THEE, THA MOULDERSOME SKIRT DRAGGER!

CLEAN WE ARE! BOTHER US NOT, THA BLUNDEROAF! UNTOUCHABLE LAW-ABIDING CITIZENLY PERSON WE!

GA!

NO, YOU ARE A CRIMINAL.

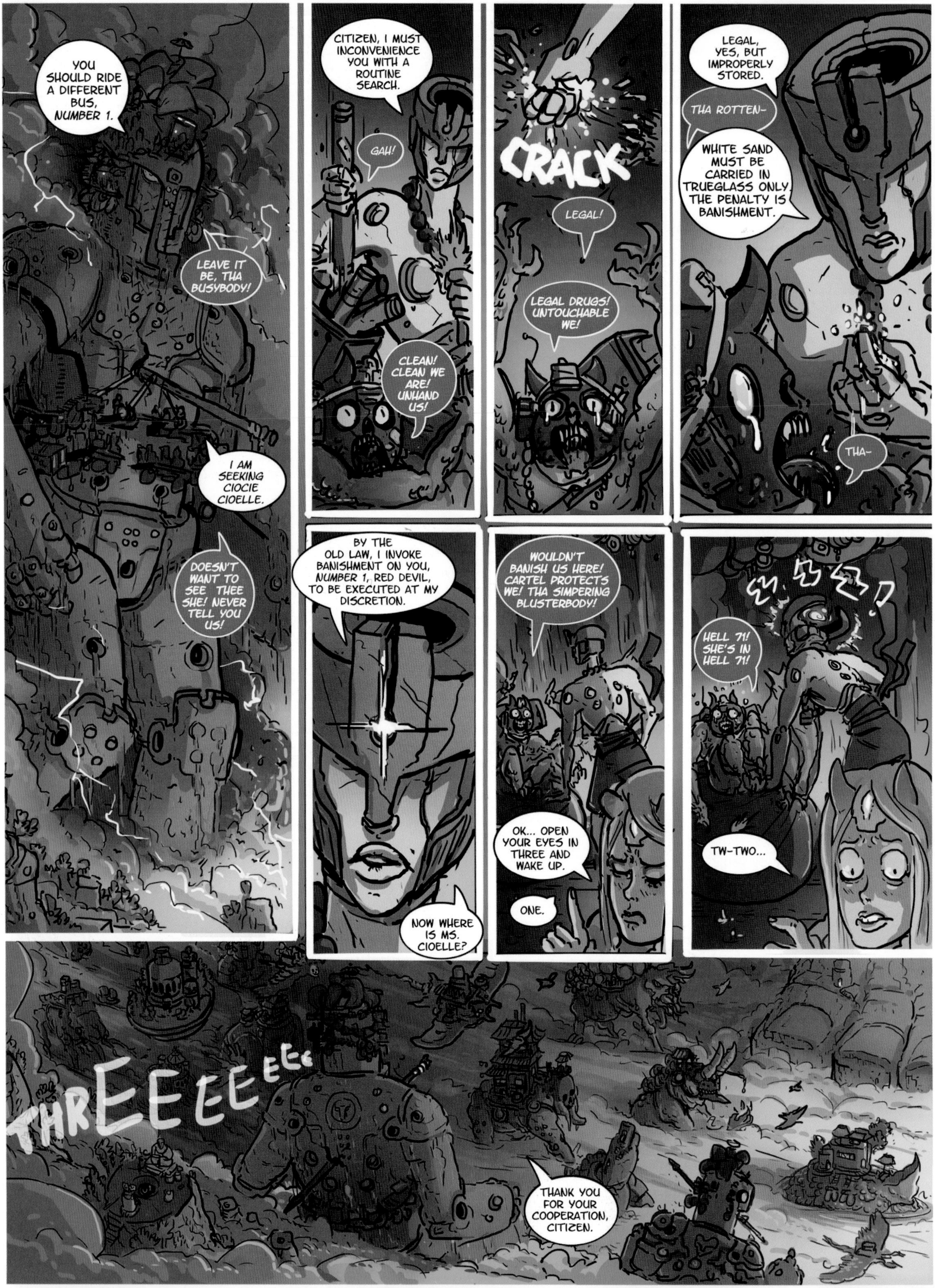
YOU SHOULD RIDE A DIFFERENT BUS, NUMBER 1.
LEAVE IT BE, THA BUSYBODY!
I AM SEEKING CIOCIE CIOELLE.
DOESN'T WANT TO SEE THEE SHE! NEVER TELL YOU US!
CITIZEN, I MUST INCONVENIENCE YOU WITH A ROUTINE SEARCH.
GAH!
CLEAN! CLEAN WE ARE! UNHAND US!
CRACK
LEGAL!
LEGAL DRUGS! UNTOUCHABLE WE!
LEGAL, YES, BUT IMPROPERLY STORED.
THA ROTTEN-
WHITE SAND MUST BE CARRIED IN TRUEGLASS ONLY. THE PENALTY IS BANISHMENT.
THA-
BY THE OLD LAW, I INVOKE BANISHMENT ON YOU, NUMBER 1, RED DEVIL, TO BE EXECUTED AT MY DISCRETION.
NOW WHERE IS MS. CIOELLE?
WOULDN'T BANISH US HERE! CARTEL PROTECTS WE! THA SIMPERING BLUSTERBODY!
OK... OPEN YOUR EYES IN THREE AND WAKE UP.
ONE.
HELL 71! SHE'S IN HELL 71!
TW-TWO...
THREEEEEEE
THANK YOU FOR YOUR COOPERATION, CITIZEN.

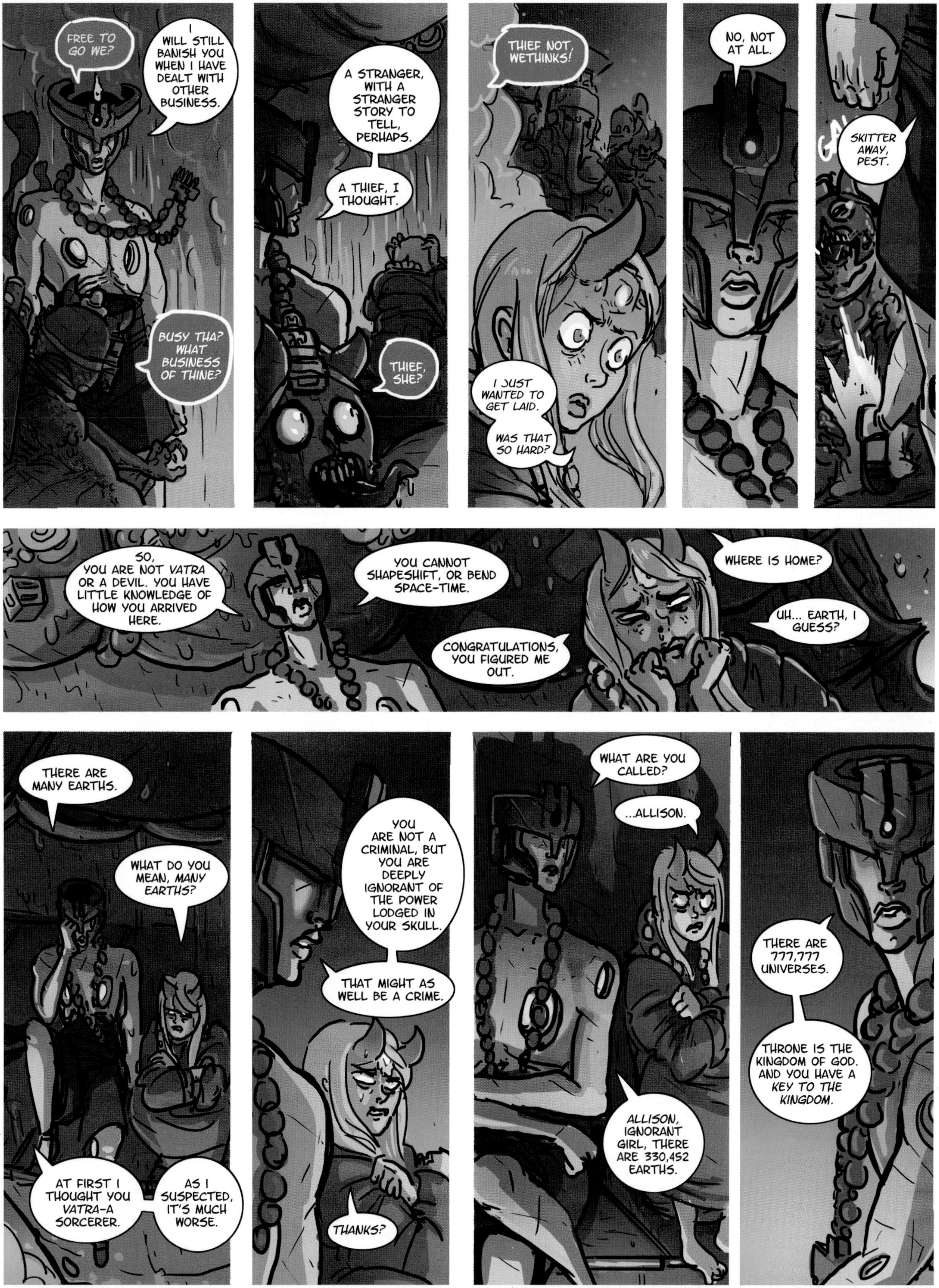
FREE TO GO WE?
I WILL STILL BANISH YOU WHEN I HAVE DEALT WITH OTHER BUSINESS.
BUSY THA? WHAT BUSINESS OF THINE?
A STRANGER, WITH A STRANGER STORY TO TELL, PERHAPS.
A THIEF, I THOUGHT.
THIEF, SHE?
THIEF NOT, WETHINKS!
I JUST WANTED TO GET LAID.
WAS THAT SO HARD?
NO, NOT AT ALL.
SKITTER AWAY, PEST.
SO, YOU ARE NOT VATRA OR A DEVIL. YOU HAVE LITTLE KNOWLEDGE OF HOW YOU ARRIVED HERE.
YOU CANNOT SHAPESHIFT, OR BEND SPACE-TIME.
CONGRATULATIONS, YOU FIGURED ME OUT.
WHERE IS HOME?
UH... EARTH, I GUESS?
THERE ARE MANY EARTHS.
WHAT DO YOU MEAN, MANY EARTHS?
AT FIRST I THOUGHT YOU VATRA—A SORCERER.
AS I SUSPECTED, IT'S MUCH WORSE.
YOU ARE NOT A CRIMINAL, BUT YOU ARE DEEPLY IGNORANT OF THE POWER LODGED IN YOUR SKULL.
THAT MIGHT AS WELL BE A CRIME.
THANKS?
WHAT ARE YOU CALLED?
...ALLISON.
ALLISON, IGNORANT GIRL, THERE ARE 330,452 EARTHS.
THERE ARE 777,777 UNIVERSES.
THRONE IS THE KINGDOM OF GOD. AND YOU HAVE A KEY TO THE KINGDOM.

SO THIS IS... HEAVEN?

IT WAS ONCE CALLED THAT, YES.

NOW...

NOW IT IS A FETID RUIN, RULED BY SEVEN BLACK KINGS FROM SEVEN TOWERS.

THEY ARE... UNKIND.

RECLUSIVE, THEY BROOD IN THEIR CITADELS, SWOLLEN WITH POWER.

USURPERS OF THE TRUE KING.

AND BENEATH THEM THE CITY ROTS.

THE SEVEN DO NOT CARE FOR CREATION. GREAT WORLD-SPANNING CRIMINAL SYNDICATES RULE THE CITY IN THEIR STEAD. THE GUILDS.

THEY HAVE GROWN FAT AND RICH.

GLUTTING THEMSELVES ON WEALTH—

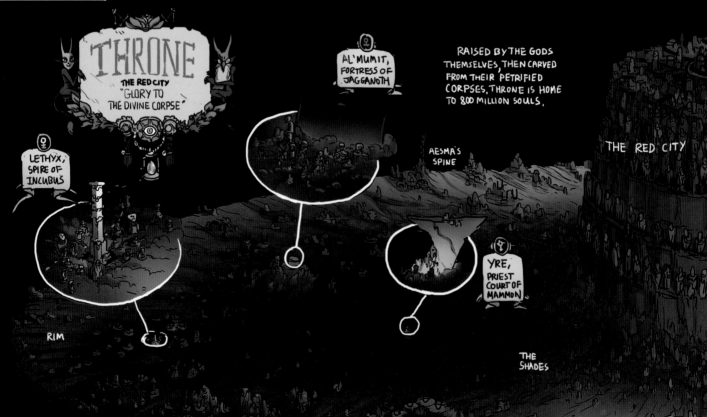

THRONE
THE RED CITY
"GLORY TO THE DIVINE CORPSE"

AL'MUMIT, FORTRESS OF JAGGANOTH

LETHYX, SPIRE OF INCUBUS

RAISED BY THE GODS THEMSELVES, THEN CARVED FROM THEIR PETRIFIED CORPSES, THRONE IS HOME TO 800 MILLION SOULS.

AESMA'S SPINE

THE RED CITY

YRE, PRIEST COURT OF MAMMON

RIM

THE SHADES

WATCHERS

OGAM'S MISTAKE

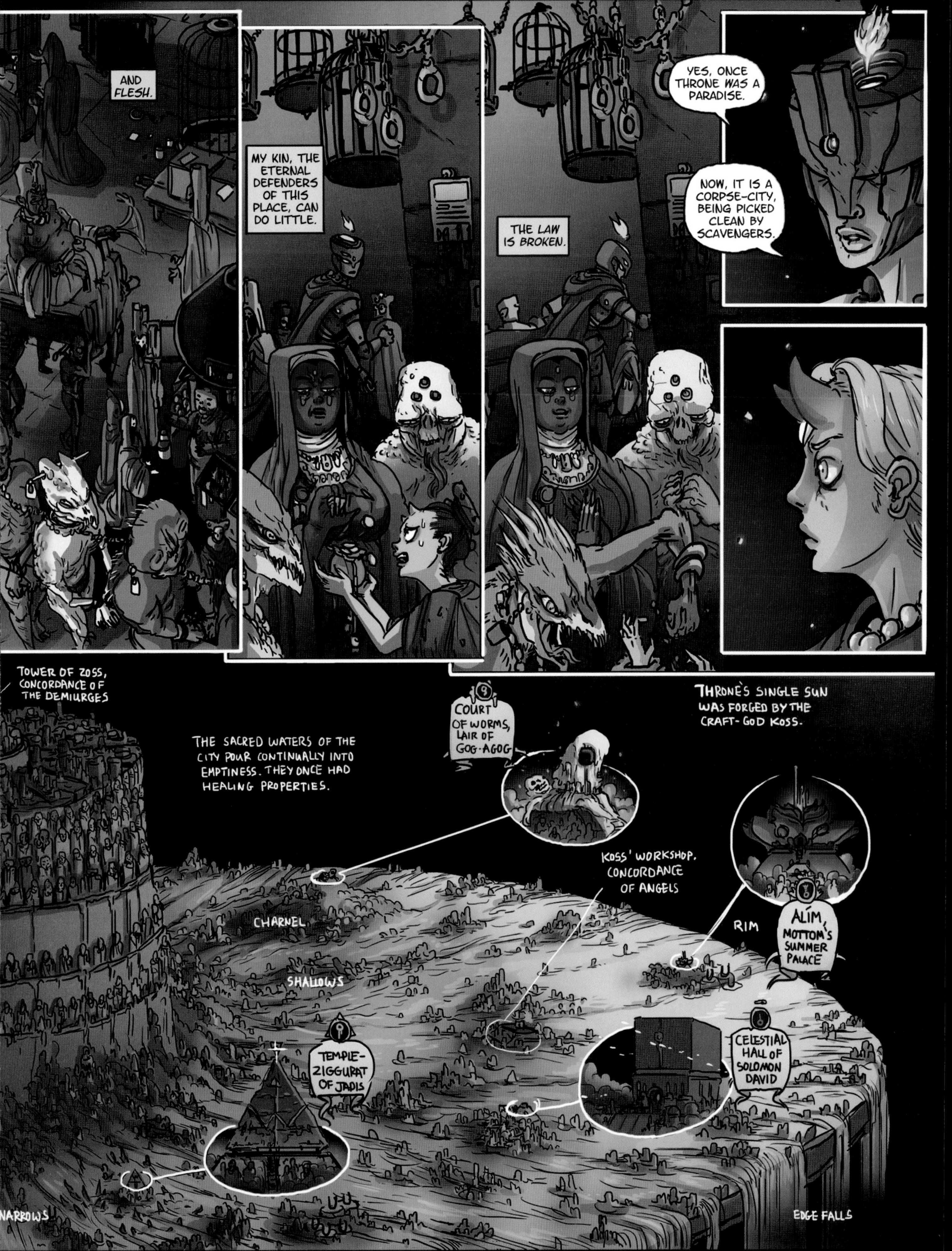

AND FLESH.
MY KIN, THE ETERNAL DEFENDERS OF THIS PLACE, CAN DO LITTLE.
THE LAW IS BROKEN.
YES, ONCE THRONE WAS A PARADISE.
NOW, IT IS A CORPSE-CITY, BEING PICKED CLEAN BY SCAVENGERS.
TOWER OF ZOSS, CONCORDANCE OF THE DEMIURGES
THE SACRED WATERS OF THE CITY POUR CONTINUALLY INTO EMPTINESS. THEY ONCE HAD HEALING PROPERTIES.
COURT OF WORMS, LAIR OF GOG-AGOG
THRONE'S SINGLE SUN WAS FORGED BY THE CRAFT-GOD KOSS.
KOSS' WORKSHOP, CONCORDANCE OF ANGELS
CHARNEL
RIM
ALÍM, MOTTOM'S SUMMER PALACE
SHALLOWS
TEMPLE-ZIGGURAT OF JADIS
CELESTIAL HALL OF SOLOMON DAVID
NARROWS
EDGE FALLS

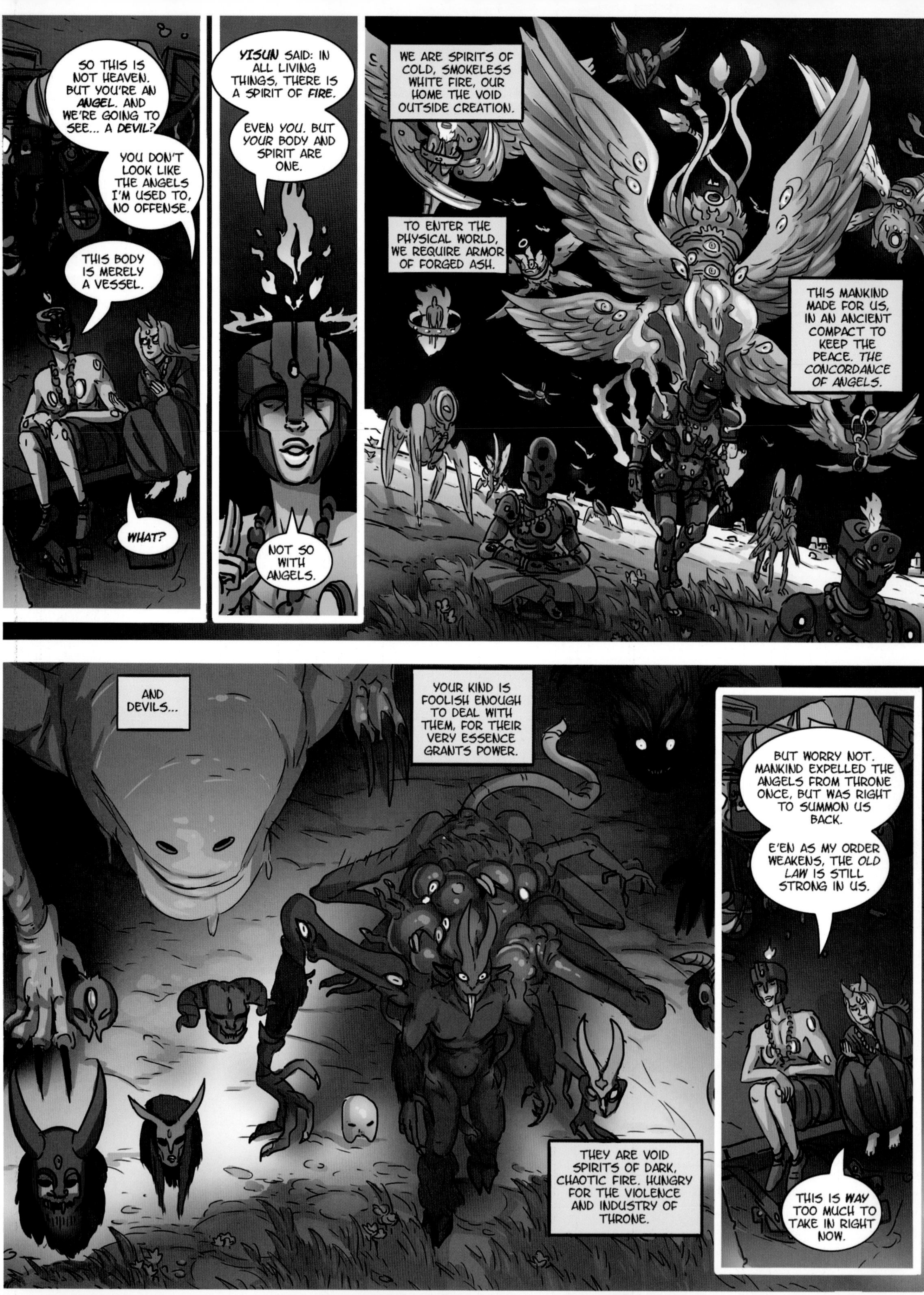

SO THIS IS NOT HEAVEN. BUT YOU'RE AN ANGEL. AND WE'RE GOING TO SEE... A DEVIL?
YOU DON'T LOOK LIKE THE ANGELS I'M USED TO, NO OFFENSE.
THIS BODY IS MERELY A VESSEL.
WHAT?
YISUN SAID: IN ALL LIVING THINGS, THERE IS A SPIRIT OF FIRE.
EVEN YOU. BUT YOUR BODY AND SPIRIT ARE ONE.
NOT SO WITH ANGELS.
WE ARE SPIRITS OF COLD, SMOKELESS WHITE FIRE, OUR HOME THE VOID OUTSIDE CREATION.
TO ENTER THE PHYSICAL WORLD, WE REQUIRE ARMOR OF FORGED ASH.
THIS MANKIND MADE FOR US, IN AN ANCIENT COMPACT TO KEEP THE PEACE. THE CONCORDANCE OF ANGELS.
AND DEVILS...
YOUR KIND IS FOOLISH ENOUGH TO DEAL WITH THEM, FOR THEIR VERY ESSENCE GRANTS POWER.
THEY ARE VOID SPIRITS OF DARK, CHAOTIC FIRE. HUNGRY FOR THE VIOLENCE AND INDUSTRY OF THRONE.
BUT WORRY NOT. MANKIND EXPELLED THE ANGELS FROM THRONE ONCE, BUT WAS RIGHT TO SUMMON US BACK.
E'EN AS MY ORDER WEAKENS, THE OLD LAW IS STILL STRONG IN US.
THIS IS WAY TOO MUCH TO TAKE IN RIGHT NOW.

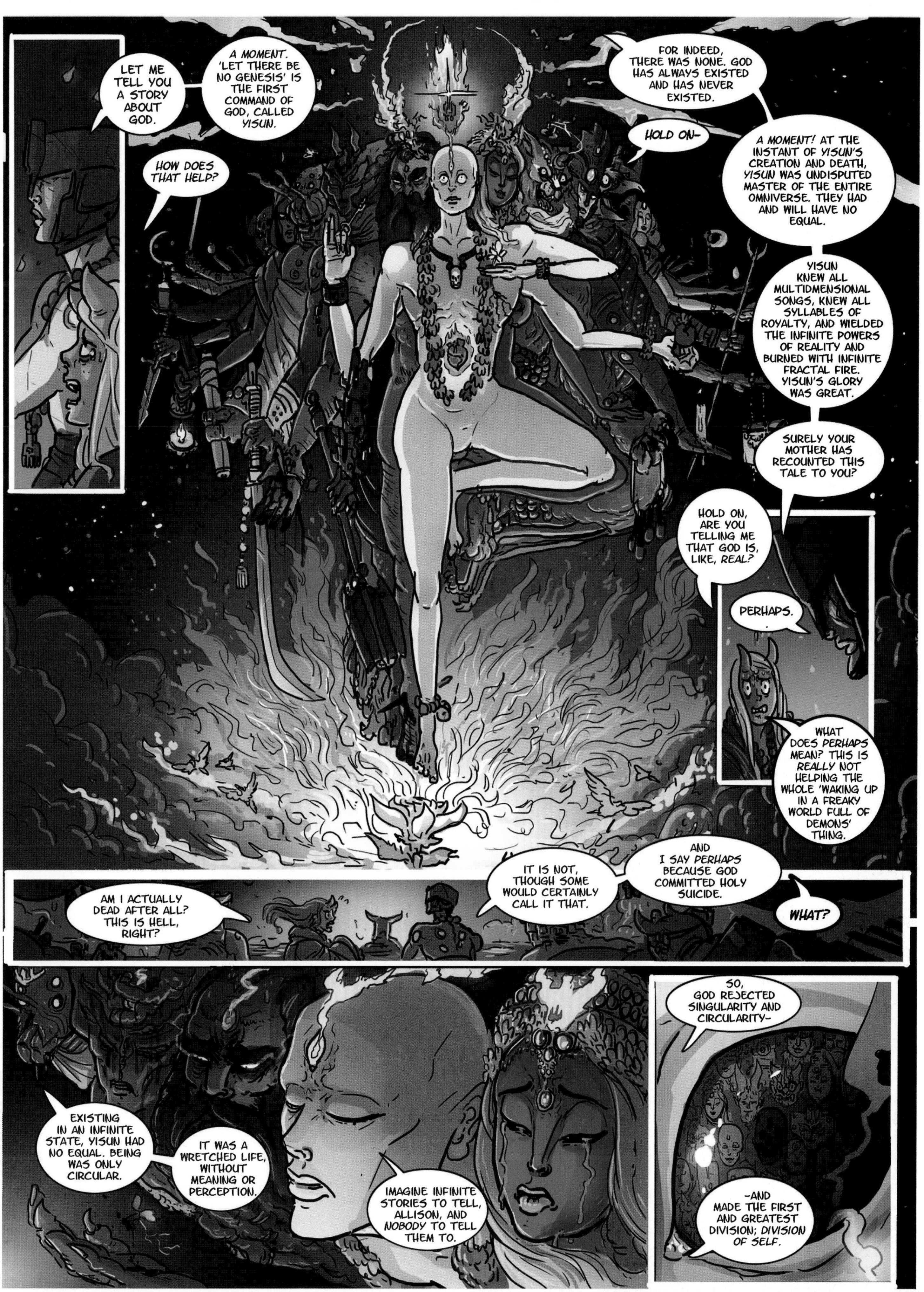

LET ME TELL YOU A STORY ABOUT GOD.
A MOMENT. 'LET THERE BE NO GENESIS' IS THE FIRST COMMAND OF GOD, CALLED YISUN.
HOW DOES THAT HELP?
FOR INDEED, THERE WAS NONE. GOD HAS ALWAYS EXISTED AND HAS NEVER EXISTED.
HOLD ON-
A MOMENT! AT THE INSTANT OF YISUN'S CREATION AND DEATH, YISUN WAS UNDISPUTED MASTER OF THE ENTIRE OMNIVERSE. THEY HAD AND WILL HAVE NO EQUAL.
YISUN KNEW ALL MULTIDMENSIONAL SONGS, KNEW ALL SYLLABLES OF ROYALTY, AND WIELDED THE INFINITE POWERS OF REALITY AND BURNED WITH INFINITE FRACTAL FIRE. YISUN'S GLORY WAS GREAT.
SURELY YOUR MOTHER HAS RECOUNTED THIS TALE TO YOU?
HOLD ON, ARE YOU TELLING ME THAT GOD IS, LIKE, REAL?
PERHAPS.
WHAT DOES PERHAPS MEAN? THIS IS REALLY NOT HELPING THE WHOLE 'WAKING UP IN A FREAKY WORLD FULL OF DEMONS' THING.
AM I ACTUALLY DEAD AFTER ALL? THIS IS HELL, RIGHT?
IT IS NOT, THOUGH SOME WOULD CERTAINLY CALL IT THAT.
AND I SAY PERHAPS BECAUSE GOD COMMITTED HOLY SUICIDE.
WHAT?
EXISTING IN AN INFINITE STATE, YISUN HAD NO EQUAL. BEING WAS ONLY CIRCULAR.
IT WAS A WRETCHED LIFE, WITHOUT MEANING OR PERCEPTION.
IMAGINE INFINITE STORIES TO TELL, ALLISON, AND NOBODY TO TELL THEM TO.
SO, GOD REJECTED SINGULARITY AND CIRCULARITY-
-AND MADE THE FIRST AND GREATEST DIVISION; DIVISION OF SELF.

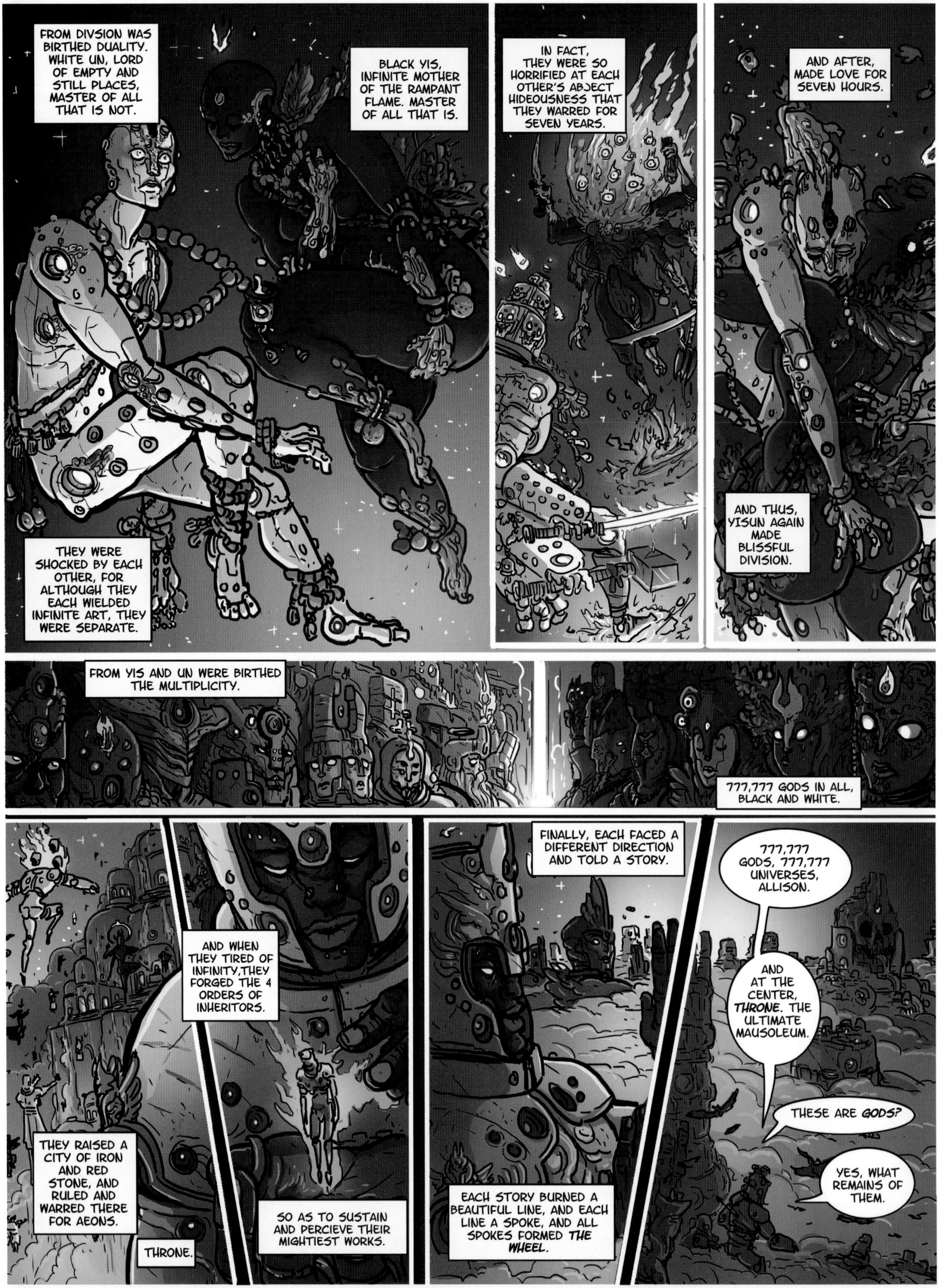
FROM DIVSION WAS BIRTHED DUALITY. WHITE UN, LORD OF EMPTY AND STILL PLACES, MASTER OF ALL THAT IS NOT.
BLACK YIS, INFINITE MOTHER OF THE RAMPANT FLAME. MASTER OF ALL THAT IS.
THEY WERE SHOCKED BY EACH OTHER, FOR ALTHOUGH THEY EACH WIELDED INFINITE ART, THEY WERE SEPARATE.
IN FACT, THEY WERE SO HORRIFIED AT EACH OTHER'S ABJECT HIDEOUSNESS THAT THEY WARRED FOR SEVEN YEARS.
AND AFTER, MADE LOVE FOR SEVEN HOURS.
AND THUS, YISUN AGAIN MADE BLISSFUL DIVISION.
FROM YIS AND UN WERE BIRTHED THE MULTIPLICITY.
777,777 GODS IN ALL, BLACK AND WHITE.
THEY RAISED A CITY OF IRON AND RED STONE, AND RULED AND WARRED THERE FOR AEONS.
THRONE.
AND WHEN THEY TIRED OF INFINITY,THEY FORGED THE 4 ORDERS OF INHERITORS.
SO AS TO SUSTAIN AND PERCIEVE THEIR MIGHTIEST WORKS.
FINALLY, EACH FACED A DIFFERENT DIRECTION AND TOLD A STORY.
EACH STORY BURNED A BEAUTIFUL LINE, AND EACH LINE A SPOKE, AND ALL SPOKES FORMED THE WHEEL.
777,777 GODS, 777,777 UNIVERSES, ALLISON.
AND AT THE CENTER, THRONE. THE ULTIMATE MAUSOLEUM.
THESE ARE GODS?
YES, WHAT REMAINS OF THEM.

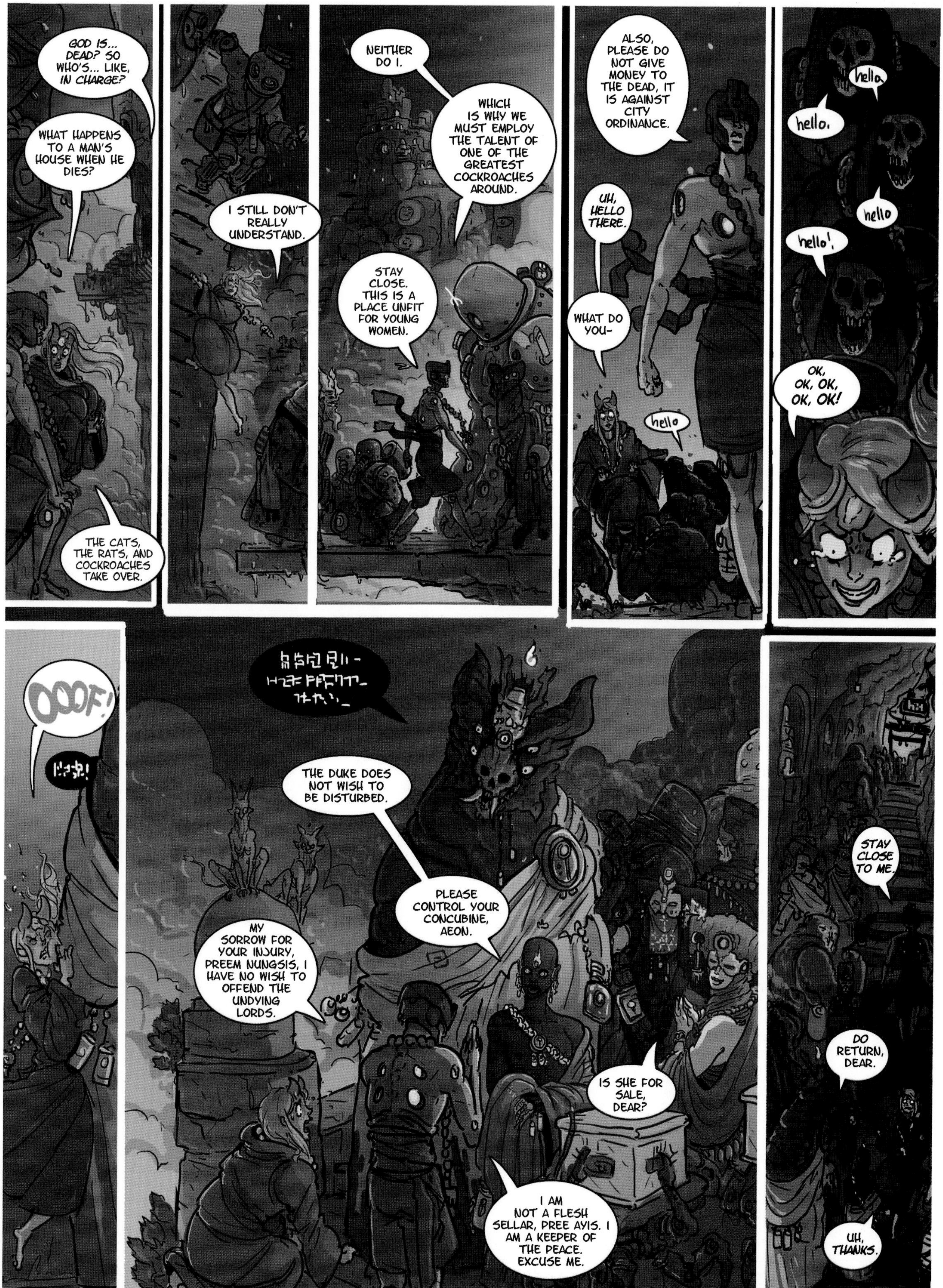
GOD IS... DEAD? SO WHO'S... LIKE, IN CHARGE?
WHAT HAPPENS TO A MAN'S HOUSE WHEN HE DIES?
THE CATS, THE RATS, AND COCKROACHES TAKE OVER.
I STILL DON'T REALLY UNDERSTAND.
NEITHER DO I.
WHICH IS WHY WE MUST EMPLOY THE TALENT OF ONE OF THE GREATEST COCKROACHES AROUND.
STAY CLOSE. THIS IS A PLACE UNFIT FOR YOUNG WOMEN.
ALSO, PLEASE DO NOT GIVE MONEY TO THE DEAD, IT IS AGAINST CITY ORDINANCE.
UH, HELLO THERE.
WHAT DO YOU-
hello
hello.
hello.
hello
hello!
OK, OK, OK, OK, OK!
OOOF!
THE DUKE DOES NOT WISH TO BE DISTURBED.
PLEASE CONTROL YOUR CONCUBINE, AEON.
MY SORROW FOR YOUR INJURY, PREEM NUNGSIS, I HAVE NO WISH TO OFFEND THE UNDYING LORDS.
IS SHE FOR SALE, DEAR?
I AM NOT A FLESH SELLAR, PREE AYIS. I AM A KEEPER OF THE PEACE. EXCUSE ME.
STAY CLOSE TO ME.
DO RETURN, DEAR.
UH, THANKS.

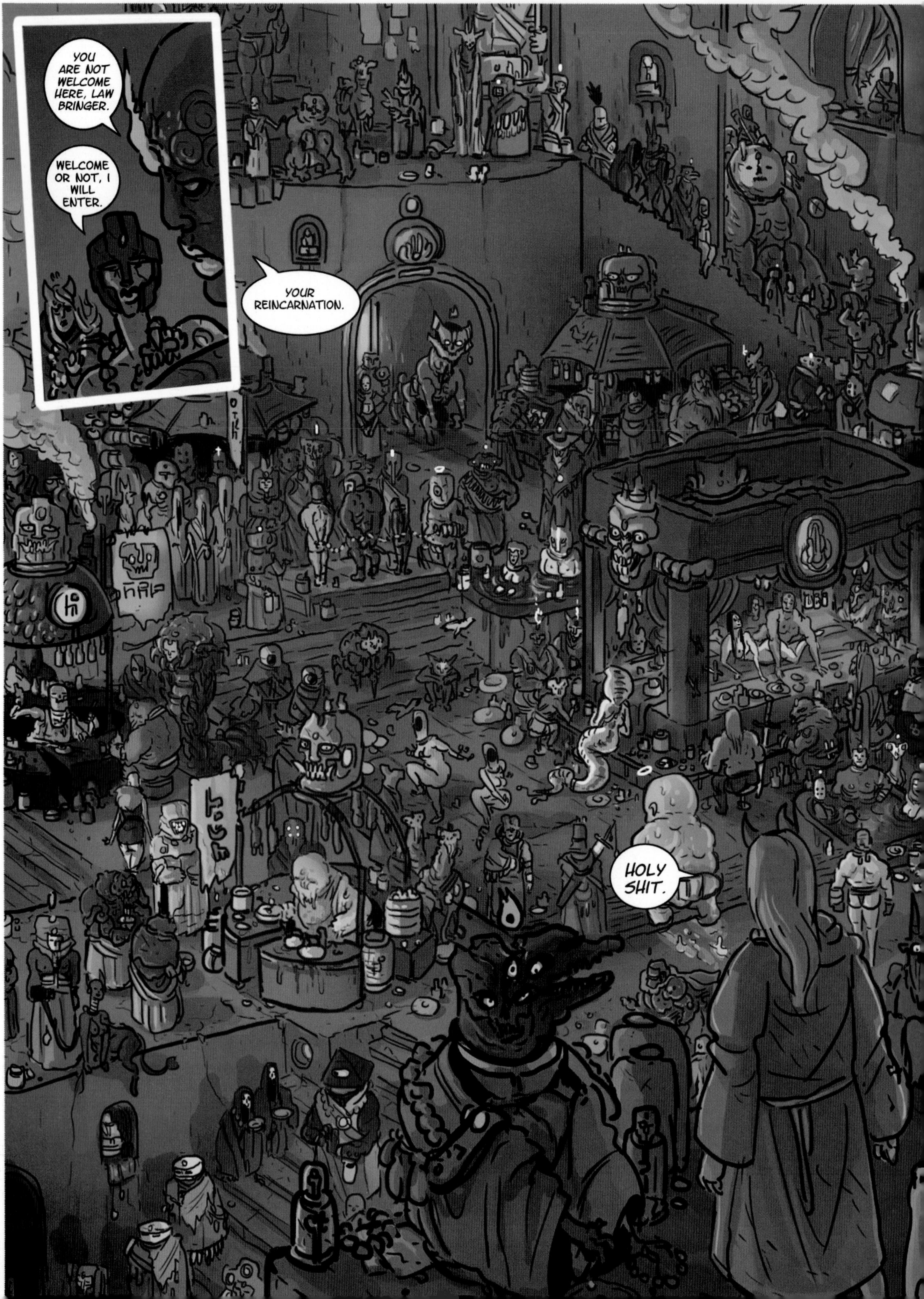
YOU ARE NOT WELCOME HERE, LAW BRINGER.
WELCOME OR NOT, I WILL ENTER.
YOUR REINCARNATION.
HOLY SHIT.

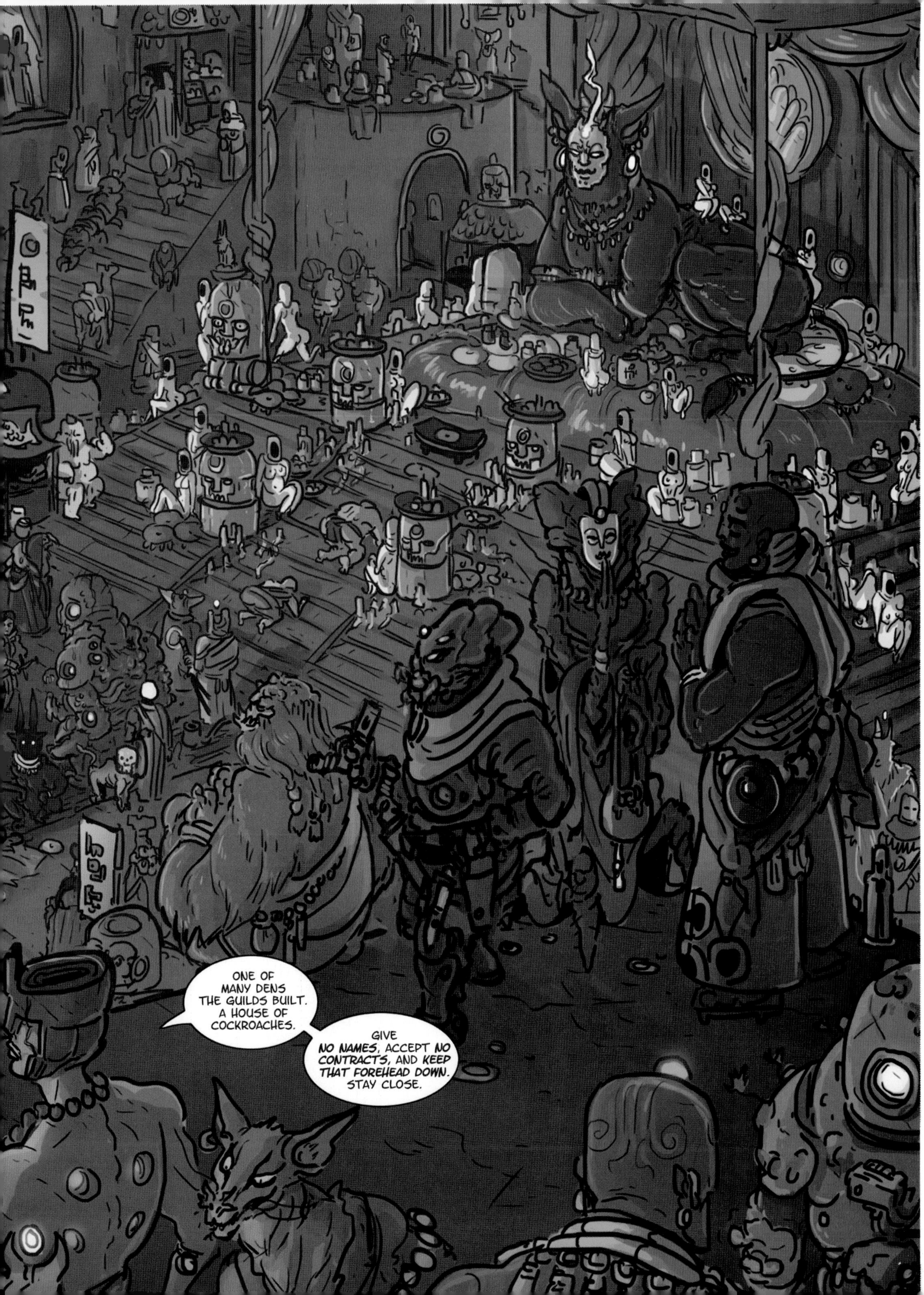
ONE OF MANY DENS THE GUILDS BUILT. A HOUSE OF COCKROACHES.
GIVE **NO NAMES**, ACCEPT **NO CONTRACTS**, AND **KEEP THAT FOREHEAD DOWN**. STAY CLOSE.

THE GRAND ENEMY CALLED I

ii. The Lie of the Iron Plum

There was once a king named UN-Payam who sat at the right hand of YISUN's throne, ruled a palace of burnished gold and fire, and dispensed justice in all things. It was made known once that Payam had grown an extraordinary plum – enormous in size, with adamant skin that was burnished as a breastplate and fifty times as impenetrable. Payam was desirous of a pillow friend of fiery heart and excellent skill with their mouth and let know that whosoever could break the skin of that plum with their teeth he would swear to share his bed with for three nights in whatever disposition they may desire.

Many gods were in attendance at Payam's hall on the first day, and even more on the second day, but by the third day of this strange contest few remained who had not tested their mettle, for the plum remained immaculate and turned many away with sore teeth and roiling frustration in their brains. A great cry rose up and YISUN was called forth from the twenty-third clockwise palace of carbon where they had been meditating on the point of a thirty-acre-long spear of crystallized time. In companionship with YISUN was Hansa, who followed along.

"See this Payam!" cried the gods, "He deceives us! He cruelly abuses our lustful hearts!"

YISUN was very fond of plums and immediately grasped the iron plum and took a long, succulent bite, praising its merits to the amazement of all.

"How?" wailed the attended.

"Why, it is a plum of flesh, and quite ripe as well," said YISUN plainly, and indeed, it was apparent to those gathered that it was the case. The plum was passed around and touched and indeed it was soft and pliant.

Hansa was not so convinced.

"It is still a plum of iron," said he, "there is some trickery here, oh master of masters."

"Indeed, it is so," said YISUN, and it was again apparent to those gathered that the flesh of that plum was as hard and impermeable as a fortress wall. "How can it be so?" said Hansa, "How comes this fickle nature? Plums and the fifty winds are not so alike, I think."

YISUN said, "I told you of this and, believing it, it was so. In truth, it is whichever you prefer. In truth, there is no plum at all, just as there is no YISUN. A plum has no shape, form, or color at all, in truth, but these are all things I find pleasing about it. A plum has no taste at all for it has no flesh or substance, but I find its sweetness intoxicating. A plum is a thing that does not exist. But it is my favorite fruit."

"A pipe is a thing that does exist, and it is my favorite past time," said Hansa, lacking understanding, and growing in cynicism.

"What a paradox!" said YISUN, smiling, "I shall share my love tenderly with Payam."

-Psalms

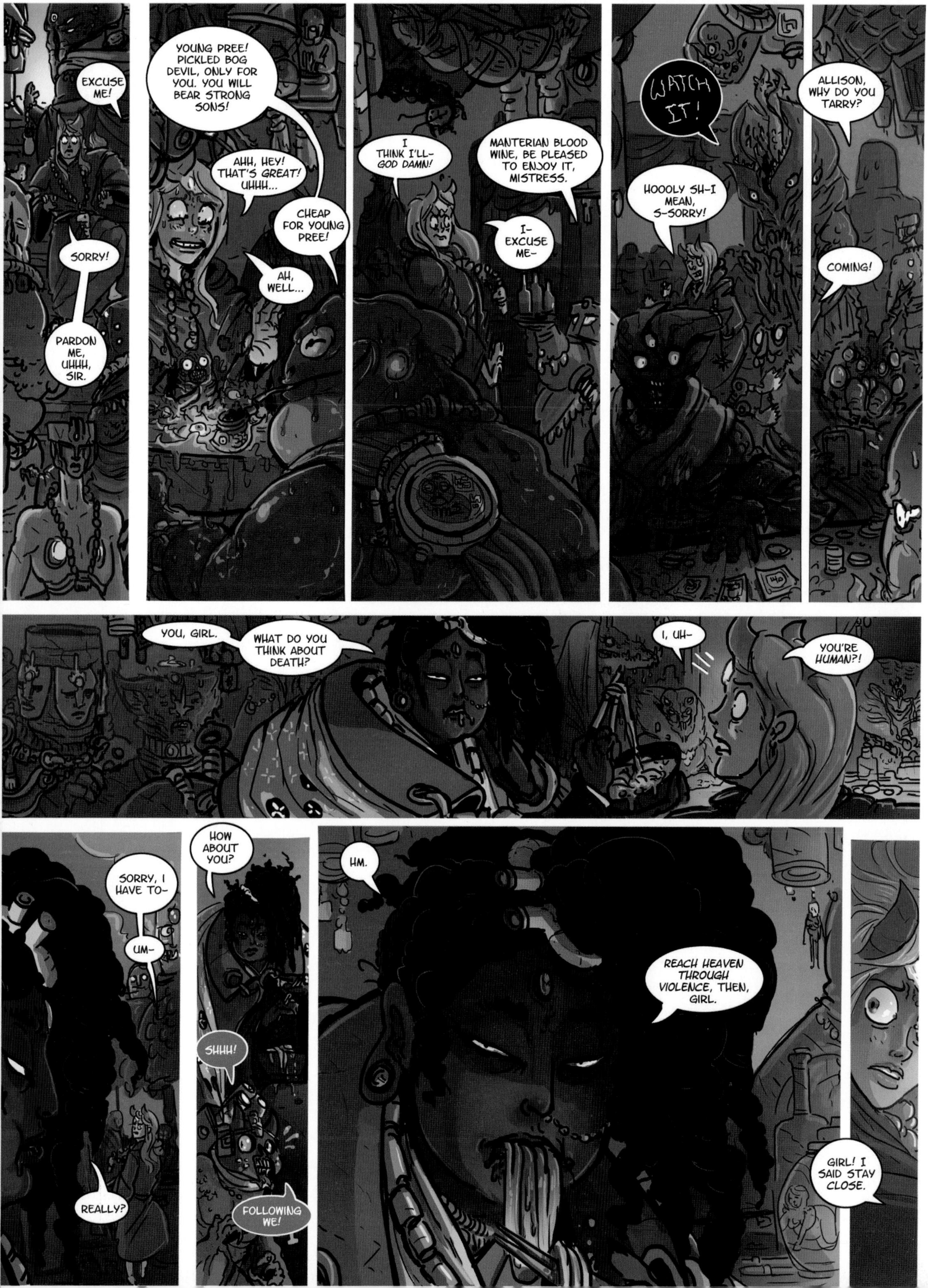
EXCUSE ME!
SORRY!
PARDON ME, UHHH, SIR.
YOUNG PREE! PICKLED BOG DEVIL, ONLY FOR YOU. YOU WILL BEAR STRONG SONS!
AHH, HEY! THAT'S GREAT! UHHH...
CHEAP FOR YOUNG PREE!
AH, WELL...
I THINK I'LL- GOD DAMN!
MANTERIAN BLOOD WINE, BE PLEASED TO ENJOY IT, MISTRESS.
I- EXCUSE ME-
WATCH IT!
HOOOLY SH-I MEAN, S-SORRY!
ALLISON, WHY DO YOU TARRY?
COMING!
YOU, GIRL.
WHAT DO YOU THINK ABOUT DEATH?
I, UH-
YOU'RE HUMAN?!
SORRY, I HAVE TO-
UM-
REALLY?
HOW ABOUT YOU?
SHHH!
FOLLOWING WE!
HM.
REACH HEAVEN THROUGH VIOLENCE, THEN, GIRL.
GIRL! I SAID STAY CLOSE.

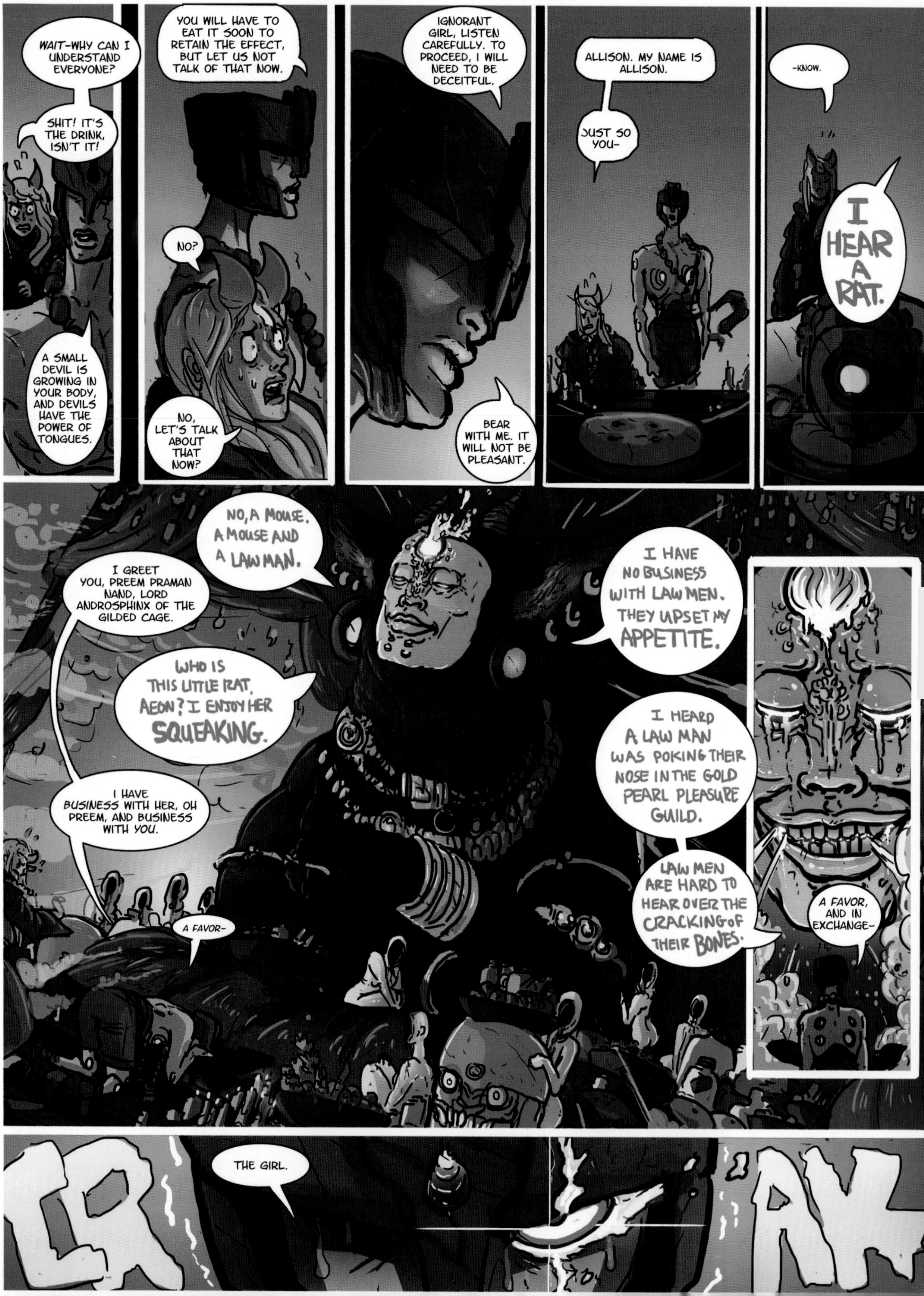

WAIT-WHY CAN I UNDERSTAND EVERYONE?
SHIT! IT'S THE DRINK, ISN'T IT!
A SMALL DEVIL IS GROWING IN YOUR BODY, AND DEVILS HAVE THE POWER OF TONGUES.
YOU WILL HAVE TO EAT IT SOON TO RETAIN THE EFFECT, BUT LET US NOT TALK OF THAT NOW.
NO?
NO, LET'S TALK ABOUT THAT NOW?
IGNORANT GIRL, LISTEN CAREFULLY. TO PROCEED, I WILL NEED TO BE DECEITFUL.
BEAR WITH ME. IT WILL NOT BE PLEASANT.
ALLISON. MY NAME IS ALLISON.
JUST SO YOU-
-KNOW.
I HEAR A RAT.
NO, A MOUSE. A MOUSE AND A LAWMAN.
I GREET YOU, PREEM PRAMAN NAND, LORD ANDROSPHINX OF THE GILDED CAGE.
I HAVE NO BUSINESS WITH LAWMEN. THEY UPSET MY APPETITE.
WHO IS THIS LITTLE RAT, AEON? I ENJOY HER SQUEAKING.
I HAVE BUSINESS WITH HER, OH PREEM, AND BUSINESS WITH YOU.
I HEARD A LAW MAN WAS POKING THEIR NOSE IN THE GOLD PEARL PLEASURE GUILD.
LAW MEN ARE HARD TO HEAR OVER THE CRACKING OF THEIR BONES.
A FAVOR-
A FAVOR, AND IN EXCHANGE-
THE GIRL.
CR AK

WHAT?

OH?

YOUR SQUIRMING EXCITES ME.

PRETTY MOUSE.

YES, I SHALL HAVE HER FACE MEASURED.

I LOVE BLONDES.

SILLY MOUSE FOUND A CAT AND THOUGHT SHE WAS SAFE.

SHE FORGOT ABOUT DOGS.

...AND WORSE.

WHAT SAY YOU, LAWMAN?

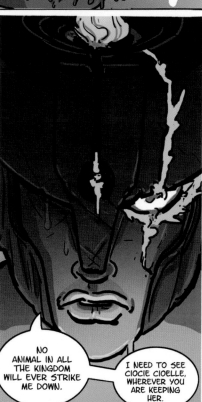

NO ANIMAL IN ALL THE KINGDOM WILL EVER STRIKE ME DOWN.

I NEED TO SEE CIOCIE CIOELLE, WHEREVER YOU ARE KEEPING HER.

YOU KNOW HOW MUCH I LOVE TO PLAY WITH MY DOLLS.

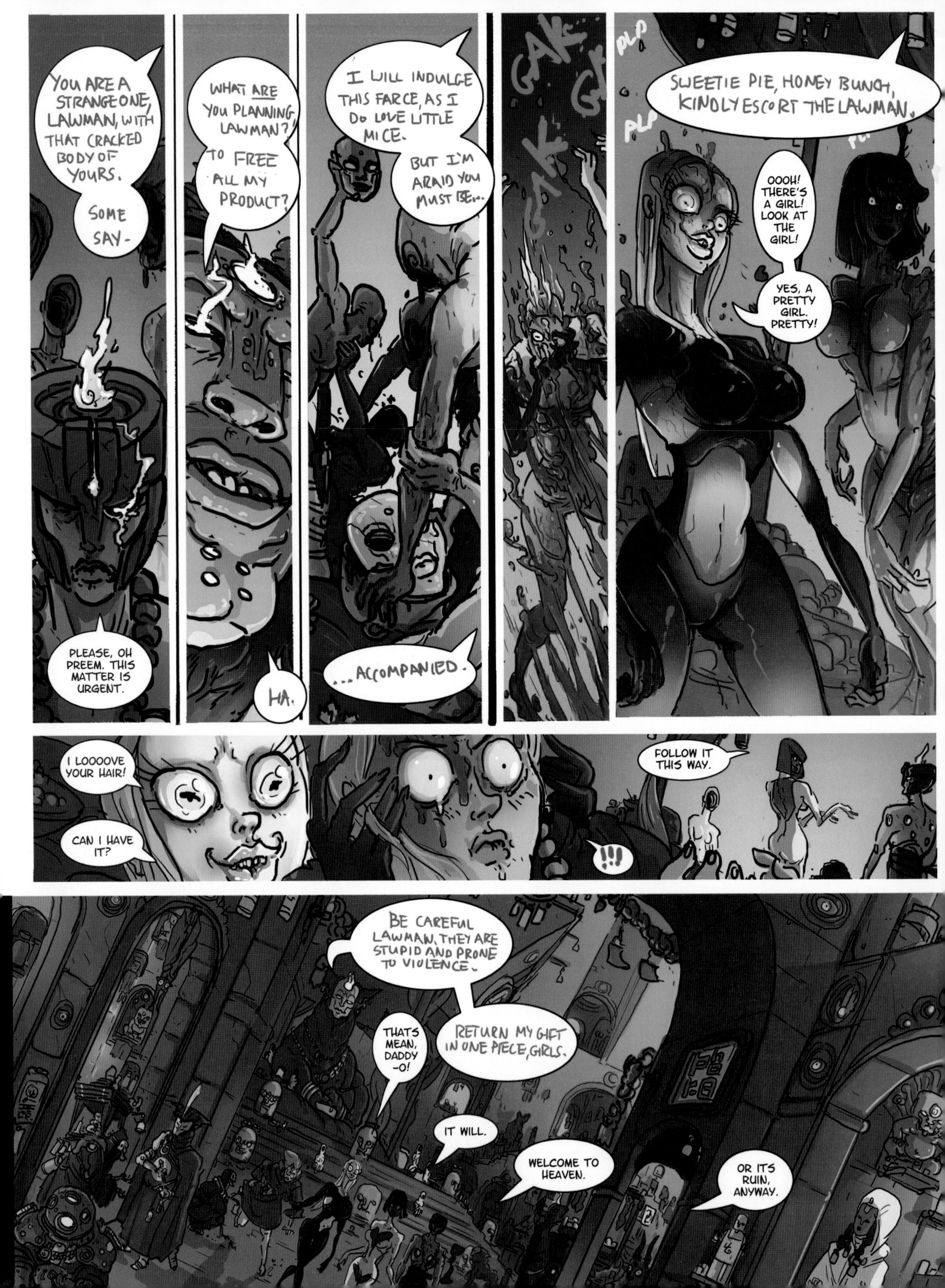
YOU ARE A STRANGE ONE, LAWMAN, WITH THAT CRACKED BODY OF YOURS.
SOME SAY-
PLEASE, OH PREEM. THIS MATTER IS URGENT.
WHAT ARE YOU PLANNING, LAWMAN?
TO FREE ALL MY PRODUCT?
HA.
I WILL INDULGE THIS FARCE, AS I DO LOVE LITTLE MICE.
BUT I'M ARAID YOU MUST BE...
...ACCOMPANIED.
GAK GAK GAK
PLP PLP PLP
SWEETIE PIE, HONEY BUNCH, KINDLY ESCORT THE LAWMAN.
OOOH! THERE'S A GIRL! LOOK AT THE GIRL!
YES, A PRETTY GIRL. PRETTY!
I LOOOOVE YOUR HAIR!
CAN I HAVE IT?
!!!
FOLLOW IT THIS WAY.
BE CAREFUL LAWMAN, THEY ARE STUPID AND PRONE TO VIOLENCE.
RETURN MY GIFT IN ONE PIECE, GIRLS.
THATS MEAN, DADDY -O!
IT WILL.
WELCOME TO HEAVEN.
OR ITS RUIN, ANYWAY.

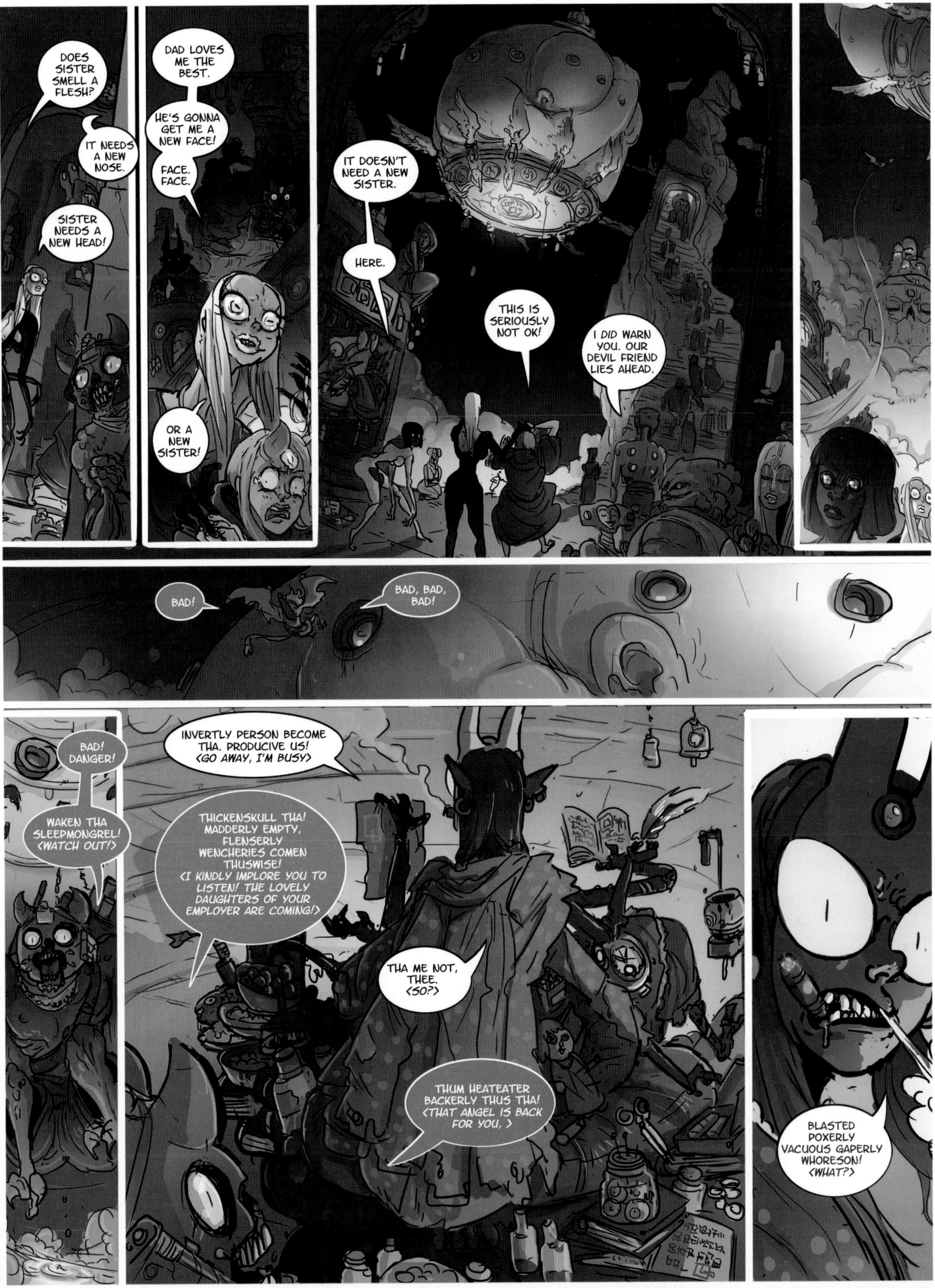

DOES SISTER SMELL A FLESH?
IT NEEDS A NEW NOSE.
SISTER NEEDS A NEW HEAD!
DAD LOVES ME THE BEST.
HE'S GONNA GET ME A NEW FACE!
FACE. FACE.
OR A NEW SISTER!
IT DOESN'T NEED A NEW SISTER.
HERE.
THIS IS SERIOUSLY NOT OK!
I DID WARN YOU. OUR DEVIL FRIEND LIES AHEAD.
BAD!
BAD, BAD, BAD!
BAD! DANGER!
WAKEN THA SLEEPMONGREL! <WATCH OUT!>
INVERTLY PERSON BECOME THA. PRODUCIVE US! <GO AWAY, I'M BUSY>
THICKENSKULL THA! MADDERLY EMPTY, FLENSERLY WENCHERIES COMEN THUSWISE! <I KINDLY IMPLORE YOU TO LISTEN! THE LOVELY DAUGHTERS OF YOUR EMPLOYER ARE COMING!>
THA ME NOT, THEE. <SO?>
THUM HEATEATER BACKERLY THUS THA! <THAT ANGEL IS BACK FOR YOU, >
BLASTED POXERLY VACUOUS GAPERLY WHORESON! <WHAT?>

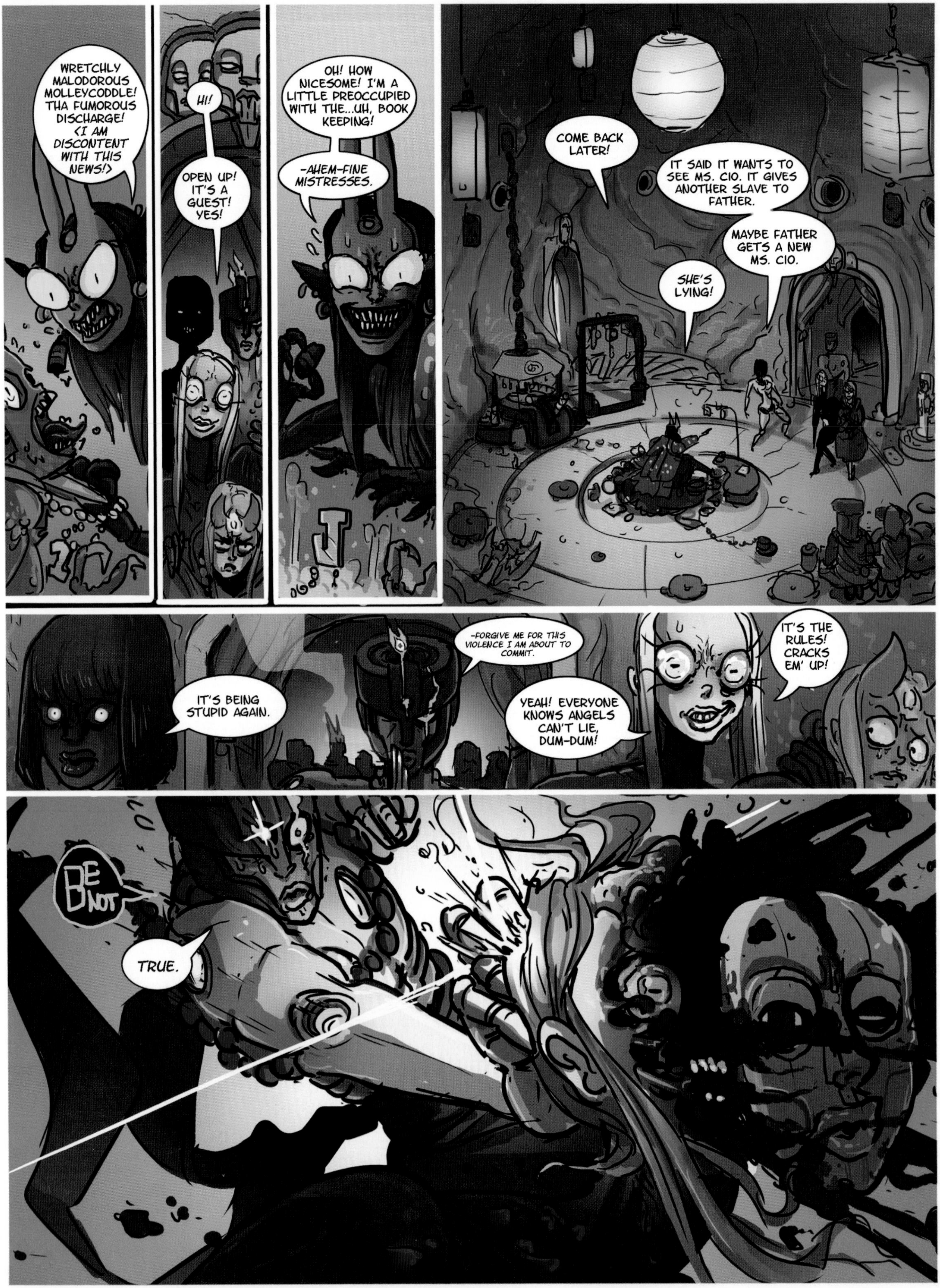
WRETCHLY MALODOROUS MOLLEYCODDLE! THA FUMOROUS DISCHARGE! <I AM DISCONTENT WITH THIS NEWS!>
HI!
OPEN UP! IT'S A GUEST! YES!
OH! HOW NICESOME! I'M A LITTLE PREOCCUPIED WITH THE...UH, BOOK KEEPING!
-AHEM-FINE MISTRESSES.
COME BACK LATER!
IT SAID IT WANTS TO SEE MS. CIO. IT GIVES ANOTHER SLAVE TO FATHER.
MAYBE FATHER GETS A NEW MS. CIO.
SHE'S LYING!
IT'S BEING STUPID AGAIN.
-FORGIVE ME FOR THIS VIOLENCE I AM ABOUT TO COMMIT.
YEAH! EVERYONE KNOWS ANGELS CAN'T LIE, DUM-DUM!
IT'S THE RULES! CRACKS EM' UP!
BE NOT
TRUE.

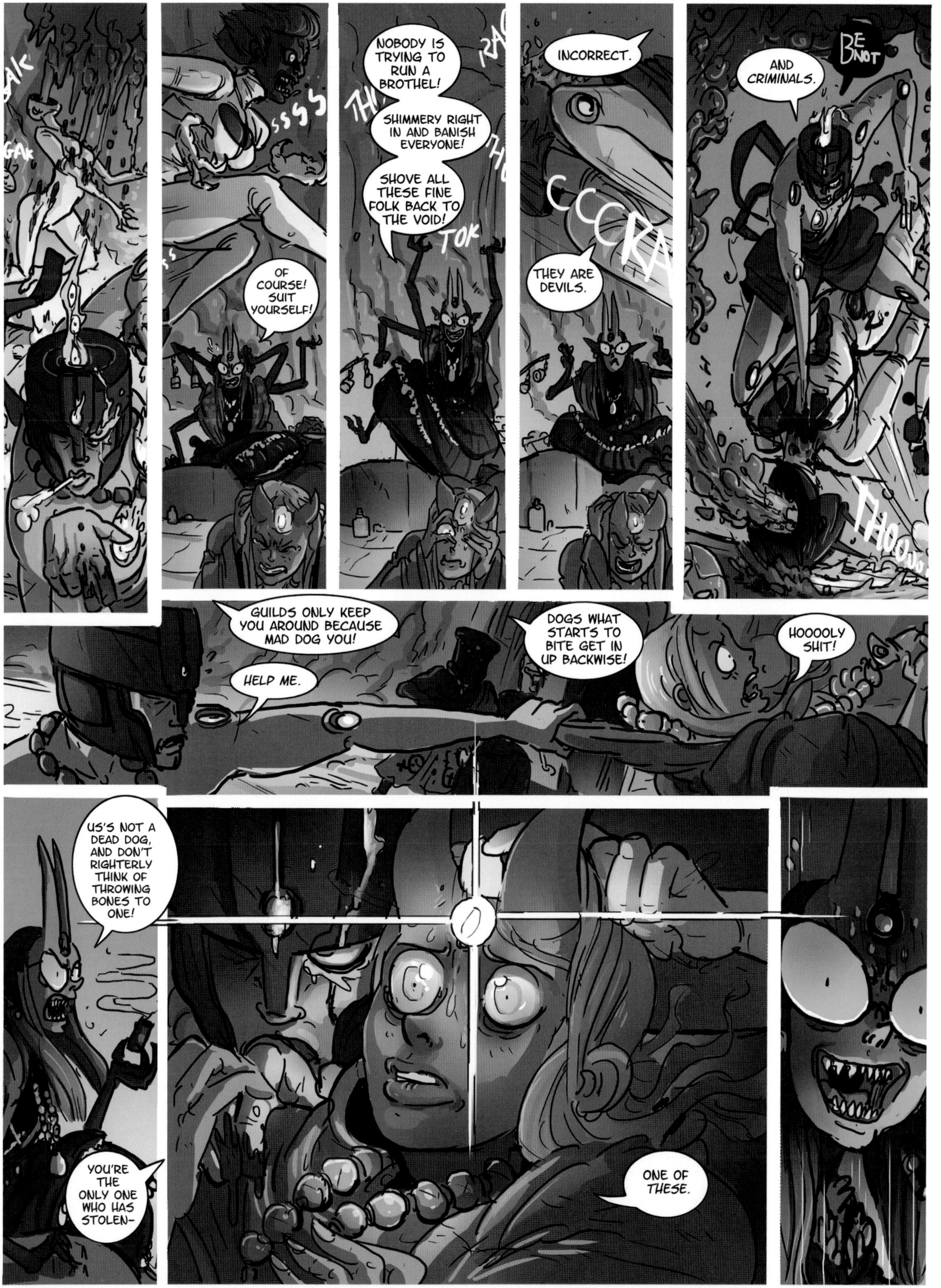
GAK
GAK
SSSSS
OF COURSE! SUIT YOURSELF!
NOBODY IS TRYING TO RUN A BROTHEL!
SHIMMERY RIGHT IN AND BANISH EVERYONE!
SHOVE ALL THESE FINE FOLK BACK TO THE VOID!
TOK
INCORRECT.
CCCRA
THEY ARE DEVILS.
AND CRIMINALS.
BE NOT
THOOOO
GUILDS ONLY KEEP YOU AROUND BECAUSE MAD DOG YOU!
HELP ME.
DOGS WHAT STARTS TO BITE GET IN UP BACKWISE!
HOOOOLY SHIT!
US'S NOT A DEAD DOG, AND DON'T RIGHTERLY THINK OF THROWING BONES TO ONE!
YOU'RE THE ONLY ONE WHO HAS STOLEN-
ONE OF THESE.

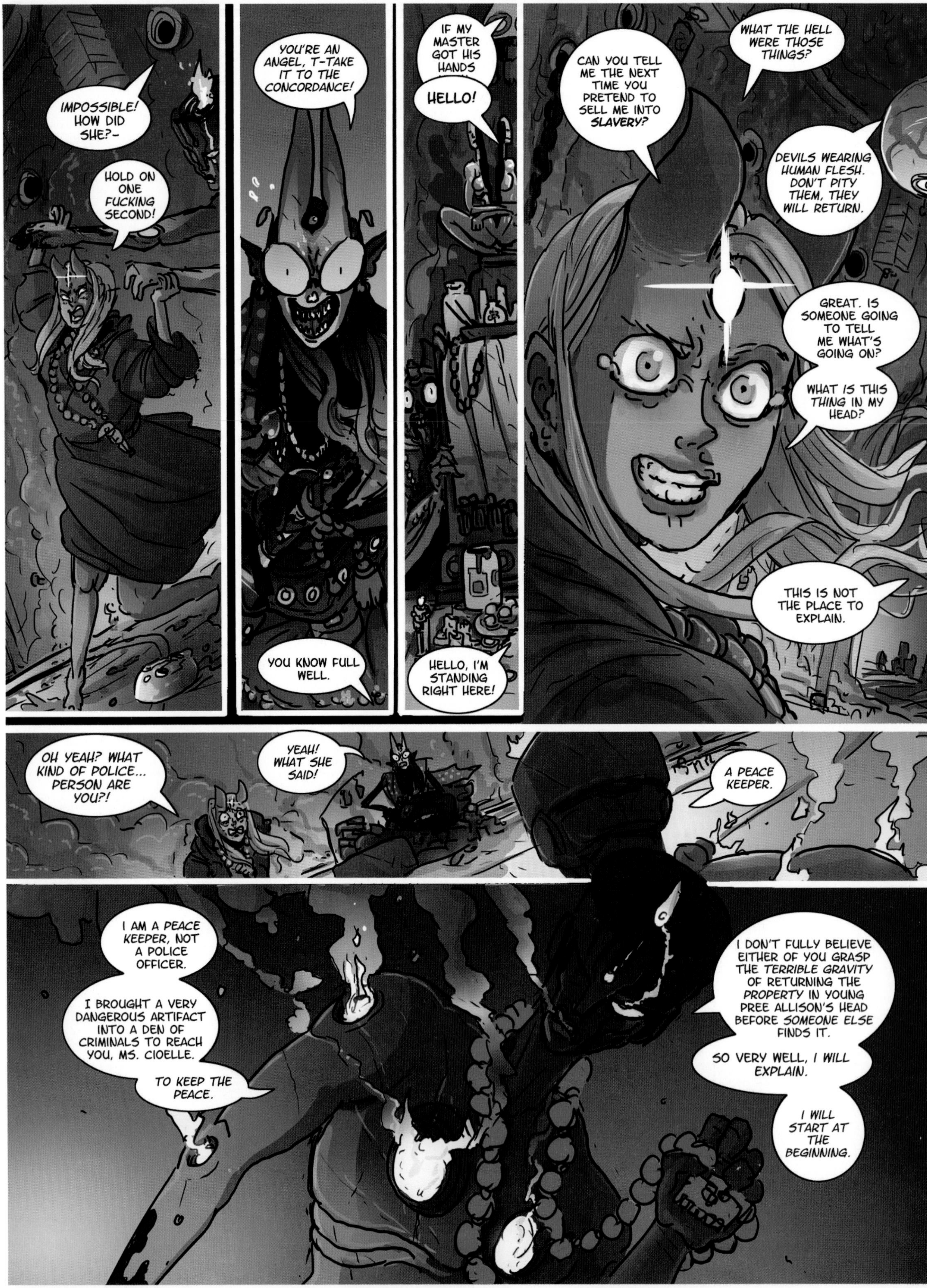
IMPOSSIBLE! HOW DID SHE?-
HOLD ON ONE FUCKING SECOND!
YOU'RE AN ANGEL, T-TAKE IT TO THE CONCORDANCE!
YOU KNOW FULL WELL.
IF MY MASTER GOT HIS HANDS
HELLO!
HELLO, I'M STANDING RIGHT HERE!
CAN YOU TELL ME THE NEXT TIME YOU PRETEND TO SELL ME INTO SLAVERY?
WHAT THE HELL WERE THOSE THINGS?
DEVILS WEARING HUMAN FLESH. DON'T PITY THEM, THEY WILL RETURN.
GREAT. IS SOMEONE GOING TO TELL ME WHAT'S GOING ON?
WHAT IS THIS THING IN MY HEAD?
THIS IS NOT THE PLACE TO EXPLAIN.
OH YEAH? WHAT KIND OF POLICE... PERSON ARE YOU?!-
YEAH! WHAT SHE SAID!
A PEACE KEEPER.
I AM A PEACE KEEPER, NOT A POLICE OFFICER.
I BROUGHT A VERY DANGEROUS ARTIFACT INTO A DEN OF CRIMINALS TO REACH YOU, MS. CIOELLE.
TO KEEP THE PEACE.
I DON'T FULLY BELIEVE EITHER OF YOU GRASP THE TERRIBLE GRAVITY OF RETURNING THE PROPERTY IN YOUNG PREE ALLISON'S HEAD BEFORE SOMEONE ELSE FINDS IT.
SO VERY WELL, I WILL EXPLAIN.
I WILL START AT THE BEGINNING.

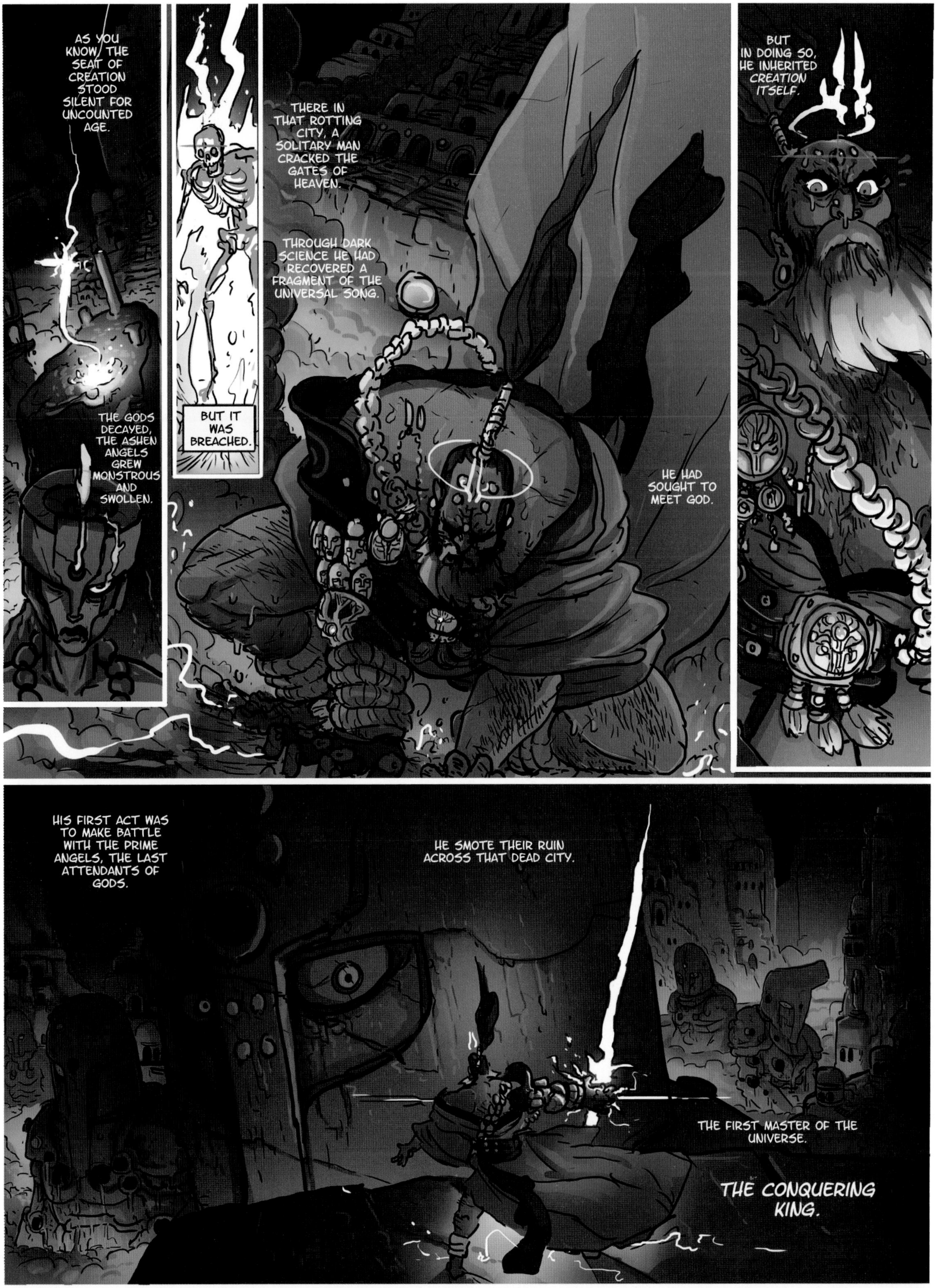
AS YOU KNOW, THE SEAT OF CREATION STOOD SILENT FOR UNCOUNTED AGE.
BUT IT WAS BREACHED.
THERE IN THAT ROTTING CITY, A SOLITARY MAN CRACKED THE GATES OF HEAVEN.
THROUGH DARK SCIENCE HE HAD RECOVERED A FRAGMENT OF THE UNIVERSAL SONG.
THE GODS DECAYED, THE ASHEN ANGELS GREW MONSTROUS AND SWOLLEN.
HE HAD SOUGHT TO MEET GOD.
BUT IN DOING SO, HE INHERITED CREATION ITSELF.
HIS FIRST ACT WAS TO MAKE BATTLE WITH THE PRIME ANGELS, THE LAST ATTENDANTS OF GODS.
HE SMOTE THEIR RUIN ACROSS THAT DEAD CITY.
THE FIRST MASTER OF THE UNIVERSE.
THE CONQUERING KING.

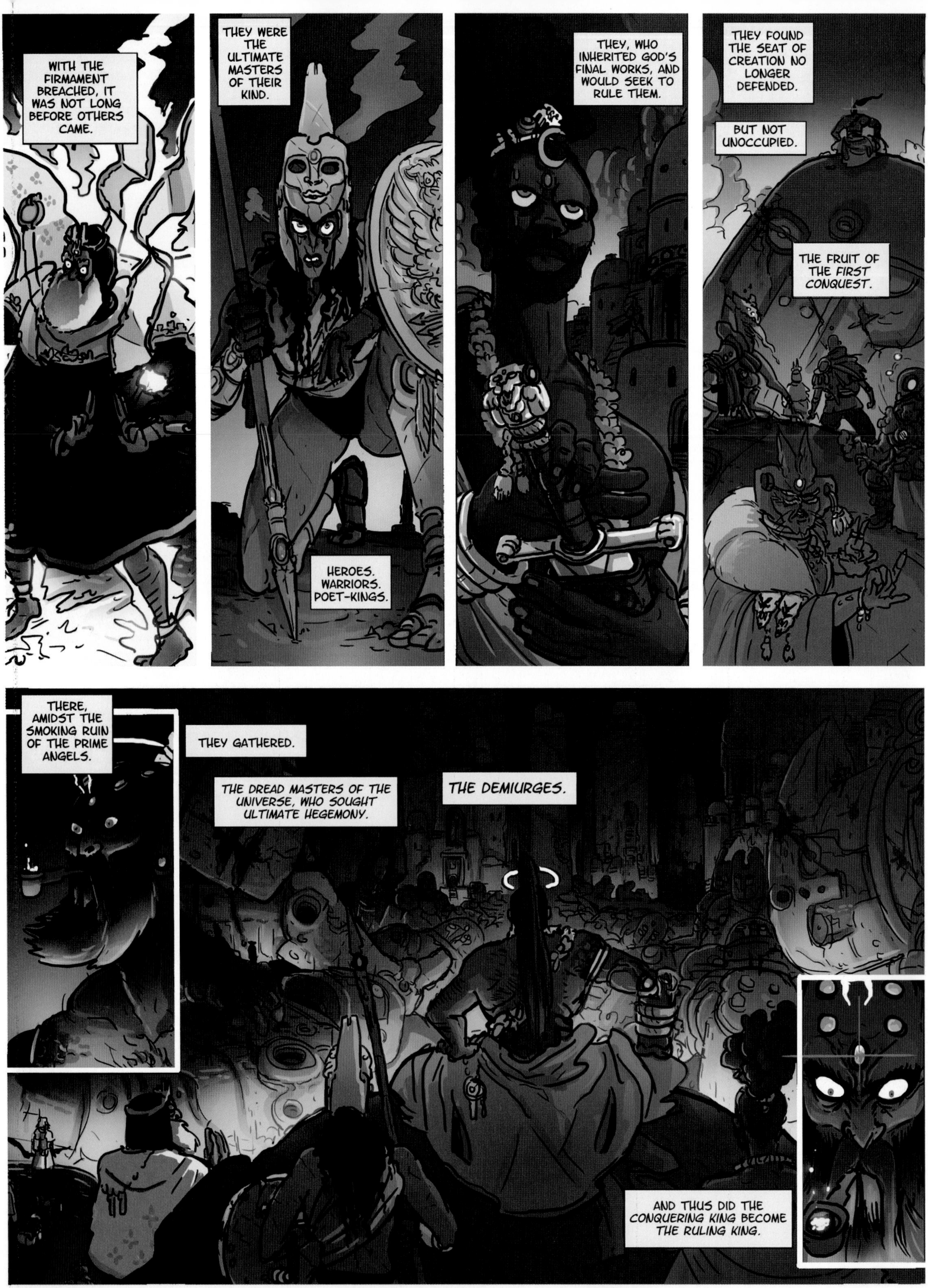

WITH THE FIRMAMENT BREACHED, IT WAS NOT LONG BEFORE OTHERS CAME.
THEY WERE THE ULTIMATE MASTERS OF THEIR KIND.
HEROES. WARRIORS. POET-KINGS.
THEY, WHO INHERITED GOD'S FINAL WORKS, AND WOULD SEEK TO RULE THEM.
THEY FOUND THE SEAT OF CREATION NO LONGER DEFENDED.
BUT NOT UNOCCUPIED.
THE FRUIT OF THE FIRST CONQUEST.
THERE, AMIDST THE SMOKING RUIN OF THE PRIME ANGELS.
THEY GATHERED.
THE DREAD MASTERS OF THE UNIVERSE, WHO SOUGHT ULTIMATE HEGEMONY.
THE DEMIURGES.
AND THUS DID THE CONQUERING KING BECOME THE RULING KING.

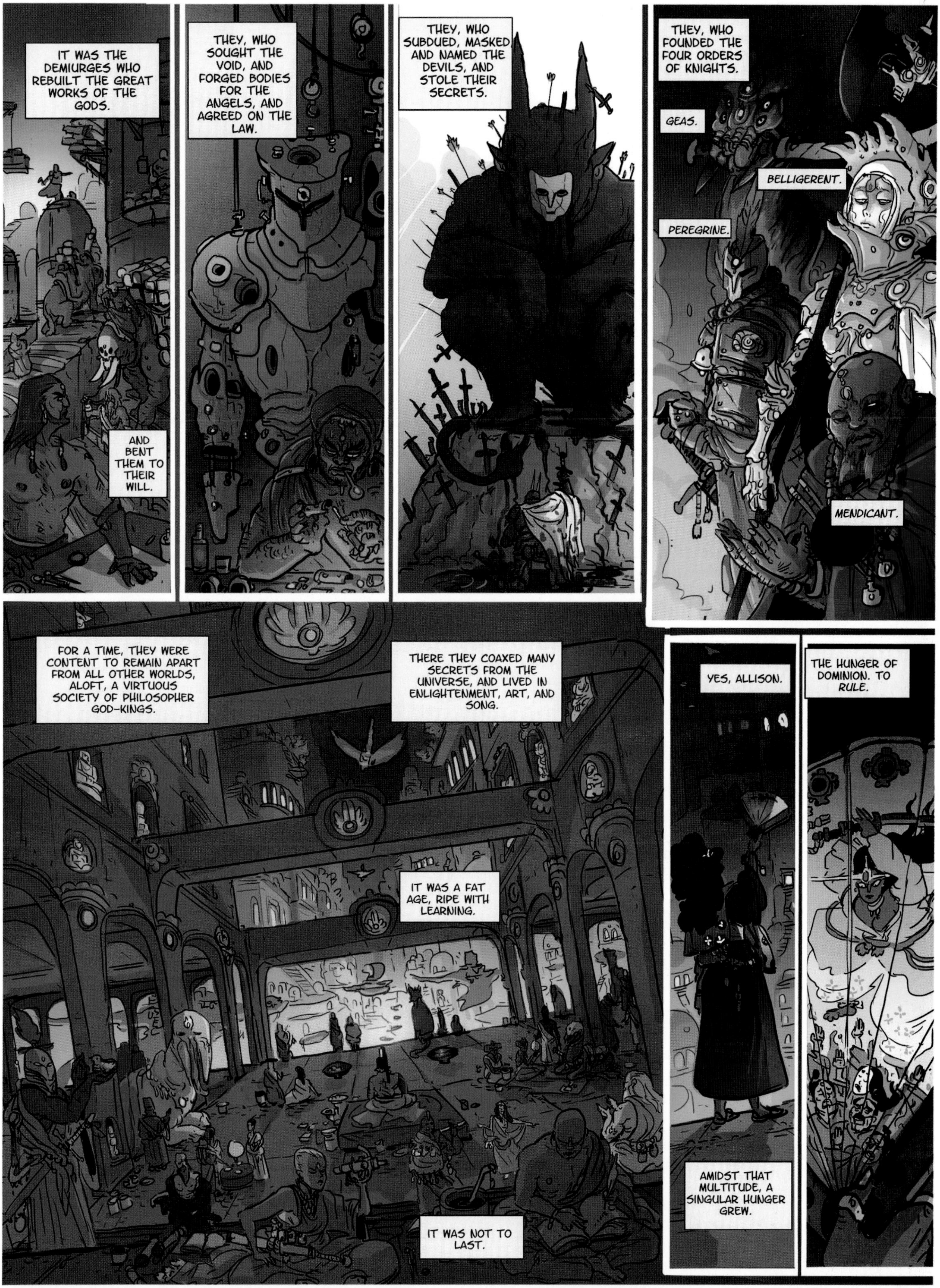
IT WAS THE DEMIURGES WHO REBUILT THE GREAT WORKS OF THE GODS.
AND BENT THEM TO THEIR WILL.
THEY, WHO SOUGHT THE VOID, AND FORGED BODIES FOR THE ANGELS, AND AGREED ON THE LAW.
THEY, WHO SUBDUED, MASKED AND NAMED THE DEVILS, AND STOLE THEIR SECRETS.
THEY, WHO FOUNDED THE FOUR ORDERS OF KNIGHTS.
GEAS.
BELLIGERENT.
PEREGRINE.
MENDICANT.
FOR A TIME, THEY WERE CONTENT TO REMAIN APART FROM ALL OTHER WORLDS, ALOFT, A VIRTUOUS SOCIETY OF PHILOSOPHER GOD-KINGS.
THERE THEY COAXED MANY SECRETS FROM THE UNIVERSE, AND LIVED IN ENLIGHTENMENT, ART, AND SONG.
IT WAS A FAT AGE, RIPE WITH LEARNING.
IT WAS NOT TO LAST.
YES, ALLISON.
AMIDST THAT MULTITUDE, A SINGULAR HUNGER GREW.
THE HUNGER OF DOMINION. TO RULE.

NOT ALL AGREED WITH THE IDEA OF RULE.

BOOOORING!

IT... ...ED CONC... ...OR

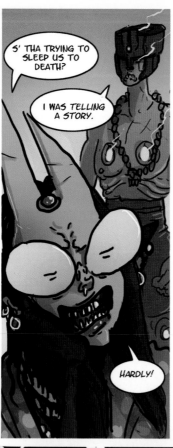

S' THA TRYING TO SLEEP US TO DEATH?

I WAS TELLING A STORY.

HARDLY!

OK... BUT WHAT DOES THIS HAVE TO DO WITH THIS THING IN MY HEAD?

ALSO, MY BOYFRIEN...

IT IS A TALE FULL OF NUANCE AND SUBTLE GESTURE. IT CANNOT BE SO—

SSSSSSS

EXPLAIN.

IT'S VERY SIMPLE!

THE KINGS OF OLD WERE WARRIORS! NOT PEACERLY SIMPERLINGS!

SO, THE NEXT THING THUM DID WAS BUILD WEAPONS!

TUNIN' FORKS FOR THE VOICE OF GOD! WEAPONS SO MIGHTISOME—

THEY COULD RIP CREATION ITSELF!

...OK...

...HOW DOES THAT...

NOT VERY SMART, THA.

IT'S A KEY, THA GORMLESS SIMPLETON! A KEY TO AN ENTIRE UNIVERSE!

TOK · TOK · TOK

WHAT!

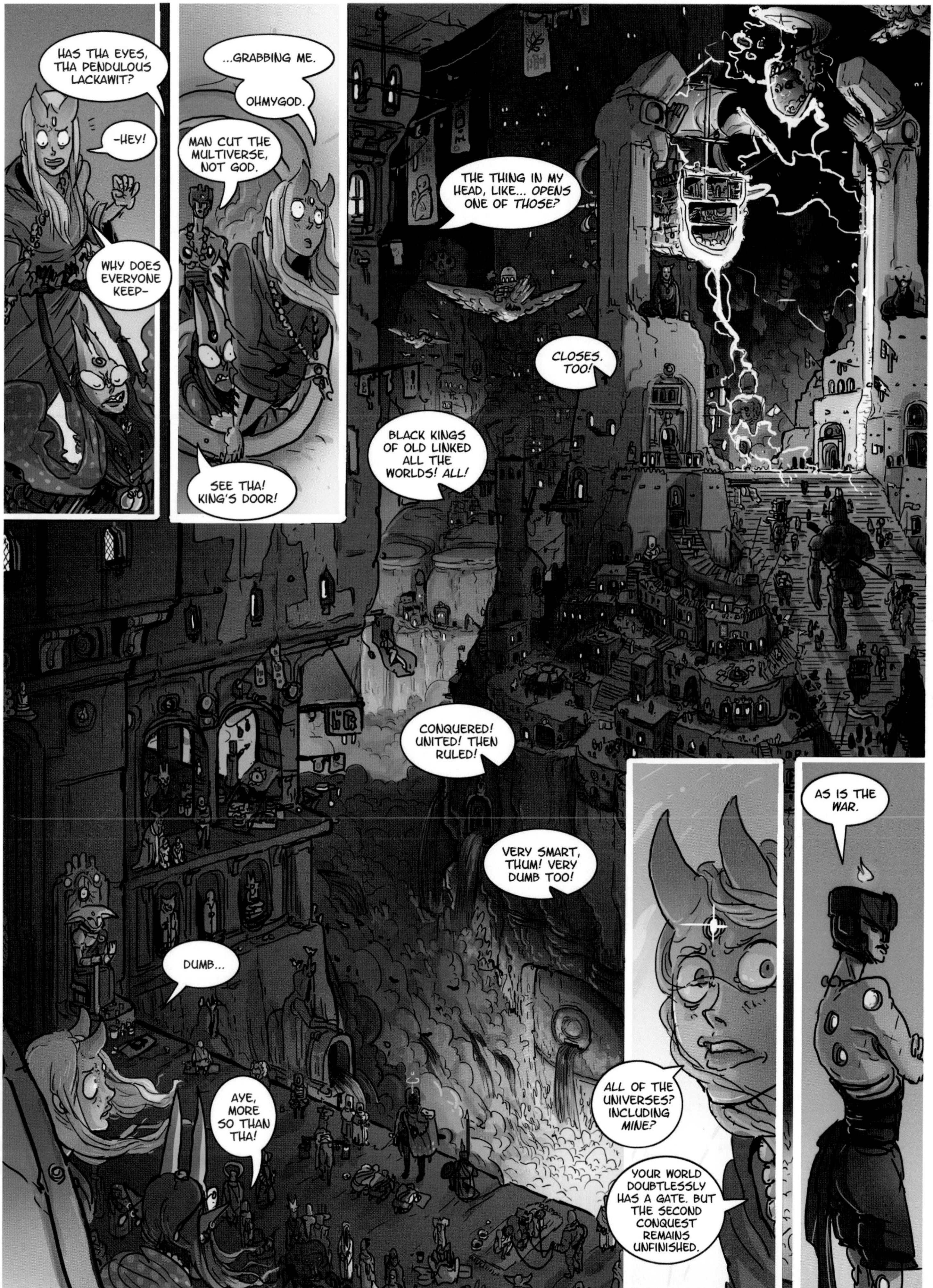
HAS THA EYES, THA PENDULOUS LACKAWIT?
-HEY!
WHY DOES EVERYONE KEEP-
...GRABBING ME.
OHMYGOD.
MAN CUT THE MULTIVERSE, NOT GOD.
SEE THA! KING'S DOOR!
THE THING IN MY HEAD, LIKE... OPENS ONE OF THOSE?
CLOSES. TOO!
BLACK KINGS OF OLD LINKED ALL THE WORLDS! ALL!
CONQUERED! UNITED! THEN RULED!
VERY SMART, THUM! VERY DUMB TOO!
DUMB...
AYE, MORE SO THAN THA!
ALL OF THE UNIVERSES? INCLUDING MINE?
YOUR WORLD DOUBTLESSLY HAS A GATE. BUT THE SECOND CONQUEST REMAINS UNFINISHED.
AS IS THE WAR.

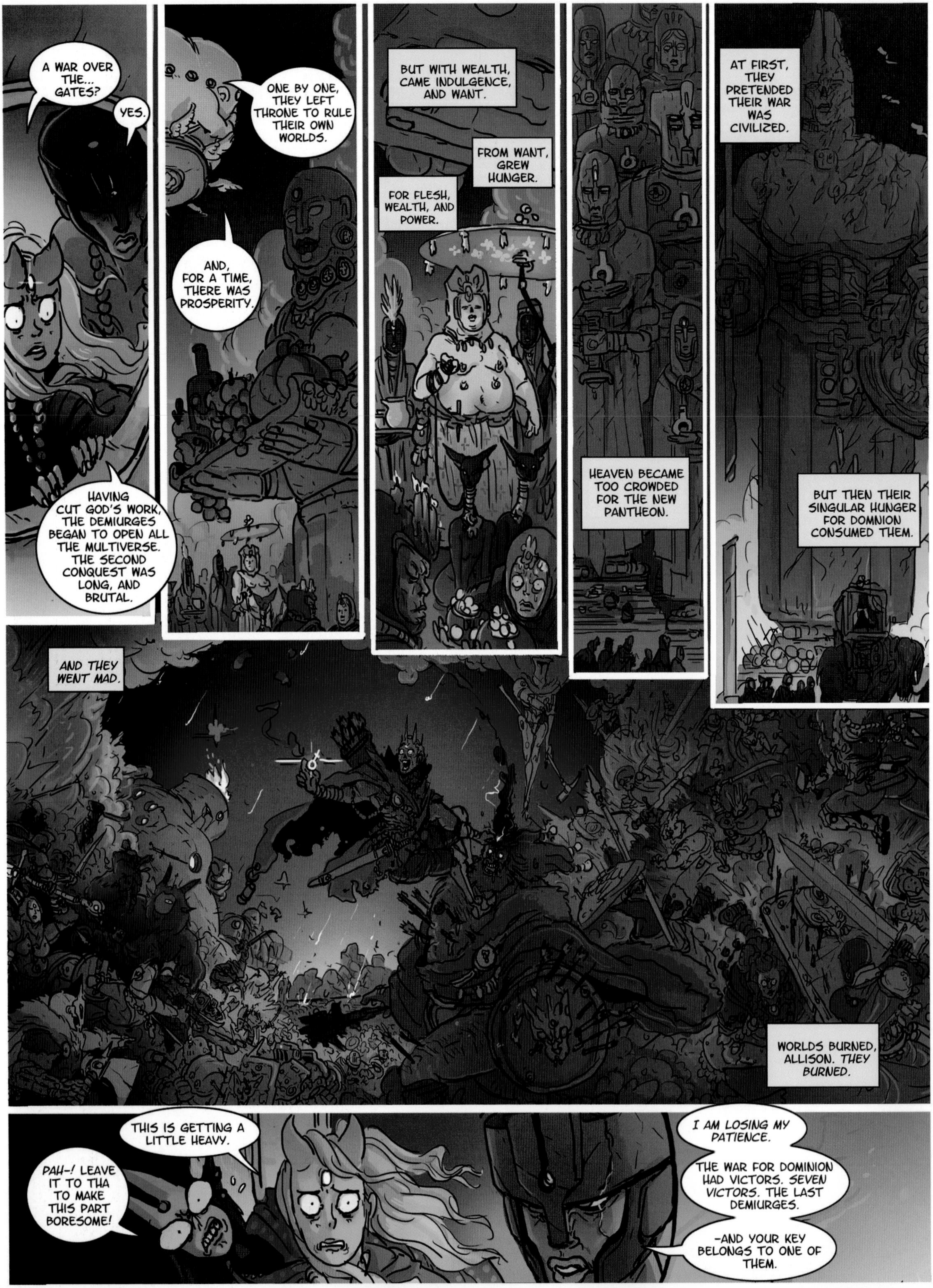
A WAR OVER THE... GATES?
YES.
HAVING CUT GOD'S WORK, THE DEMIURGES BEGAN TO OPEN ALL THE MULTIVERSE. THE SECOND CONQUEST WAS LONG, AND BRUTAL.
ONE BY ONE, THEY LEFT THRONE TO RULE THEIR OWN WORLDS.
AND, FOR A TIME, THERE WAS PROSPERITY.
BUT WITH WEALTH, CAME INDULGENCE, AND WANT.
FROM WANT, GREW HUNGER.
FOR FLESH, WEALTH, AND POWER.
HEAVEN BECAME TOO CROWDED FOR THE NEW PANTHEON.
AT FIRST, THEY PRETENDED THEIR WAR WAS CIVILIZED.
BUT THEN THEIR SINGULAR HUNGER FOR DOMNION CONSUMED THEM.
AND THEY WENT MAD.
WORLDS BURNED, ALLISON. THEY BURNED.
THIS IS GETTING A LITTLE HEAVY.
PAH-! LEAVE IT TO THA TO MAKE THIS PART BORESOME!
I AM LOSING MY PATIENCE.
THE WAR FOR DOMINION HAD VICTORS. SEVEN VICTORS. THE LAST DEMIURGES.
-AND YOUR KEY BELONGS TO ONE OF THEM.

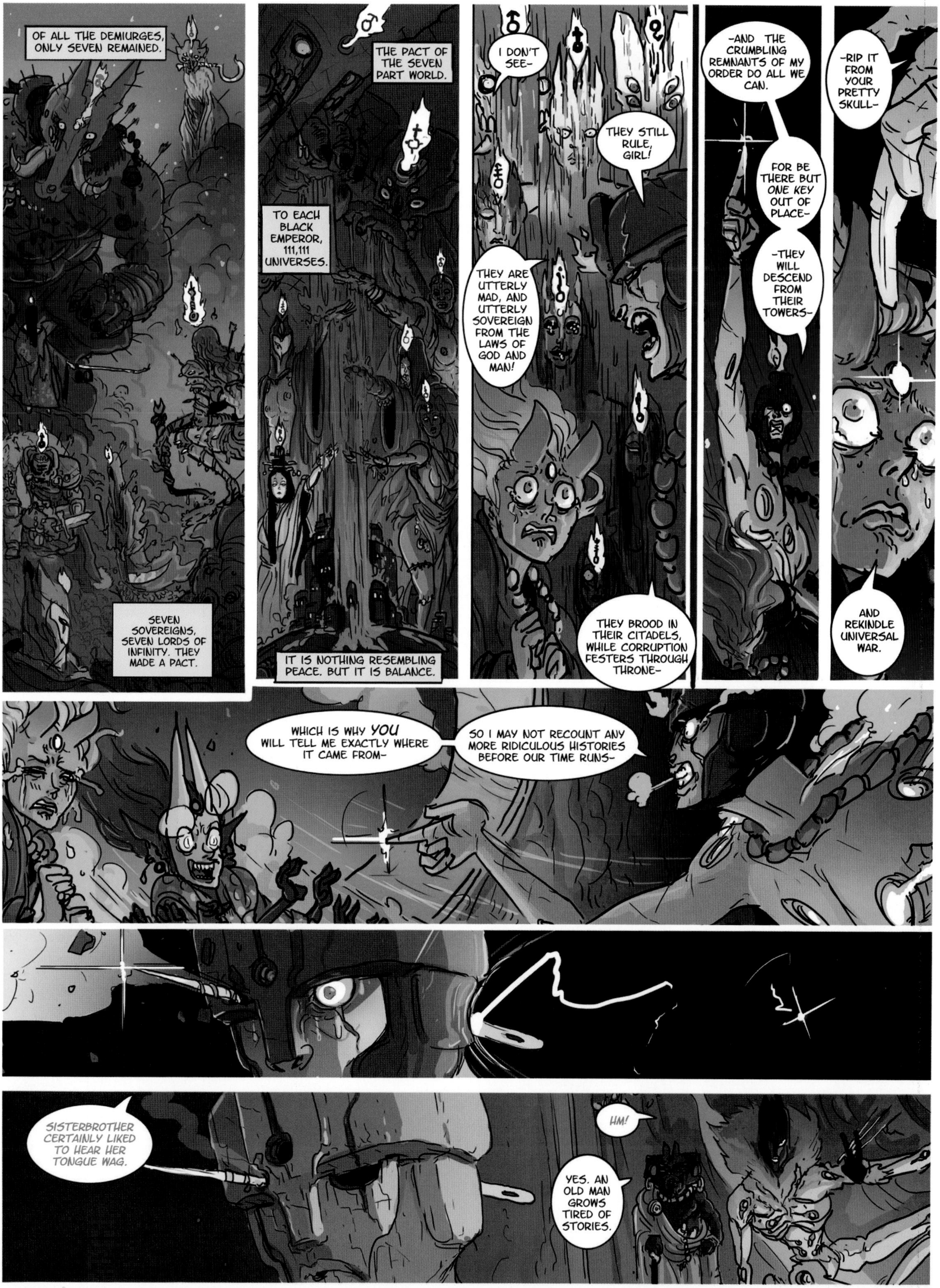
OF ALL THE DEMIURGES, ONLY SEVEN REMAINED.
SEVEN SOVEREIGNS, SEVEN LORDS OF INFINITY. THEY MADE A PACT.
THE PACT OF THE SEVEN PART WORLD.
TO EACH BLACK EMPEROR, 111,111 UNIVERSES.
IT IS NOTHING RESEMBLING PEACE. BUT IT IS BALANCE.
I DON'T SEE-
THEY STILL RULE, GIRL!
THEY ARE UTTERLY MAD, AND UTTERLY SOVEREIGN FROM THE LAWS OF GOD AND MAN!
THEY BROOD IN THEIR CITADELS, WHILE CORRUPTION FESTERS THROUGH THRONE-
-AND THE CRUMBLING REMNANTS OF MY ORDER DO ALL WE CAN.
FOR BE THERE BUT ONE KEY OUT OF PLACE-
-THEY WILL DESCEND FROM THEIR TOWERS-
-RIP IT FROM YOUR PRETTY SKULL-
AND REKINDLE UNIVERSAL WAR.
WHICH IS WHY YOU WILL TELL ME EXACTLY WHERE IT CAME FROM-
SO I MAY NOT RECOUNT ANY MORE RIDICULOUS HISTORIES BEFORE OUR TIME RUNS-
SISTERBROTHER CERTAINLY LIKED TO HEAR HER TONGUE WAG.
HM!
YES. AN OLD MAN GROWS TIRED OF STORIES.

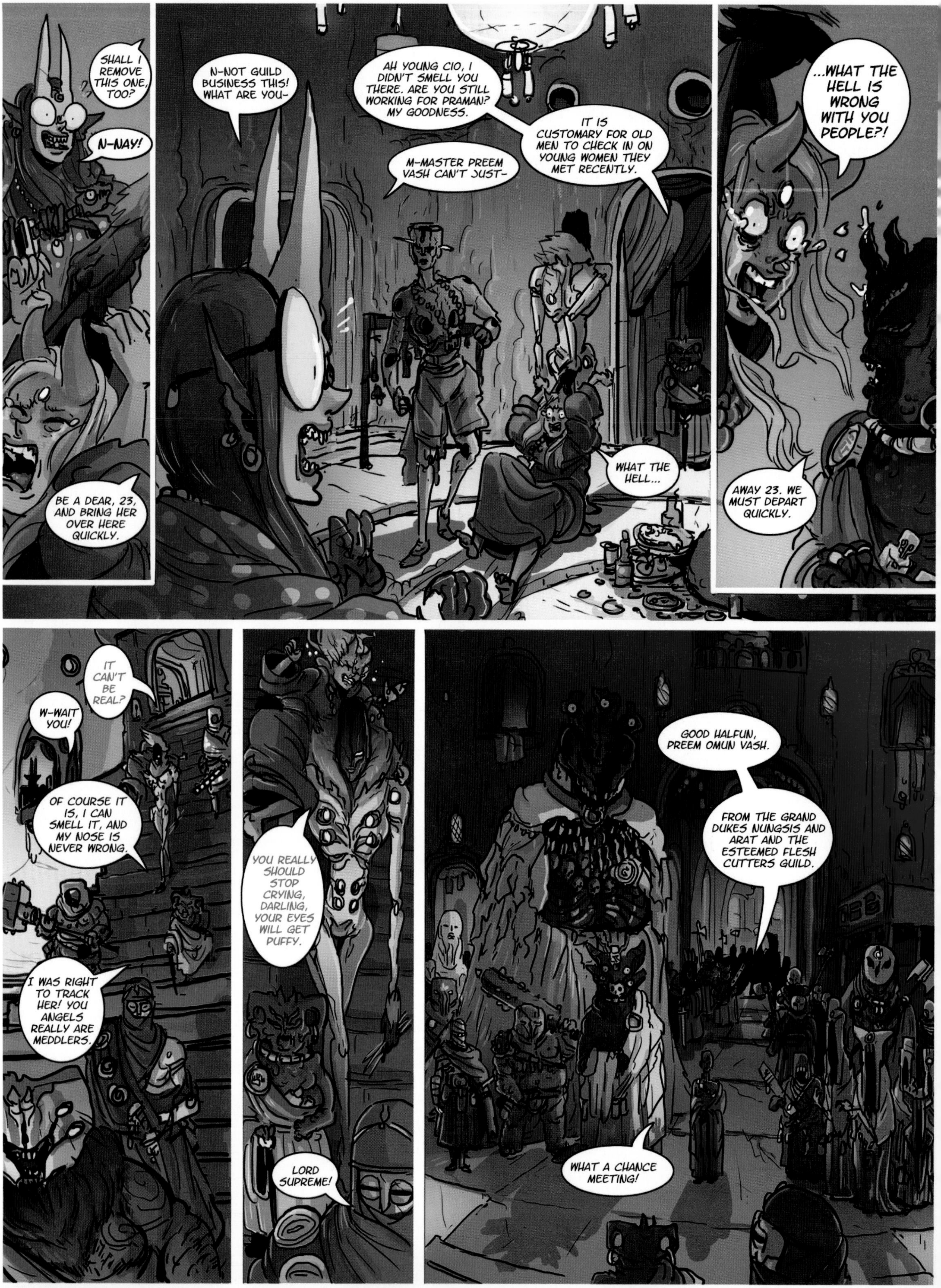
SHALL I REMOVE THIS ONE, TOO?
N-NAY!
BE A DEAR, 23, AND BRING HER OVER HERE QUICKLY.
N-NOT GUILD BUSINESS THIS! WHAT ARE YOU-
AH YOUNG CIO, I DIDN'T SMELL YOU THERE. ARE YOU STILL WORKING FOR PRAMAN? MY GOODNESS.
M-MASTER PREEM VASH CAN'T JUST-
IT IS CUSTOMARY FOR OLD MEN TO CHECK IN ON YOUNG WOMEN THEY MET RECENTLY.
WHAT THE HELL...
...WHAT THE HELL IS WRONG WITH YOU PEOPLE?!
AWAY 23. WE MUST DEPART QUICKLY.
W-WAIT YOU!
IT CAN'T BE REAL?
OF COURSE IT IS, I CAN SMELL IT, AND MY NOSE IS NEVER WRONG.
I WAS RIGHT TO TRACK HER! YOU ANGELS REALLY ARE MEDDLERS.
YOU REALLY SHOULD STOP CRYING, DARLING, YOUR EYES WILL GET PUFFY.
LORD SUPREME!
GOOD HALFUN, PREEM OMUN VASH.
FROM THE GRAND DUKES NUNGSIS AND ARAT AND THE ESTEEMED FLESH CUTTERS GUILD.
WHAT A CHANCE MEETING!

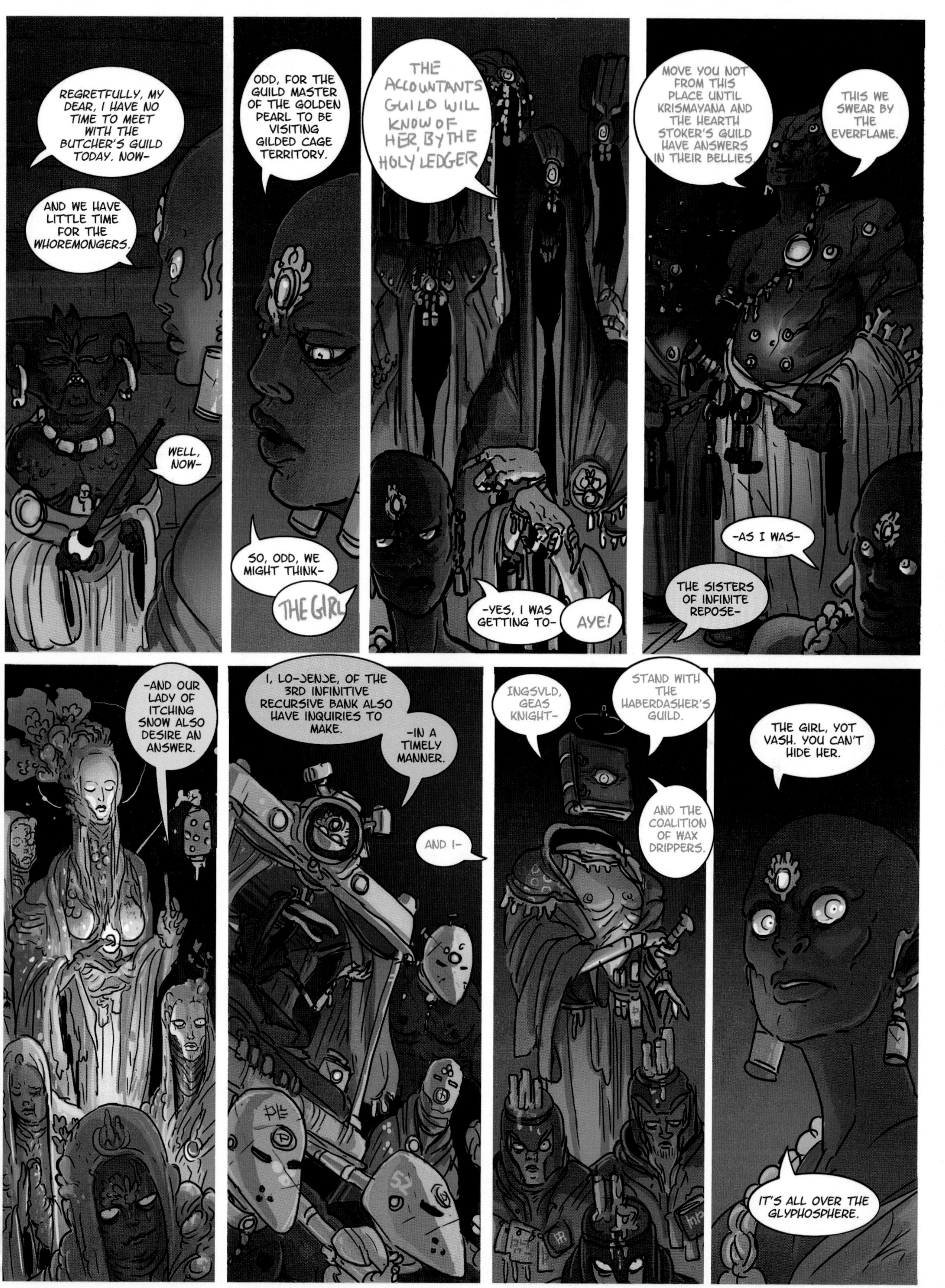
REGRETFULLY, MY DEAR, I HAVE NO TIME TO MEET WITH THE BUTCHER'S GUILD TODAY. NOW-
AND WE HAVE LITTLE TIME FOR THE WHOREMONGERS.
WELL, NOW-
ODD, FOR THE GUILD MASTER OF THE GOLDEN PEARL TO BE VISITING GILDED CAGE TERRITORY.
SO, ODD, WE MIGHT THINK-
THE GIRL
THE ACCOUNTANTS GUILD WILL KNOW OF HER, BY THE HOLY LEDGER
-YES, I WAS GETTING TO-
AYE!
MOVE YOU NOT FROM THIS PLACE UNTIL KRISMAYANA AND THE HEARTH STOKER'S GUILD HAVE ANSWERS IN THEIR BELLIES.
THIS WE SWEAR BY THE EVERFLAME.
-AS I WAS-
THE SISTERS OF INFINITE REPOSE-
-AND OUR LADY OF ITCHING SNOW ALSO DESIRE AN ANSWER.
I, LO-JENJE, OF THE 3RD INFINITIVE RECURSIVE BANK ALSO HAVE INQUIRIES TO MAKE.
-IN A TIMELY MANNER.
AND I-
INGSVLD, GEAS KNIGHT-
STAND WITH THE HABERDASHER'S GUILD.
AND THE COALITION OF WAX DRIPPERS.
THE GIRL, YOT VASH. YOU CAN'T HIDE HER.
IT'S ALL OVER THE GLYPHOSPHERE.

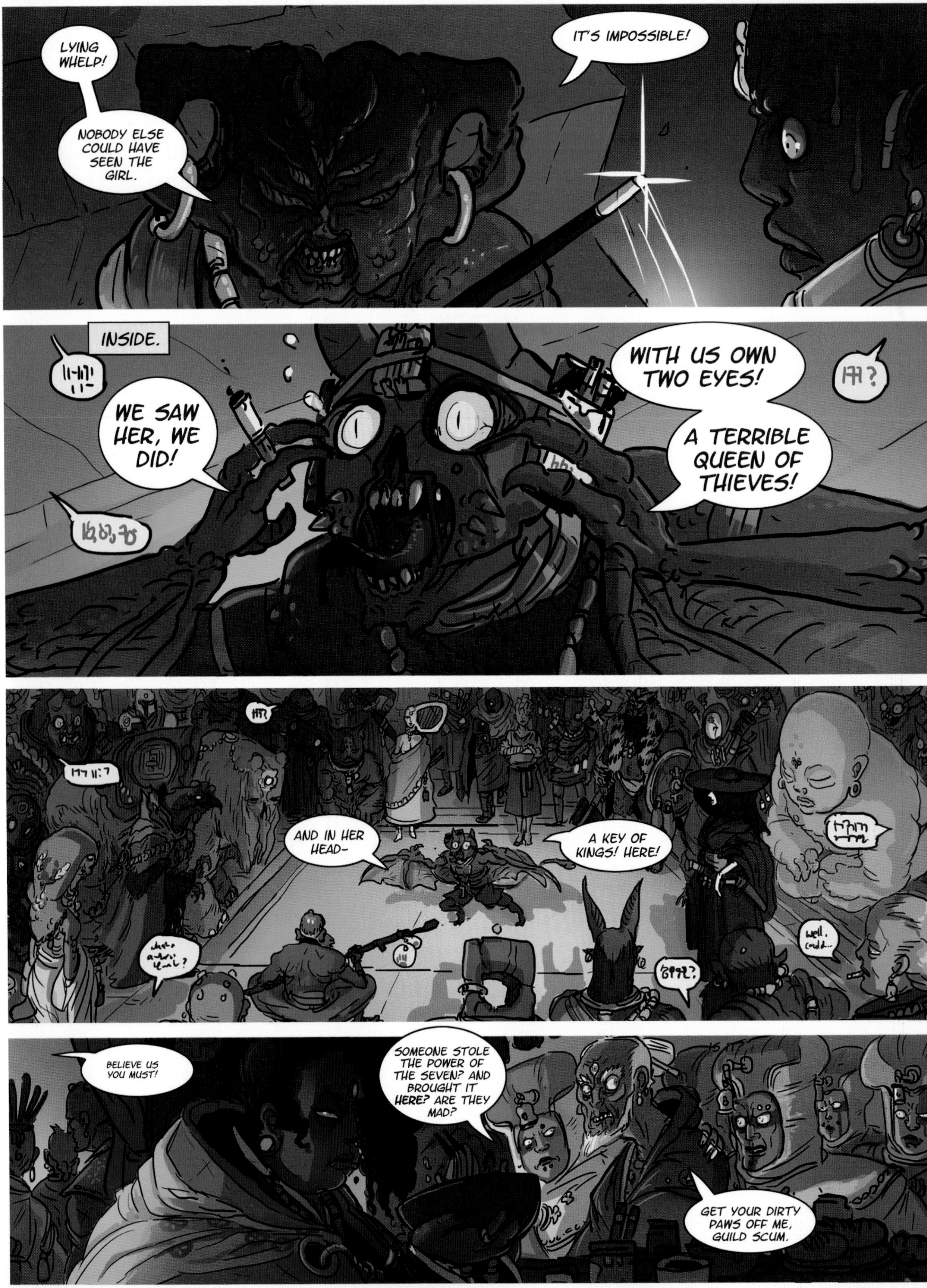
LYING WHELP!
NOBODY ELSE COULD HAVE SEEN THE GIRL.
IT'S IMPOSSIBLE!
INSIDE.
WE SAW HER, WE DID!
WITH US OWN TWO EYES!
A TERRIBLE QUEEN OF THIEVES!
AND IN HER HEAD-
A KEY OF KINGS! HERE!
Well. could...
BELIEVE US YOU MUST!
SOMEONE STOLE THE POWER OF THE SEVEN? AND BROUGHT IT HERE? ARE THEY MAD?
GET YOUR DIRTY PAWS OFF ME, GUILD SCUM.

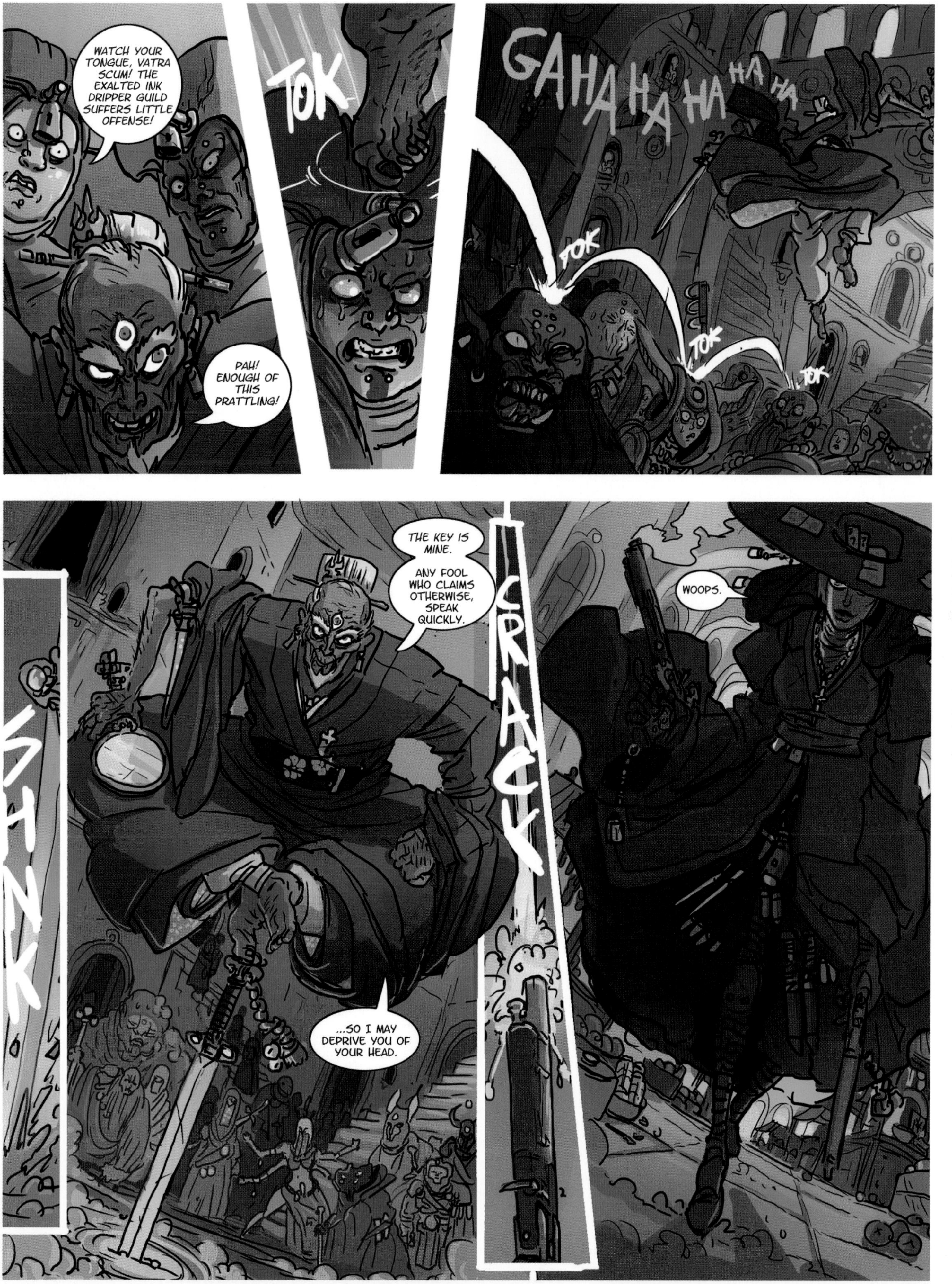
WATCH YOUR TONGUE, VATRA SCUM! THE EXALTED INK DRIPPER GUILD SUFFERS LITTLE OFFENSE!
PAH! ENOUGH OF THIS PRATTLING!
TOK
GAHAHAHAHAHA
TOK
TOK
TOK
THE KEY IS MINE.
ANY FOOL WHO CLAIMS OTHERWISE, SPEAK QUICKLY.
...SO I MAY DEPRIVE YOU OF YOUR HEAD.
SHNK
CRACK
WOOPS.

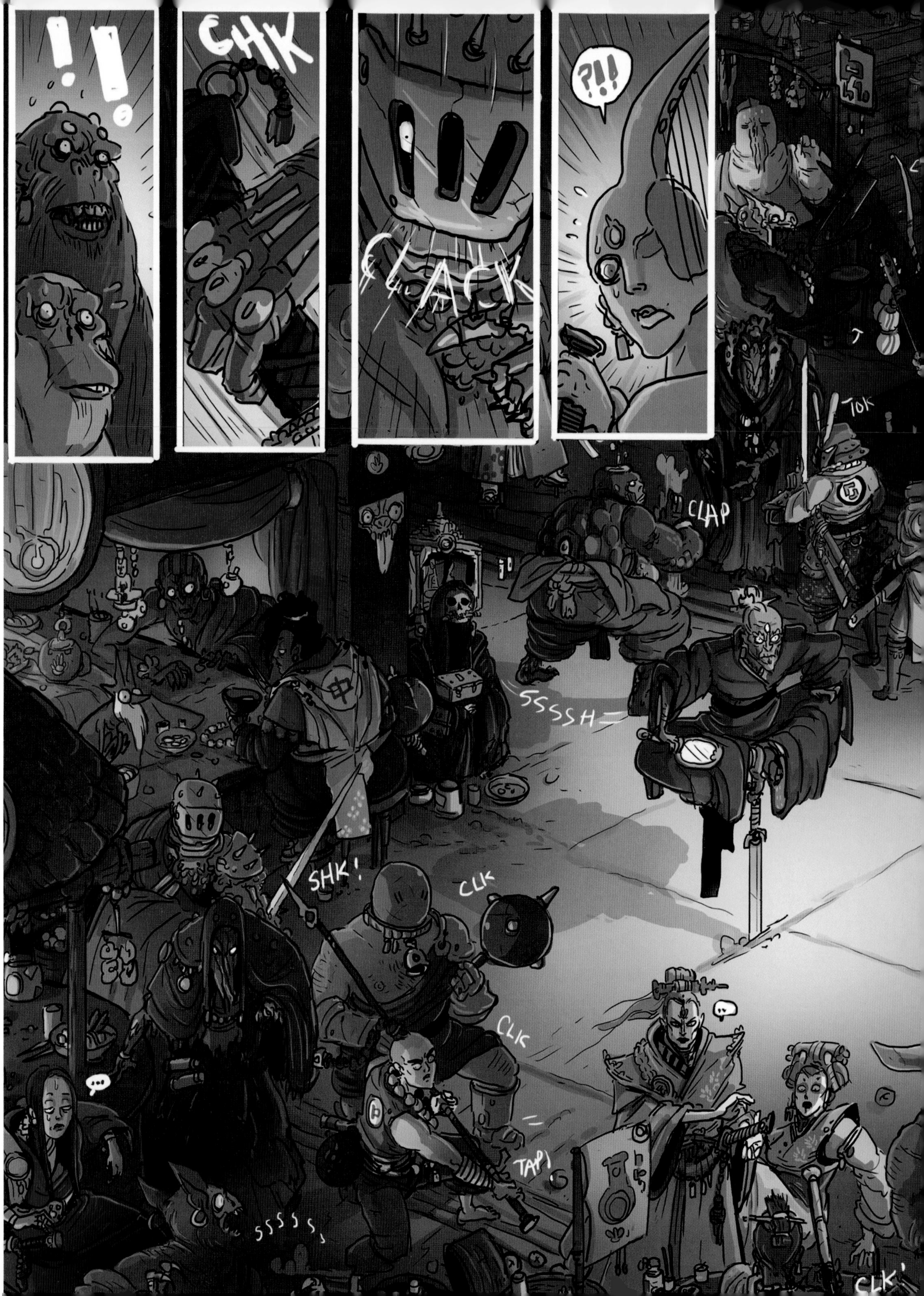
!!
CHK
CLACK
?!!
TOK
CLAP
SSSSH
SHK!
CLK
CLK
TAP!
SSSSS
CLK!

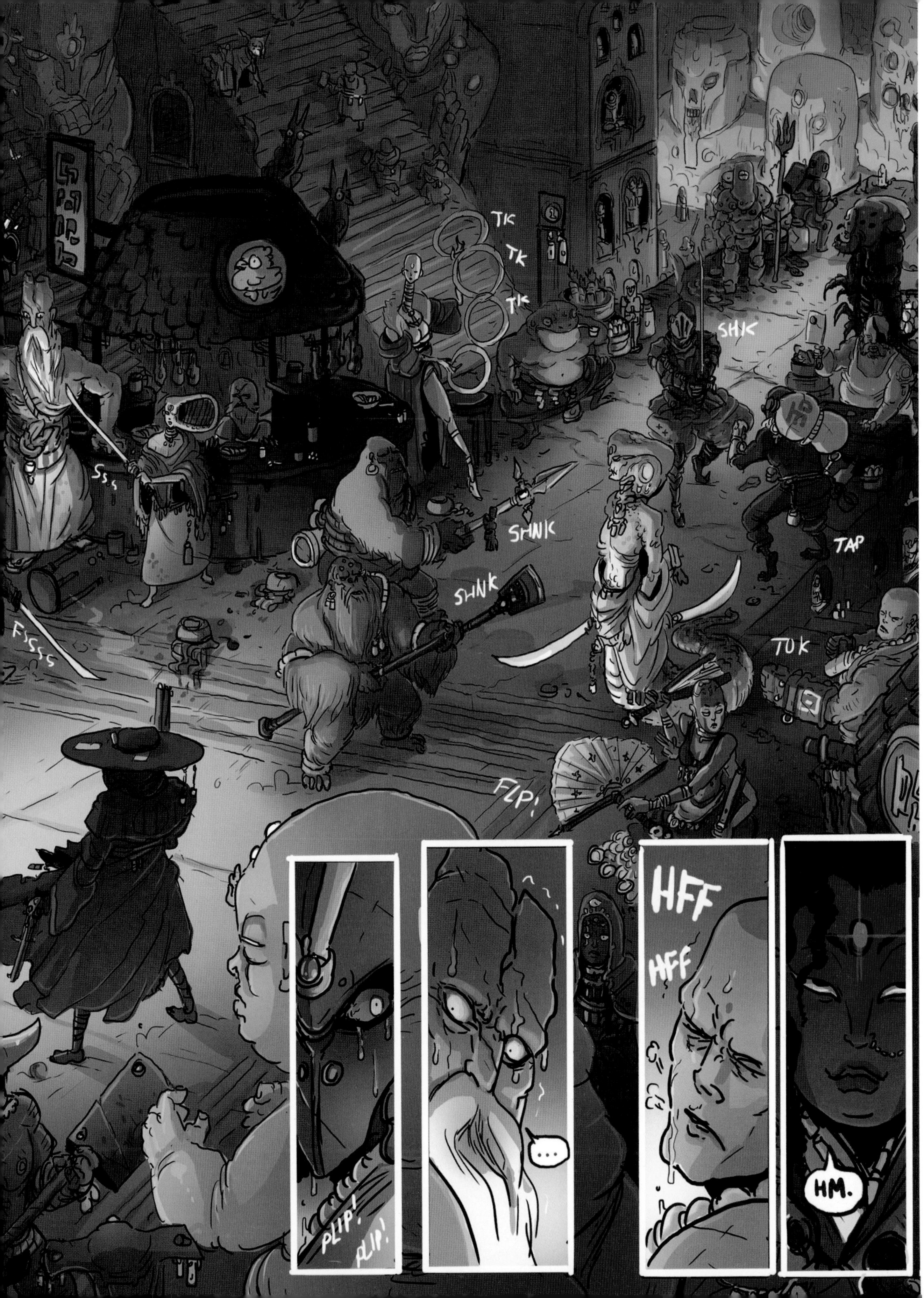
TK
TK
TK
SHK
Sss
SHNK
SHNK
TAP
FSSSS
TUK
FLP!
PLIP!
PLIP!
...
HFF
HFF
HM.

THE GRAND ENEMY CALLED I

iii. *The Lie of the Water House*

YISUN and Hansa walked the king's road once, drinking plum wine. "Dearest Un-Hansa," spoke YISUN, after a moment, as they strolled along an expanse of fractal glass and cold fire, "Art thou not flesh of my self-love? Springst thou not from my recursive womb?"

"Sprung I from your brow, for it is my lot in life to beat my hands against it in return for ejecting me," said Hansa, in jest, but in truth he listened.

"Knowst thou the meaning of my name Y-S-U-N is the true name of sovereignty?" spoke YISUN plainly.

"I do," spoke Hansa, for it was true.

YISUN then assumed a speaking form that was bright and very cold. From her breath she inhaled the void, and when she exhaled, beautiful water came forth from her pliant lips in great rushing gasps, and there was a sound like a clear bell that meant emptiness. Hansa was very moved by this display and watched as the shining water curved and bent upon itself and crystallized, and suddenly before the pair was a great, beautiful house, translucent and all filled with light of many colors.

"Observe my work," said YISUN, pleased. "It is an astounding work," said Hansa, clearly impressed. They strode inside the house at YISUN's bidding. The walls were clear and smooth as crystal, and warm to the touch. It had a wide hall, and a full hearth, and was full of light and air, and the openness of the place with the starkness of the void was incredibly pleasing. Hansa would have given half his lordship for such a house, in truth, for his own was a dark and cramped tomb of iron and dust.

"Observe again," said YISUN, with a keen eye. Hansa did, and as he looked closer, he saw the walls, the floor, the vaulted roof, the wall coverings, and even the altar with the flowers in the visiting hall were all made of water — water as clear and still and solid as smooth and perfect glass.

"Water, lord?" spoke Hansa, sensing some purpose.

"What," spoke YISUN playfully, "is the meaning of this allegory?"

They reposed for a while as Hansa thought, in the resting hall of that great water house, and gazed through the shining rim of that house across the great void, where the empty sky was perfect in its nothingness. The house rung gently like a bell and it was pleasing to Hansa as he sat in his flesh and thought.

After a while, he said this:

"The house is a man's life."

"Why this?" answered YISUN, as was the fashion.

"Because although it is very beautiful and filled with many fine things, it is only water, after all. It would be poor to rely on its existence — it is only water pretending to be a house. In truth, there is no real house here at all, just as there is no Hansa, or no plums."

"This is a good answer," said YISUN, and made a small motion with her fingers, and smiled.

"It is an infuriating answer," said Hansa, his mood darkening, and his brow furrowing, "As is common with you. How can one grant themselves the pleasure to enjoy such a fine thing? It sparkles and shines like a gorgeous jewel, but its sparkle is an intimate falsehood."

"Death is my gift to you," spoke YISUN in reply.

"What's the point," spoke Hansa, bitterly, "of such a fine house, if it is only a lie? What is the point of Hansa, if Hansa is only a lie?"

"I am a fine liar," spoke YISUN in reply.

Hansa was silent a moment.

"It is a beautiful house," he admitted, after some time. "It is a beautiful lie."

"Our self-realization is the most beautiful lie there is. I am the most conceited and prime liar. Lies are the enemy of stagnation and my self-salvation. How could we appreciate the shining beauty of my house of lies," spoke YISUN, "if there was always such a house? How could we appreciate Hansa if there was always such a Hansa?"

They sat in stillness a while longer.

"In truth, we would get very bored," said Hansa, after a while.

"In truth, we would," said YISUN.

-Psalms

THE GRAND ENEMY CALLED I

iv. The Lie of the Small Light

Hansa was of sound mind and proud soul and only once asked YISUN a conceited question, when he was
very old and his bones were set about with dust and bent with age. It was about his own death.
"Lord," said Hansa, allowing a doubt to blossom, "what is ending?"
It was said later he regretted this question but none could confirm the suspicion.
"Ending is a small light in a vast cavern growing dim," said YISUN, plainly, as was the manner.
"When the light goes out, what will happen to the cavern?"
"It and the universe will cease to exist, for how can we see anything without any light, no matter how small?"
said YISUN. Hansa was somewhat dismayed, but sensed a lesson, as was the manner.
"Darkness is the natural state of caverns," said he, vexingly. "If I were a cavern, I would be glad to be rid of
the pest of light and exist obstinately anyway!"
"Hansa is observant," said YISUN.

-Psalms

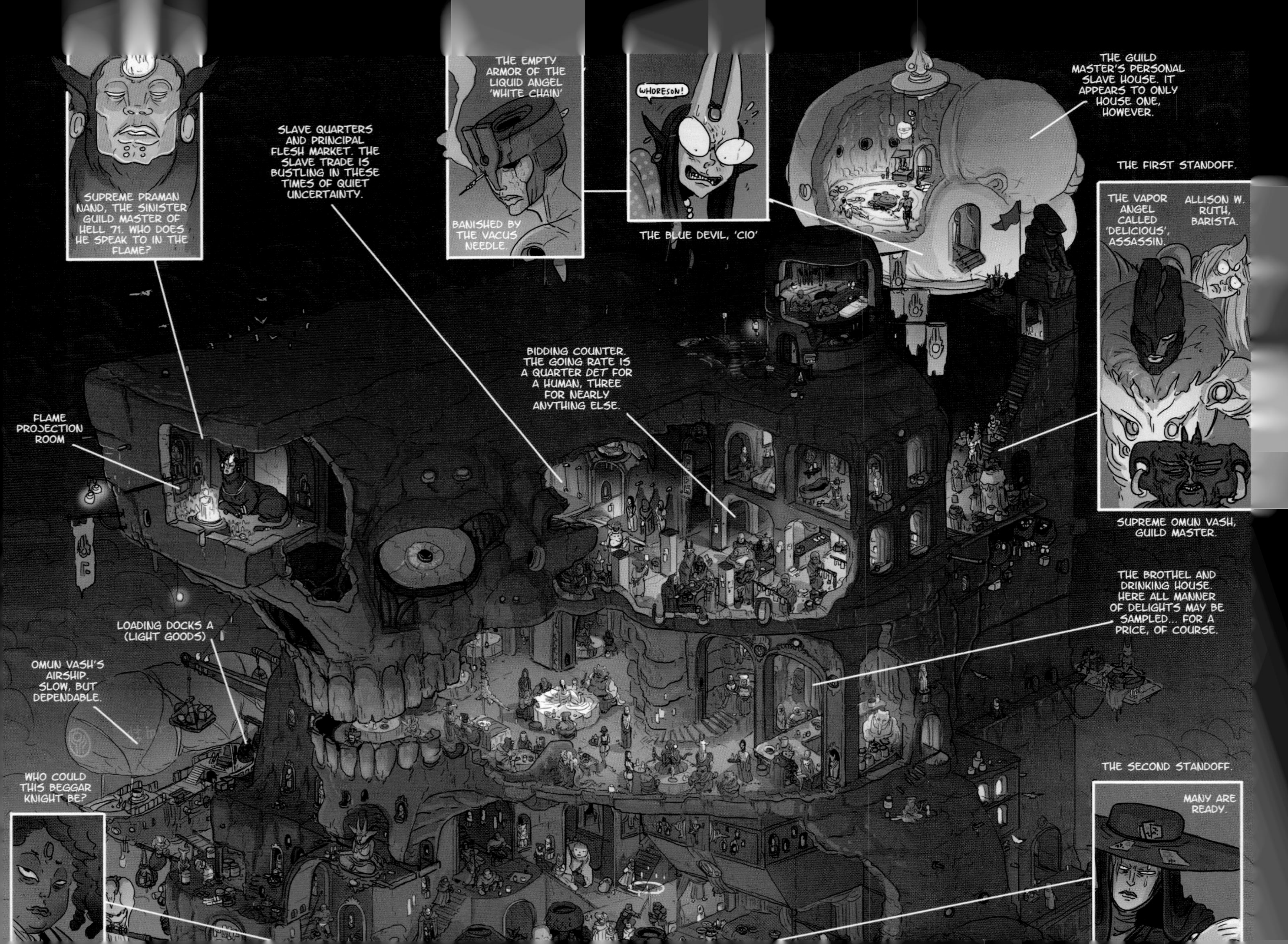
SUPREME PRAMAN NAND, THE SINISTER GUILD MASTER OF HELL 71. WHO DOES HE SPEAK TO IN THE FLAME?
THE EMPTY ARMOR OF THE LIQUID ANGEL 'WHITE CHAIN'
BANISHED BY THE VACUS NEEDLE.
WHORESON!
THE BLUE DEVIL, 'CIO'
THE GUILD MASTER'S PERSONAL SLAVE HOUSE. IT APPEARS TO ONLY HOUSE ONE, HOWEVER.
THE FIRST STANDOFF.
THE VAPOR ANGEL CALLED 'DELICIOUS', ASSASSIN.
ALLISON W. RUTH, BARISTA.
SUPREME OMUN VASH, GUILD MASTER.
SLAVE QUARTERS AND PRINCIPAL FLESH MARKET. THE SLAVE TRADE IS BUSTLING IN THESE TIMES OF QUIET UNCERTAINTY.
BIDDING COUNTER. THE GOING RATE IS A QUARTER DET FOR A HUMAN, THREE FOR NEARLY ANYTHING ELSE.
FLAME PROJECTION ROOM
THE BROTHEL AND DRINKING HOUSE. HERE ALL MANNER OF DELIGHTS MAY BE SAMPLED... FOR A PRICE, OF COURSE.
LOADING DOCKS A (LIGHT GOODS)
OMUN VASH'S AIRSHIP. SLOW, BUT DEPENDABLE.
WHO COULD THIS BEGGAR KNIGHT BE?
THE SECOND STANDOFF.
MANY ARE READY.

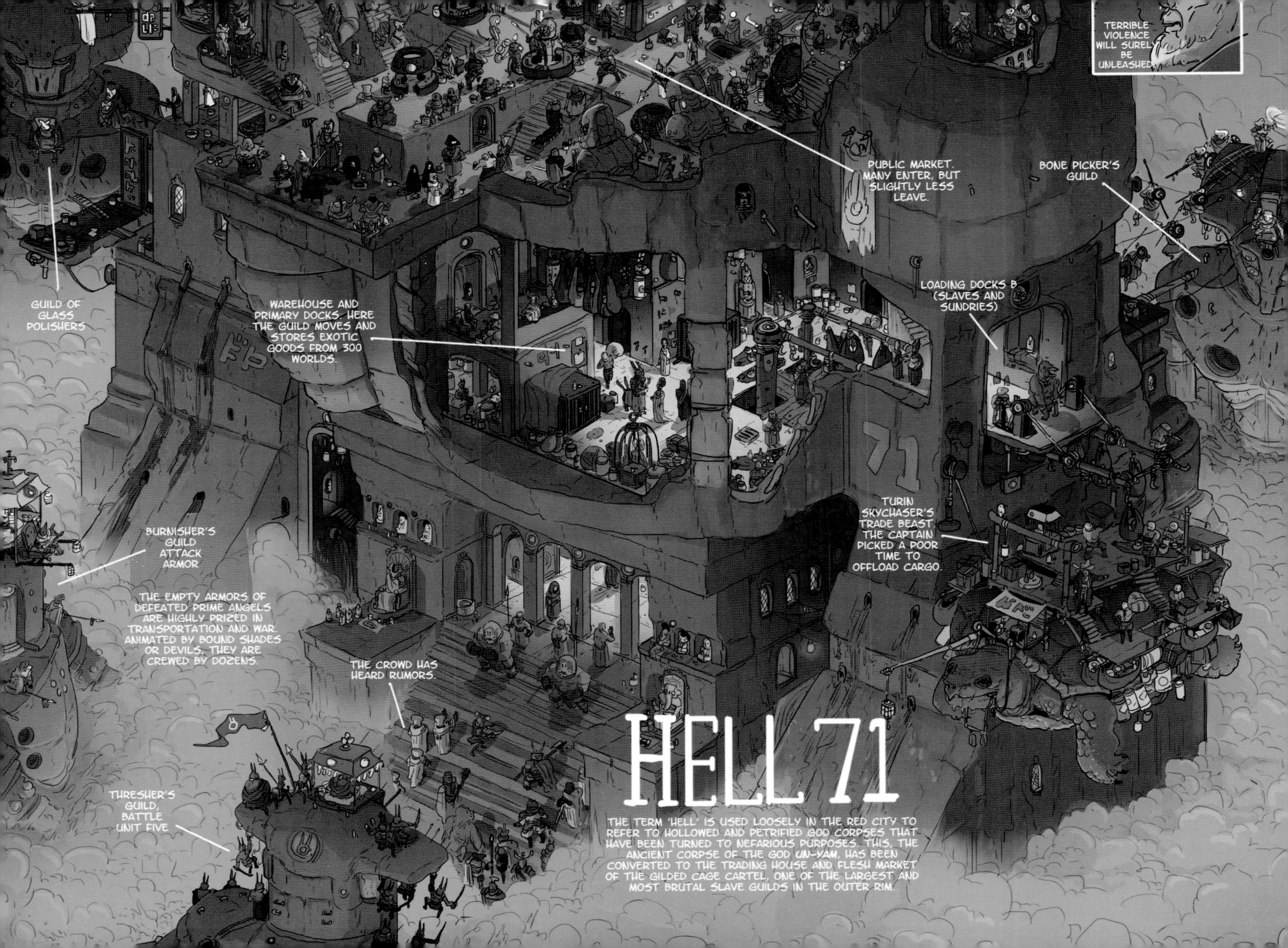
TERRIBLE VIOLENCE WILL SURELY BE UNLEASHED.
GUILD OF GLASS POLISHERS
WAREHOUSE AND PRIMARY DOCKS. HERE THE GUILD MOVES AND STORES EXOTIC GOODS FROM 300 WORLDS.
PUBLIC MARKET. MANY ENTER, BUT SLIGHTLY LESS LEAVE.
BONE PICKER'S GUILD
LOADING DOCKS B (SLAVES AND SUNDRIES)
BURNISHER'S GUILD ATTACK ARMOR
THE EMPTY ARMORS OF DEFEATED PRIME ANGELS ARE HIGHLY PRIZED IN TRANSPORTATION AND WAR. ANIMATED BY BOUND SHADES OR DEVILS. THEY ARE CREWED BY DOZENS.
TURIN SKYCHASER'S TRADE BEAST. THE CAPTAIN PICKED A POOR TIME TO OFFLOAD CARGO.
THE CROWD HAS HEARD RUMORS.
THRESHER'S GUILD, BATTLE UNIT FIVE
HELL 71
THE TERM 'HELL' IS USED LOOSELY IN THE RED CITY TO REFER TO HOLLOWED AND PETRIFIED GOD CORPSES THAT HAVE BEEN TURNED TO NEFARIOUS PURPOSES. THIS, THE ANCIENT CORPSE OF THE GOD UN-YAM, HAS BEEN CONVERTED TO THE TRADING HOUSE AND FLESH MARKET OF THE GILDED CAGE CARTEL, ONE OF THE LARGEST AND MOST BRUTAL SLAVE GUILDS IN THE OUTER RIM.

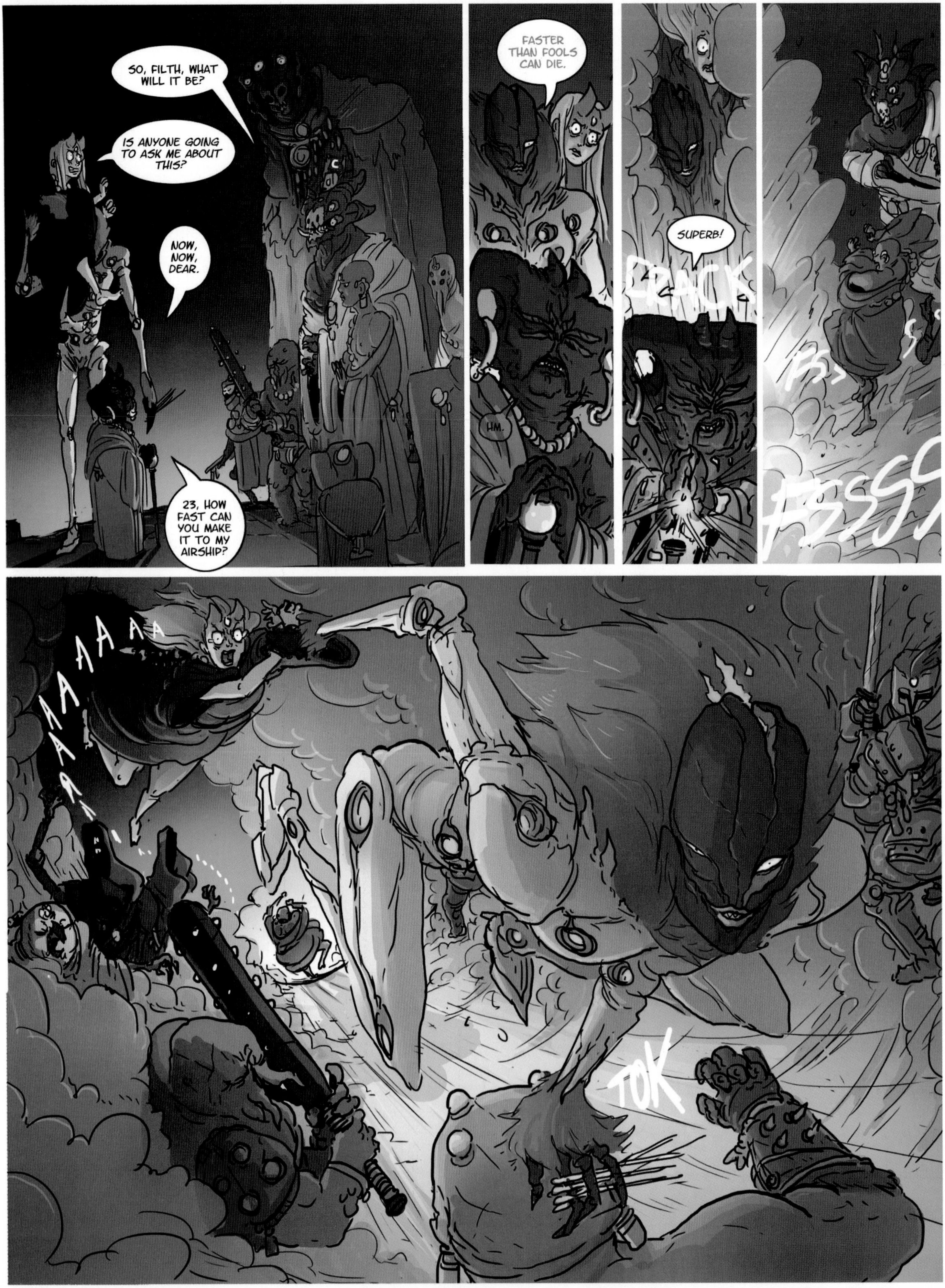

SO, FILTH, WHAT WILL IT BE?
IS ANYONE GOING TO ASK ME ABOUT THIS?
NOW, NOW, DEAR.
23, HOW FAST CAN YOU MAKE IT TO MY AIRSHIP?
FASTER THAN FOOLS CAN DIE.
HM.
SUPERB!
CRACK
FSSS
FSSSS
AAAAAA
AAAAA
TOK

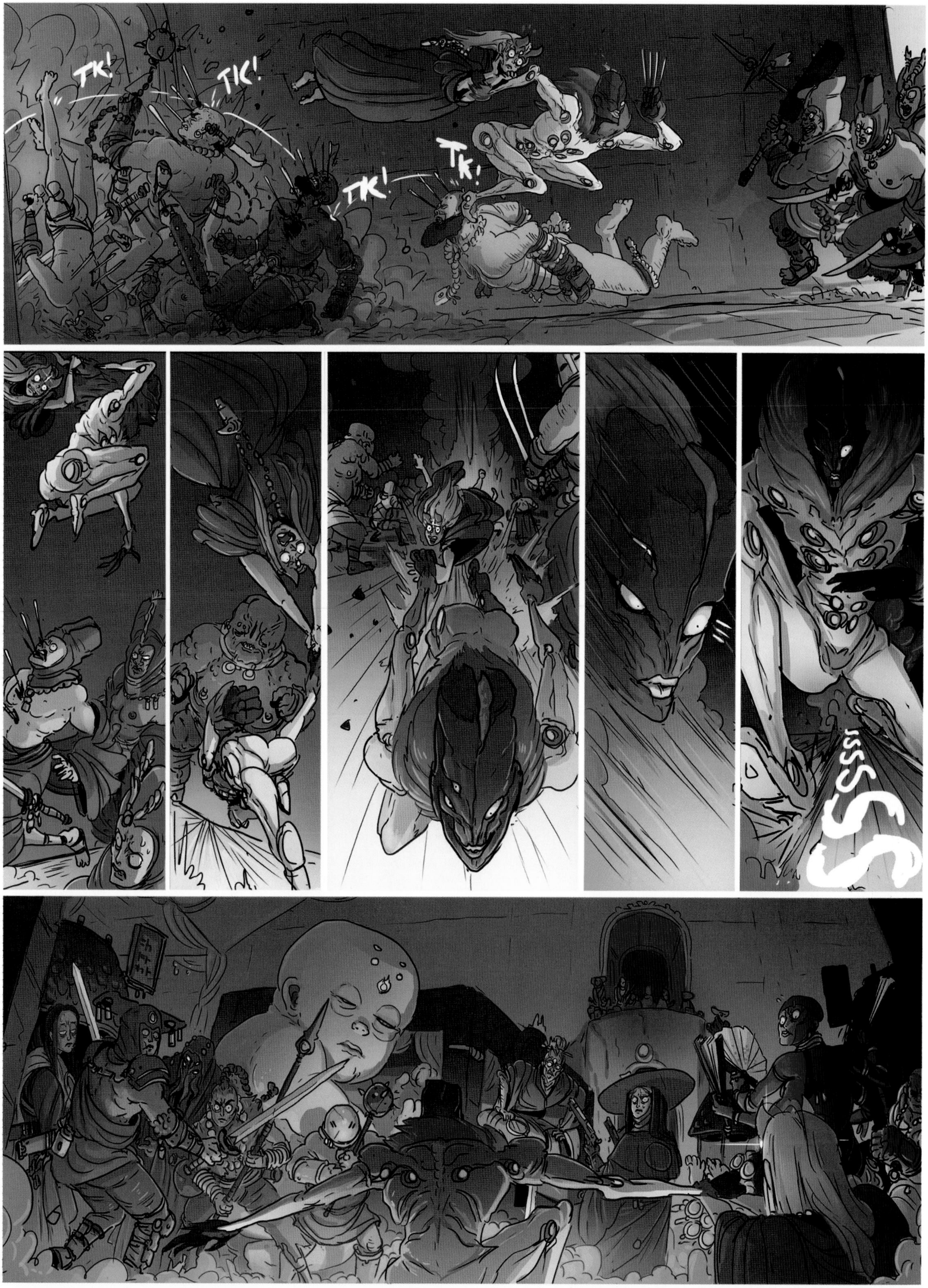
TK!
TK!
TK!
TK!
SSSS

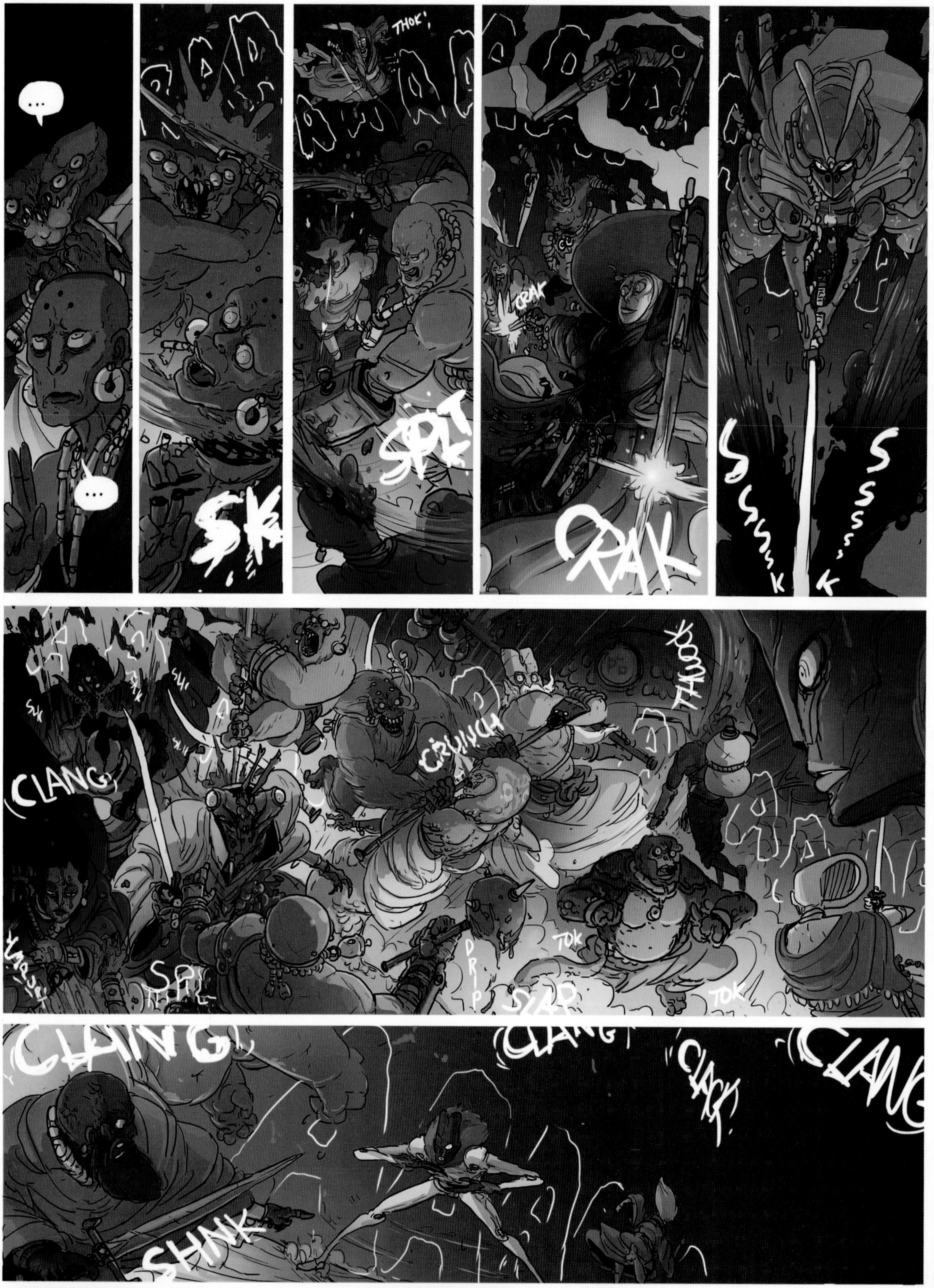

...
...
SK
THOK
SPLIT
CRAK
CRAK
SSSSSK
SSSS...K
CLANG
CRUNCH
THWOCK
SPL
DRIP
TOK
TOK
CLANG
CLANG
CLACK
CLANG
SHNK

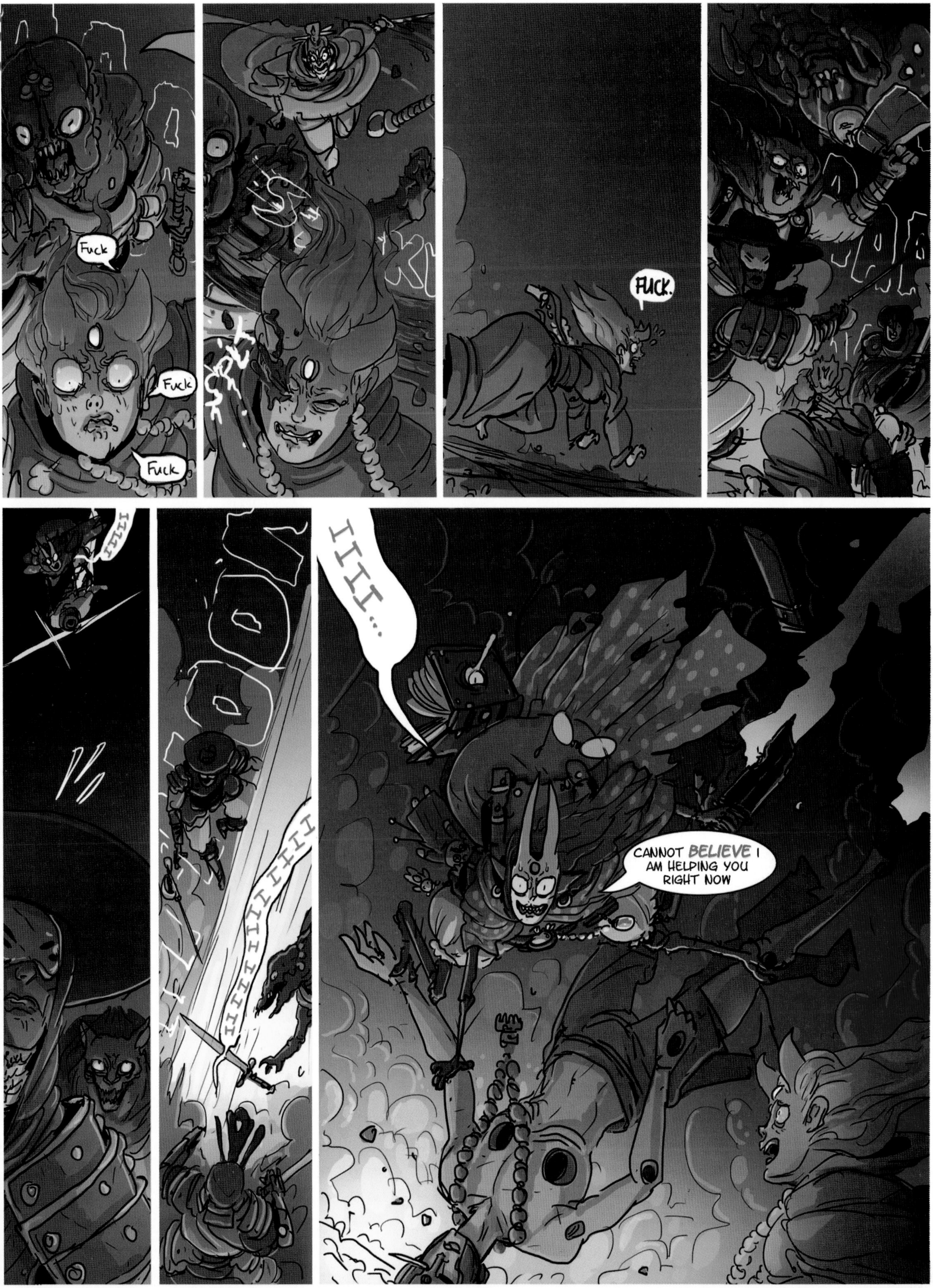

Fuck
Fuck
Fuck
FUCK.
IIIII
IIII...
IIIIIIIIIIIIIIIII
CANNOT BELIEVE I AM HELPING YOU RIGHT NOW

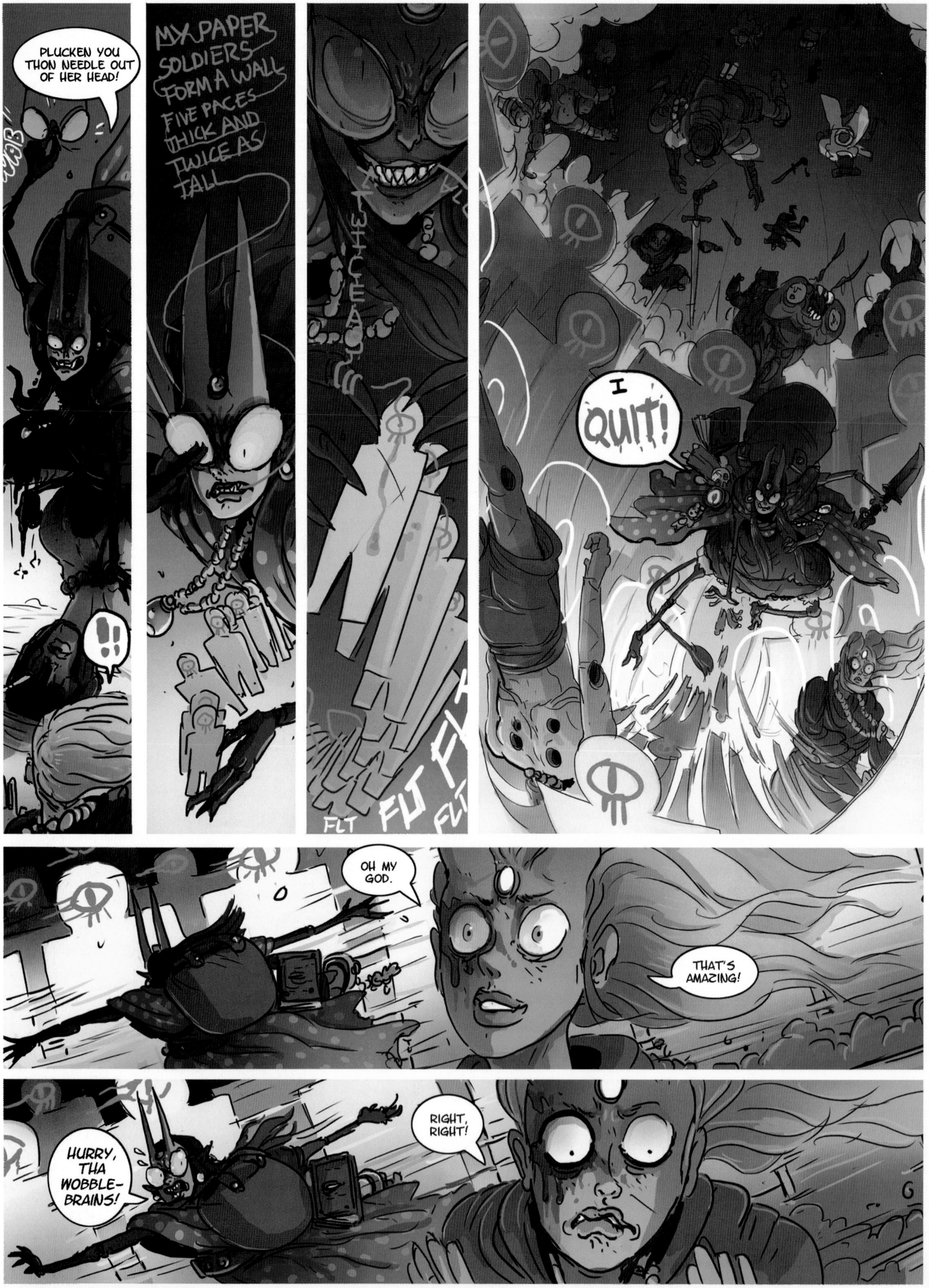
PLUCKEN YOU THON NEEDLE OUT OF HER HEAD!
!!
MY PAPER SOLDIERS FORM A WALL FIVE PACES THICK AND TWICE AS TALL
FLT FLT FLT FLT
I QUIT!
OH MY GOD.
THAT'S AMAZING!
HURRY, THA WOBBLE-BRAINS!
RIGHT, RIGHT!

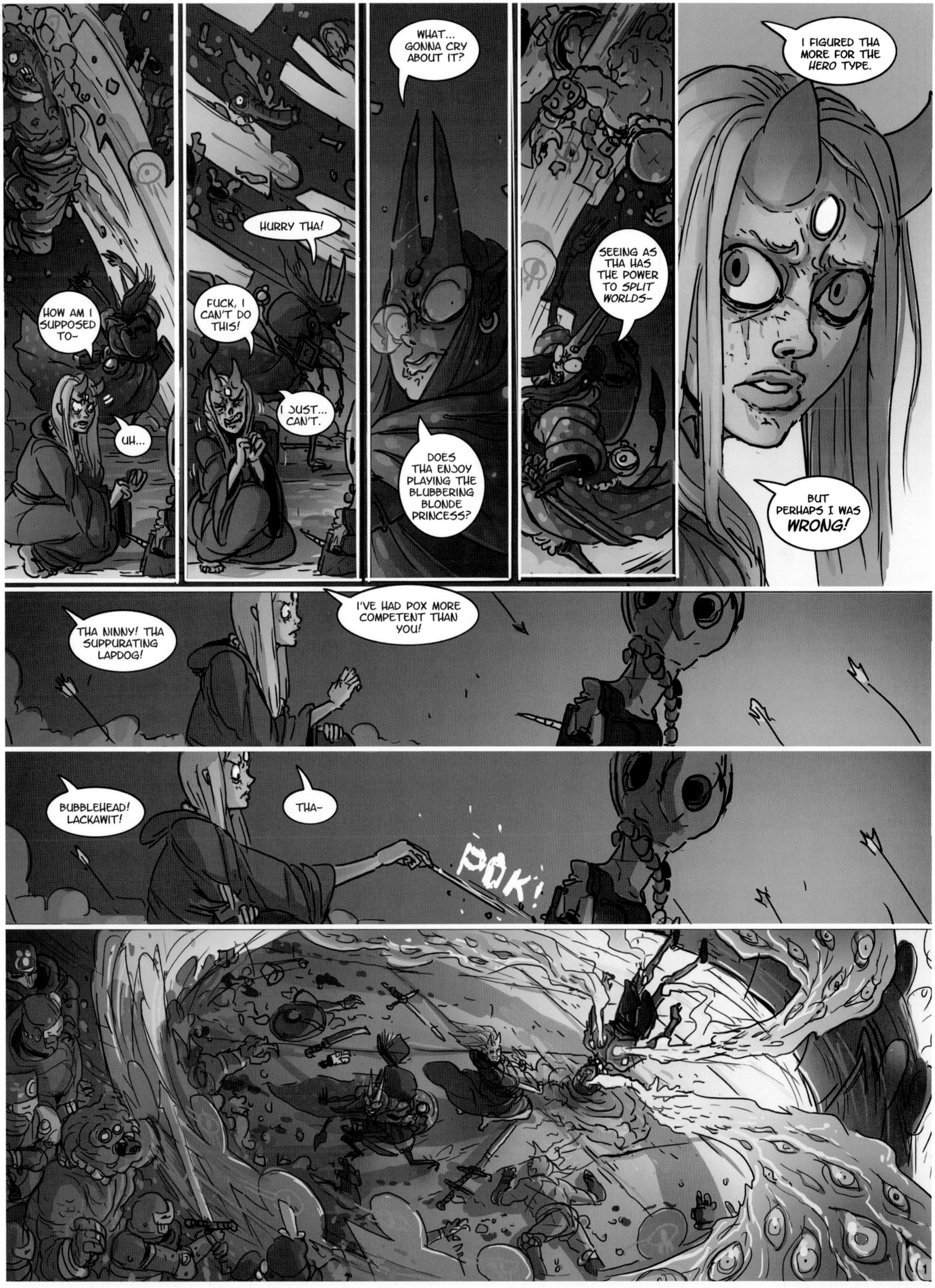
HOW AM I SUPPOSED TO-
UH...
HURRY THA!
FUCK, I CAN'T DO THIS!
I JUST... CAN'T.
WHAT... GONNA CRY ABOUT IT?
DOES THA ENJOY PLAYING THE BLUBBERING BLONDE PRINCESS?
SEEING AS THA HAS THE POWER TO SPLIT WORLDS-
I FIGURED THA MORE FOR THE HERO TYPE.
BUT PERHAPS I WAS WRONG!
THA NINNY! THA SUPPURATING LAPDOG!
I'VE HAD POX MORE COMPETENT THAN YOU!
BUBBLEHEAD! LACKAWIT!
THA-
POK!

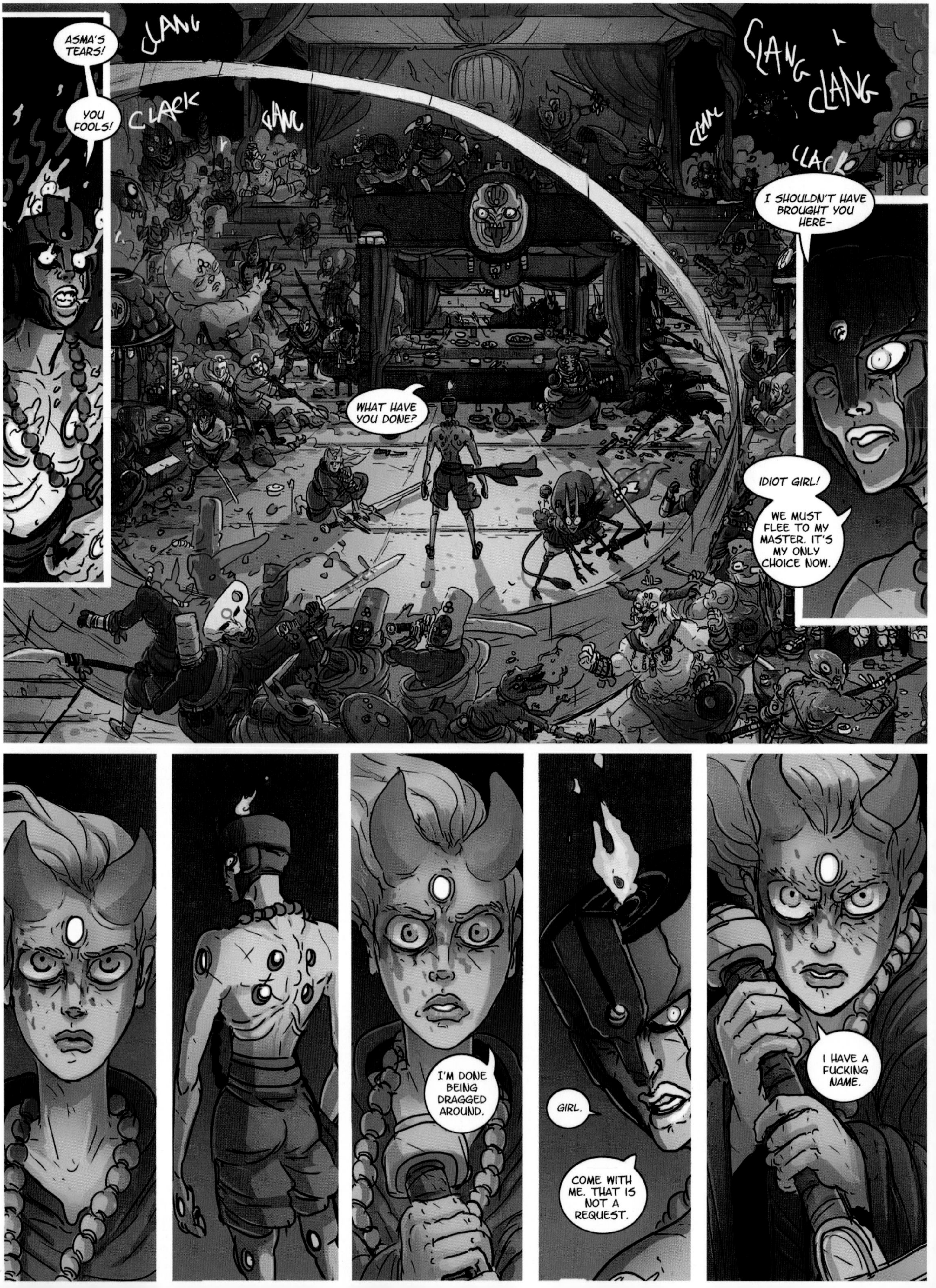
ASMA'S TEARS!
YOU FOOLS!
CLANG
CLARK
CLANG
CLANG
CLANG CLANG
CLANG
CLACK
I SHOULDN'T HAVE BROUGHT YOU HERE-
WHAT HAVE YOU DONE?
IDIOT GIRL!
WE MUST FLEE TO MY MASTER. IT'S MY ONLY CHOICE NOW.
I'M DONE BEING DRAGGED AROUND.
GIRL.
COME WITH ME. THAT IS NOT A REQUEST.
I HAVE A FUCKING NAME.

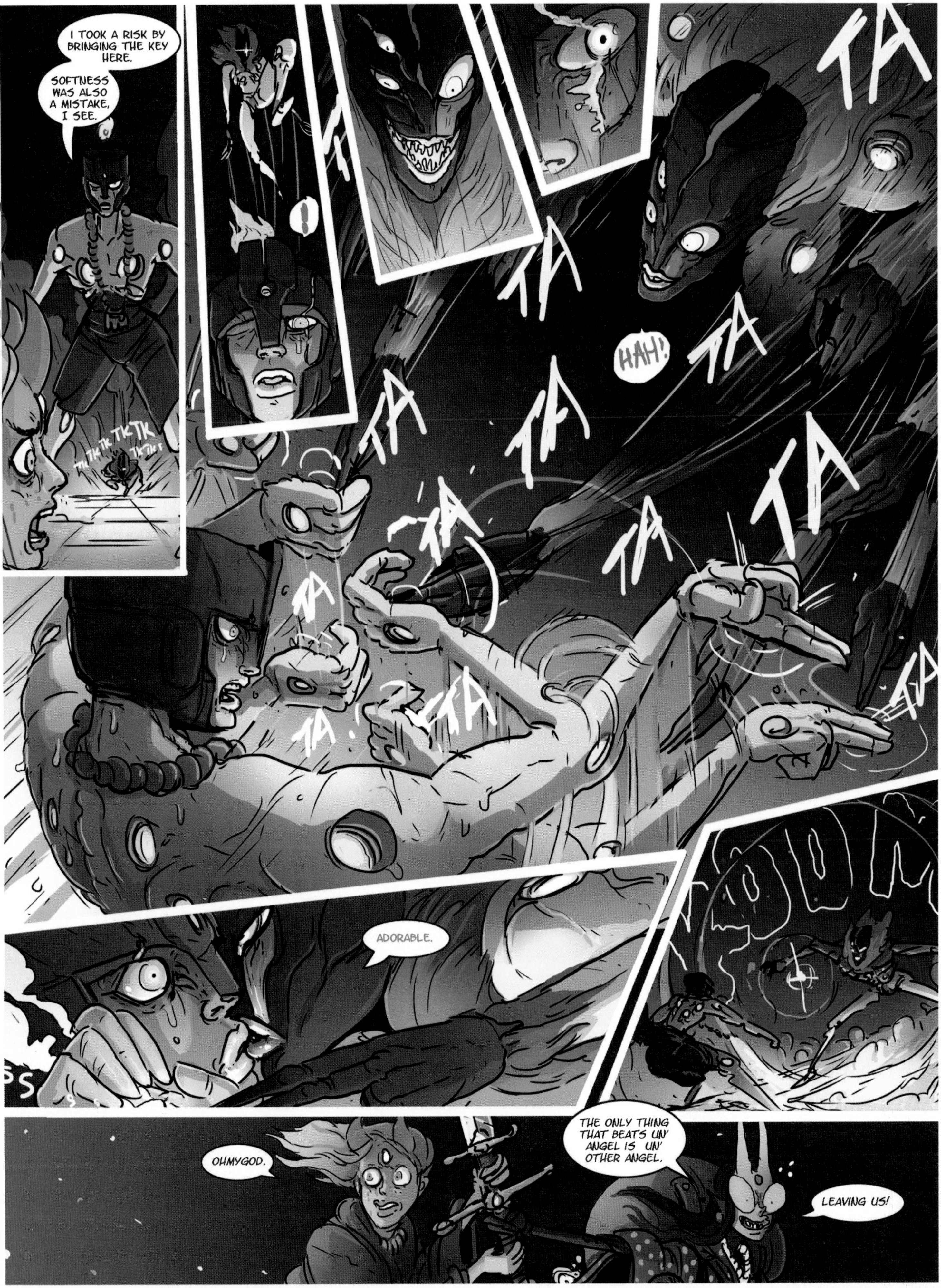
I TOOK A RISK BY BRINGING THE KEY HERE.
SOFTNESS WAS ALSO A MISTAKE, I SEE.
TKTKTK
!
TA TA TA TA TA TA TA TA TA TA TA TA TA TA
HAH!
ADORABLE.
OHMYGOD.
THE ONLY THING THAT BEATS UN' ANGEL IS UN' OTHER ANGEL.
LEAVING US!

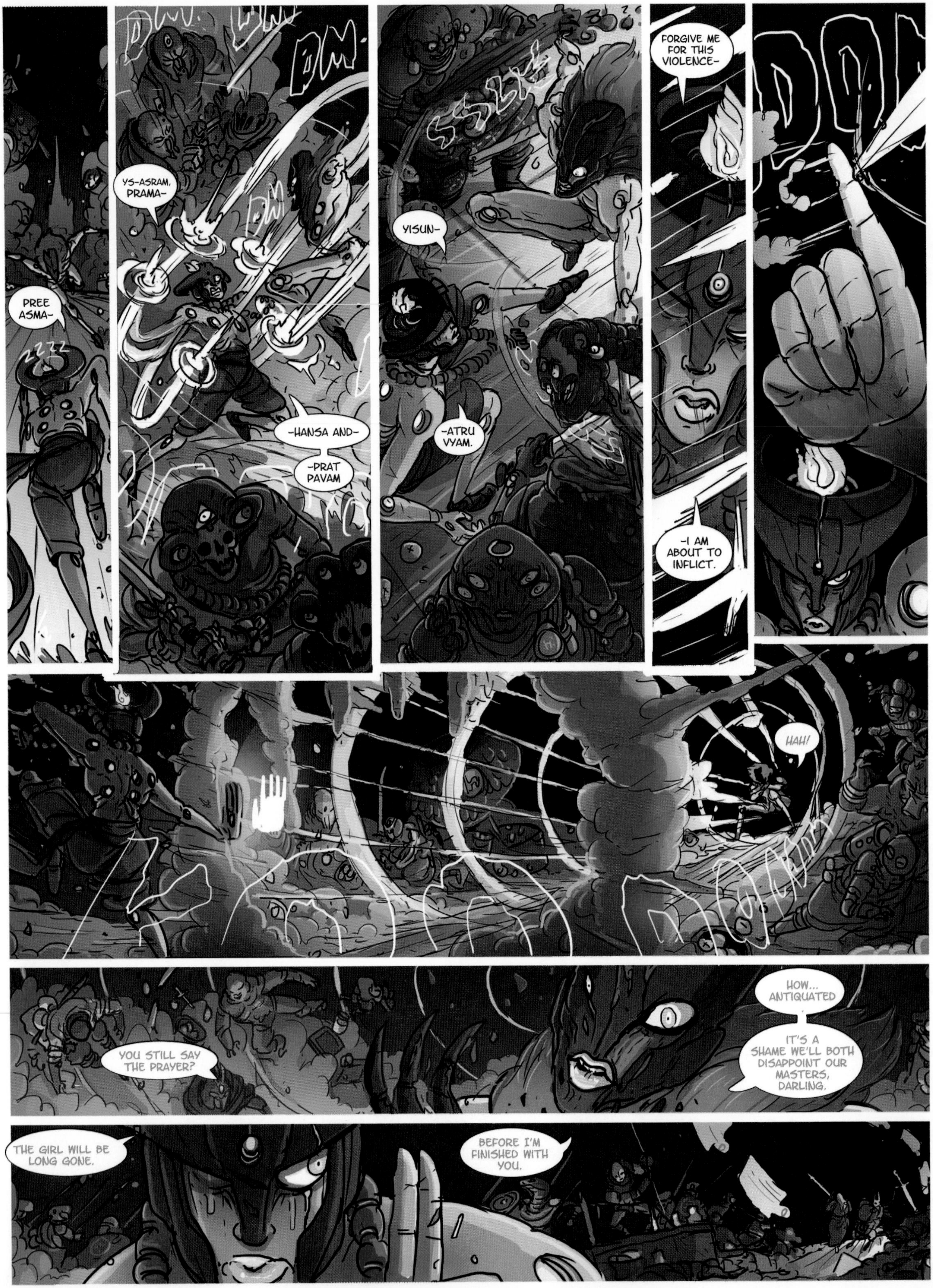
PREE ASMA-
ZZZZ
DM. DM. DM.
YS-ASRAM, PRAMA-
DM
-HANSA AND-
-PRAT PAVAM
SSZZKE
YISUN-
-ATRU VYAM.
FORGIVE ME FOR THIS VIOLENCE-
-I AM ABOUT TO INFLICT.
DOOM
HAH!
HOW... ANTIQUATED.
YOU STILL SAY THE PRAYER?
IT'S A SHAME WE'LL BOTH DISAPPOINT OUR MASTERS, DARLING.
THE GIRL WILL BE LONG GONE.
BEFORE I'M FINISHED WITH YOU.

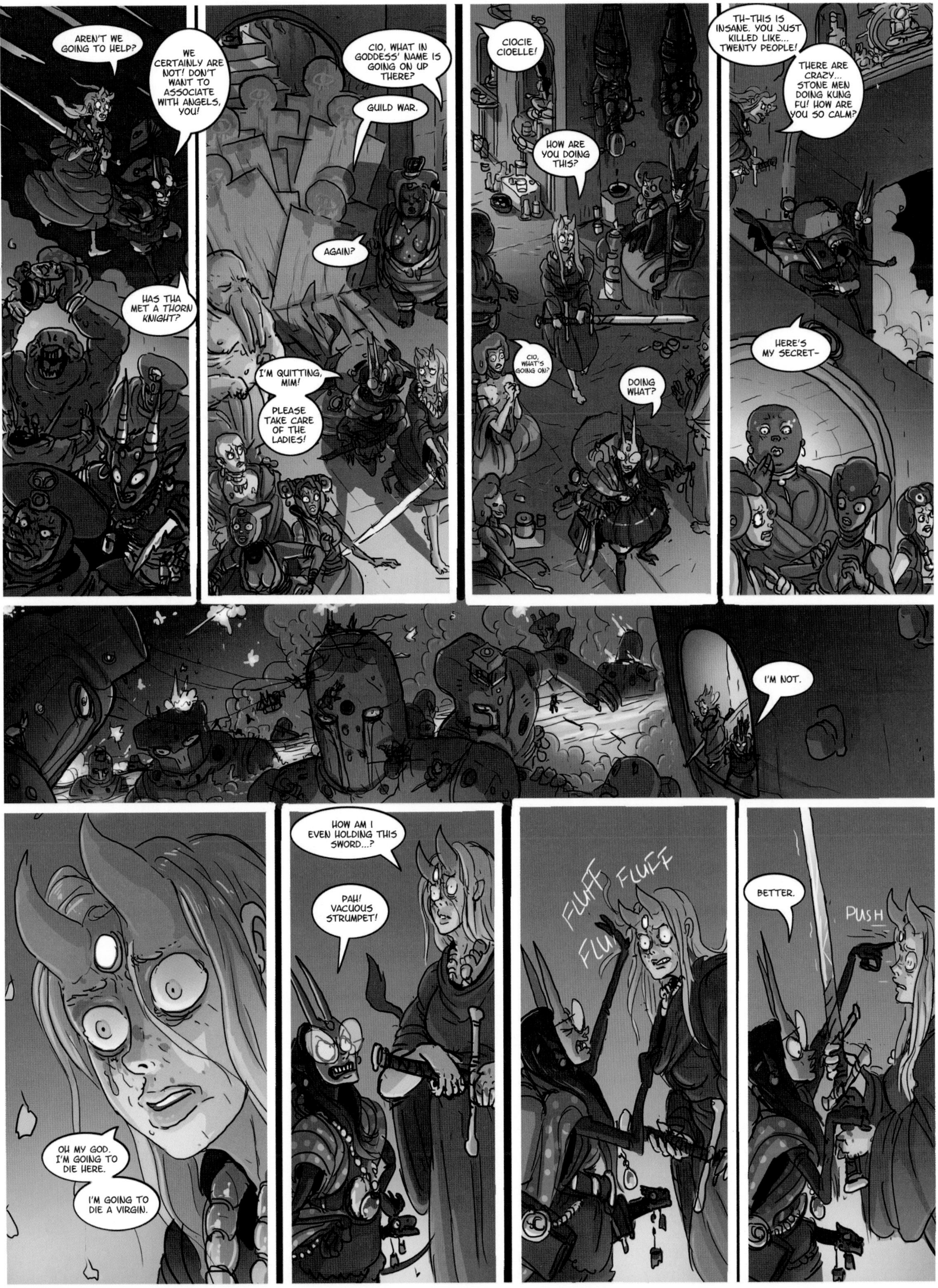

AREN'T WE GOING TO HELP?
WE CERTAINLY ARE NOT! DON'T WANT TO ASSOCIATE WITH ANGELS, YOU!
HAS THA MET A THORN KNIGHT?
CIO, WHAT IN GODDESS' NAME IS GOING ON UP THERE?
GUILD WAR.
AGAIN?
I'M QUITTING, MIM!
PLEASE TAKE CARE OF THE LADIES!
CIOCIE CIOELLE!
HOW ARE YOU DOING THIS?
CIO, WHAT'S GOING ON?
DOING WHAT?
TH-THIS IS INSANE. YOU JUST KILLED LIKE... TWENTY PEOPLE!
THERE ARE CRAZY... STONE MEN DOING KUNG FU! HOW ARE YOU SO CALM?
HERE'S MY SECRET-
I'M NOT.
OH MY GOD. I'M GOING TO DIE HERE.
I'M GOING TO DIE A VIRGIN.
HOW AM I EVEN HOLDING THIS SWORD...?
PAH! VACUOUS STRUMPET!
FLUFF FLUFF
FLU
BETTER.
PUSH

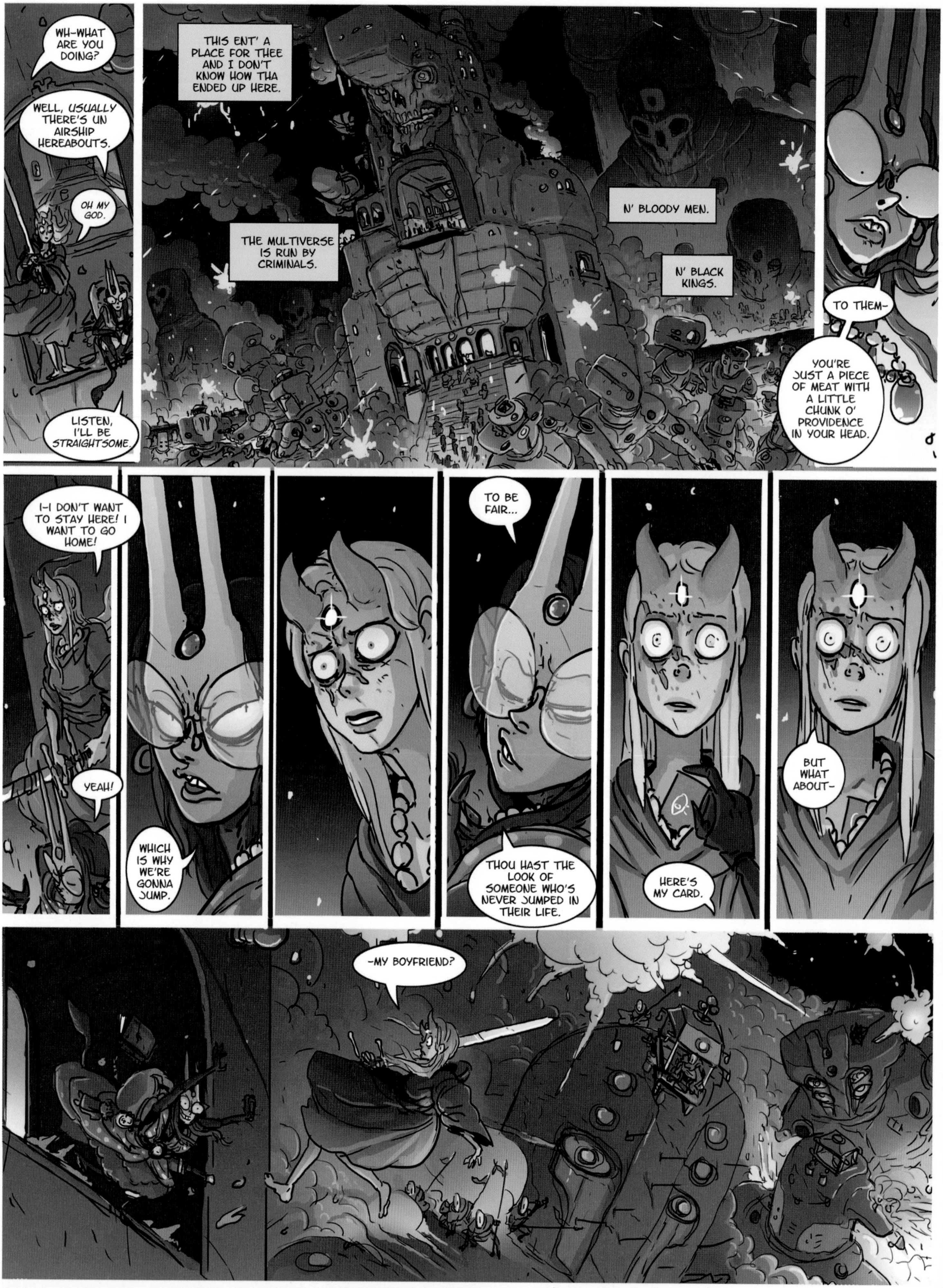
WH-WHAT ARE YOU DOING?
WELL, USUALLY THERE'S UN AIRSHIP HEREABOUTS.
OH MY GOD.
LISTEN, I'LL BE STRAIGHTSOME.
THIS ENT' A PLACE FOR THEE AND I DON'T KNOW HOW THA ENDED UP HERE.
THE MULTIVERSE IS RUN BY CRIMINALS.
N' BLOODY MEN.
N' BLACK KINGS.
TO THEM-
YOU'RE JUST A PIECE OF MEAT WITH A LITTLE CHUNK O' PROVIDENCE IN YOUR HEAD.
I-I DON'T WANT TO STAY HERE! I WANT TO GO HOME!
YEAH!
WHICH IS WHY WE'RE GONNA JUMP.
TO BE FAIR...
THOU HAST THE LOOK OF SOMEONE WHO'S NEVER JUMPED IN THEIR LIFE.
HERE'S MY CARD.
BUT WHAT ABOUT-
-MY BOYFRIEND?

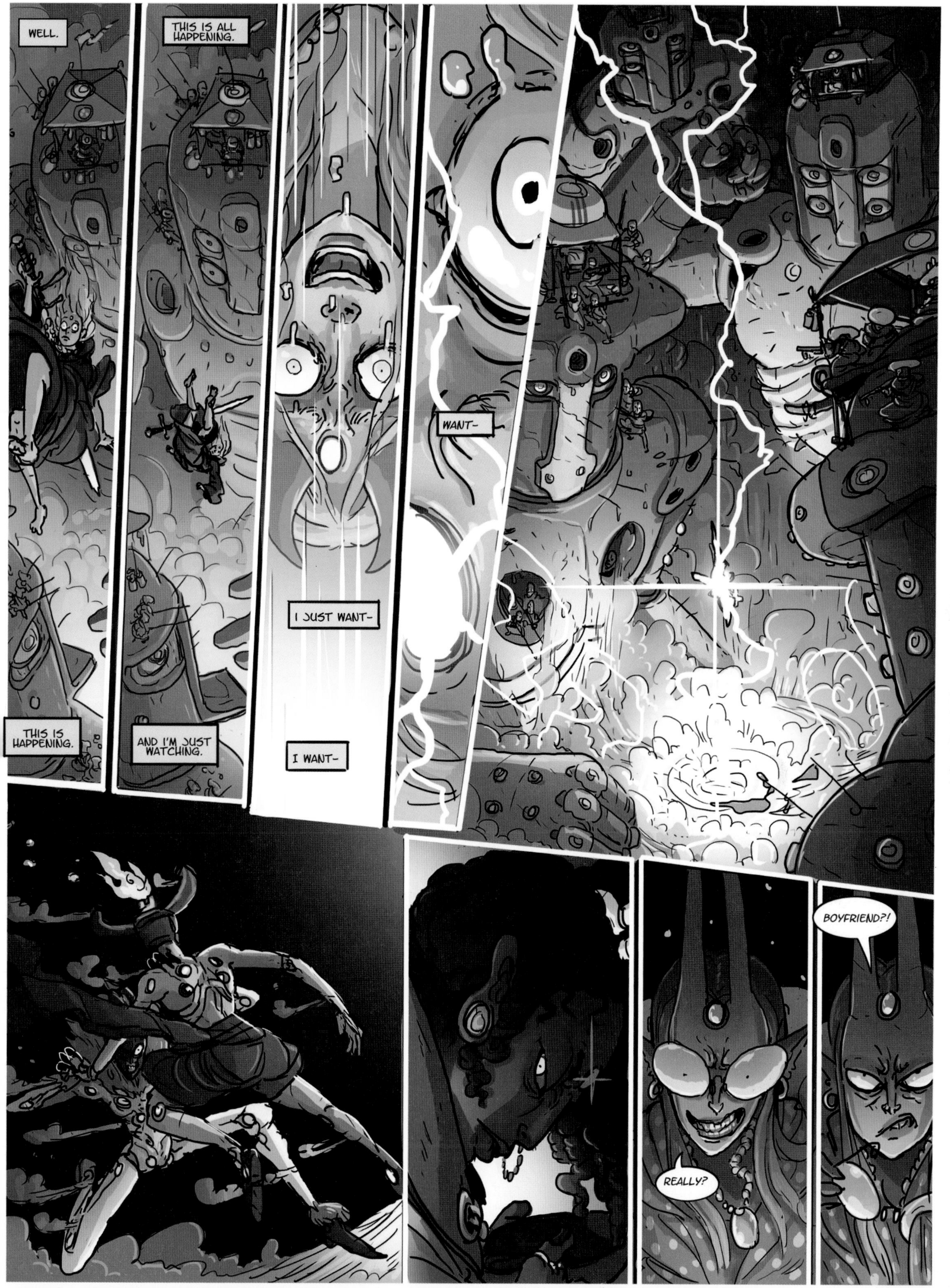
WELL.
THIS IS HAPPENING.
THIS IS ALL HAPPENING.
AND I'M JUST WATCHING.
I JUST WANT-
I WANT-
WANT-
REALLY?
BOYFRIEND?!

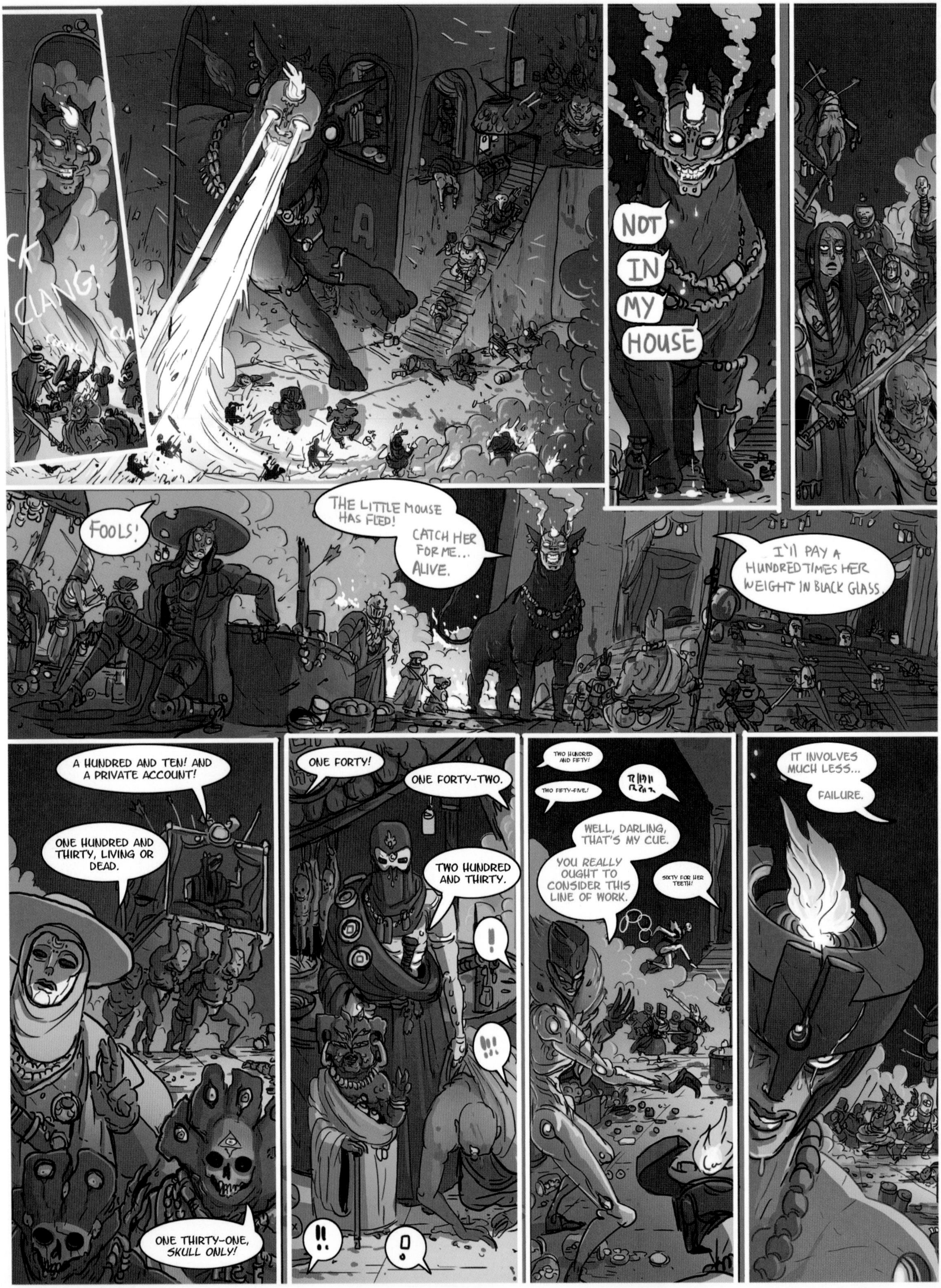
CLANG!
NOT IN MY HOUSE
FOOLS!
THE LITTLE MOUSE HAS FLED!
CATCH HER FOR ME... ALIVE.
I'LL PAY A HUNDRED TIMES HER WEIGHT IN BLACK GLASS.
A HUNDRED AND TEN! AND A PRIVATE ACCOUNT!
ONE HUNDRED AND THIRTY, LIVING OR DEAD.
ONE THIRTY-ONE, SKULL ONLY!
ONE FORTY!
ONE FORTY-TWO.
TWO HUNDRED AND THIRTY.
!
!!!
!!
!?
TWO HUNDRED AND FIFTY!
TWO FIFTY-FIVE!
WELL, DARLING, THAT'S MY CUE.
YOU REALLY OUGHT TO CONSIDER THIS LINE OF WORK.
SIXTY FOR HER TEETH!
IT INVOLVES MUCH LESS...
FAILURE.

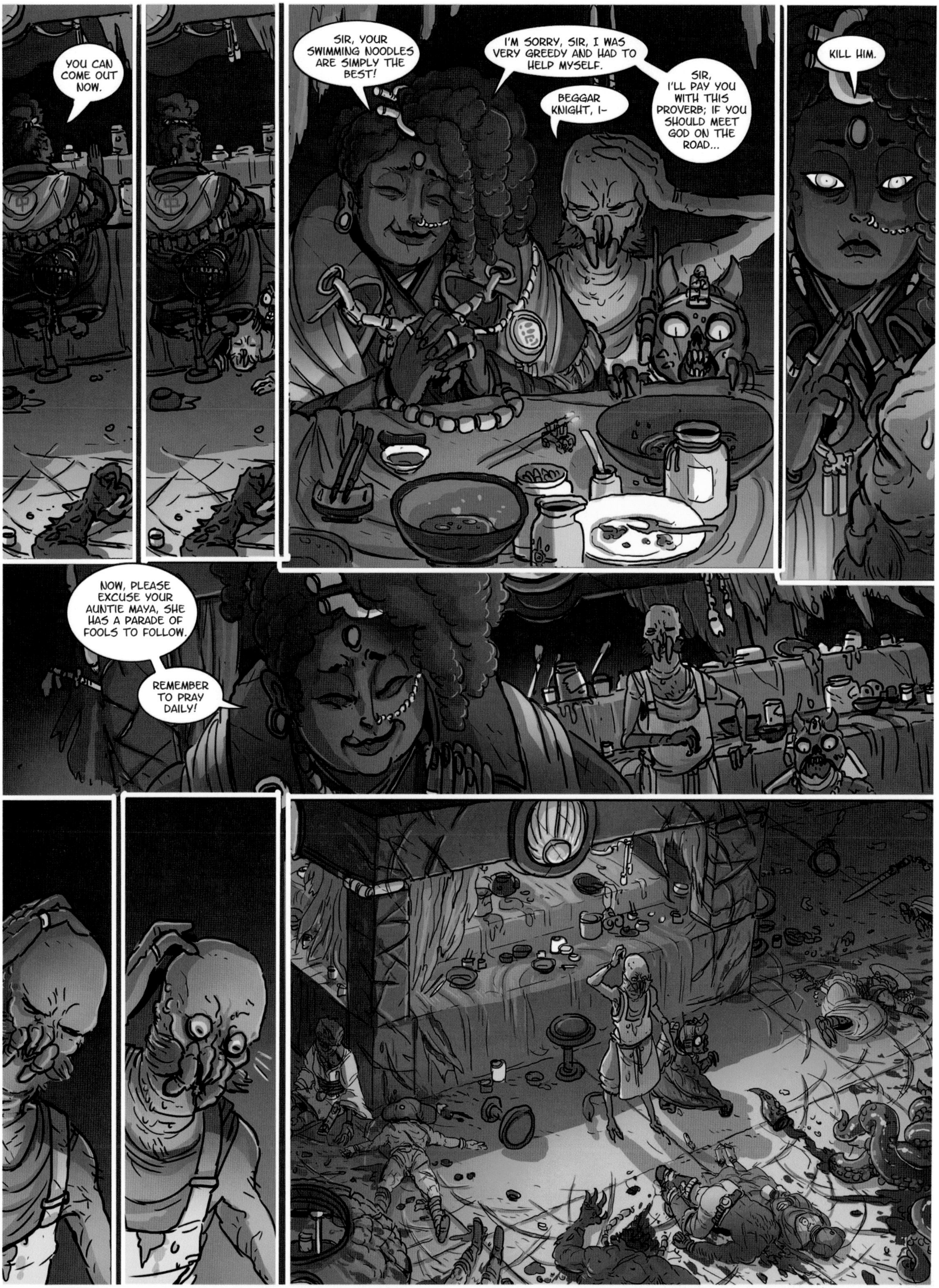
YOU CAN COME OUT NOW.
SIR, YOUR SWIMMING NOODLES ARE SIMPLY THE BEST!
I'M SORRY, SIR, I WAS VERY GREEDY AND HAD TO HELP MYSELF.
BEGGAR KNIGHT, I-
SIR, I'LL PAY YOU WITH THIS PROVERB; IF YOU SHOULD MEET GOD ON THE ROAD...
KILL HIM.
NOW, PLEASE EXCUSE YOUR AUNTIE MAYA, SHE HAS A PARADE OF FOOLS TO FOLLOW.
REMEMBER TO PRAY DAILY!

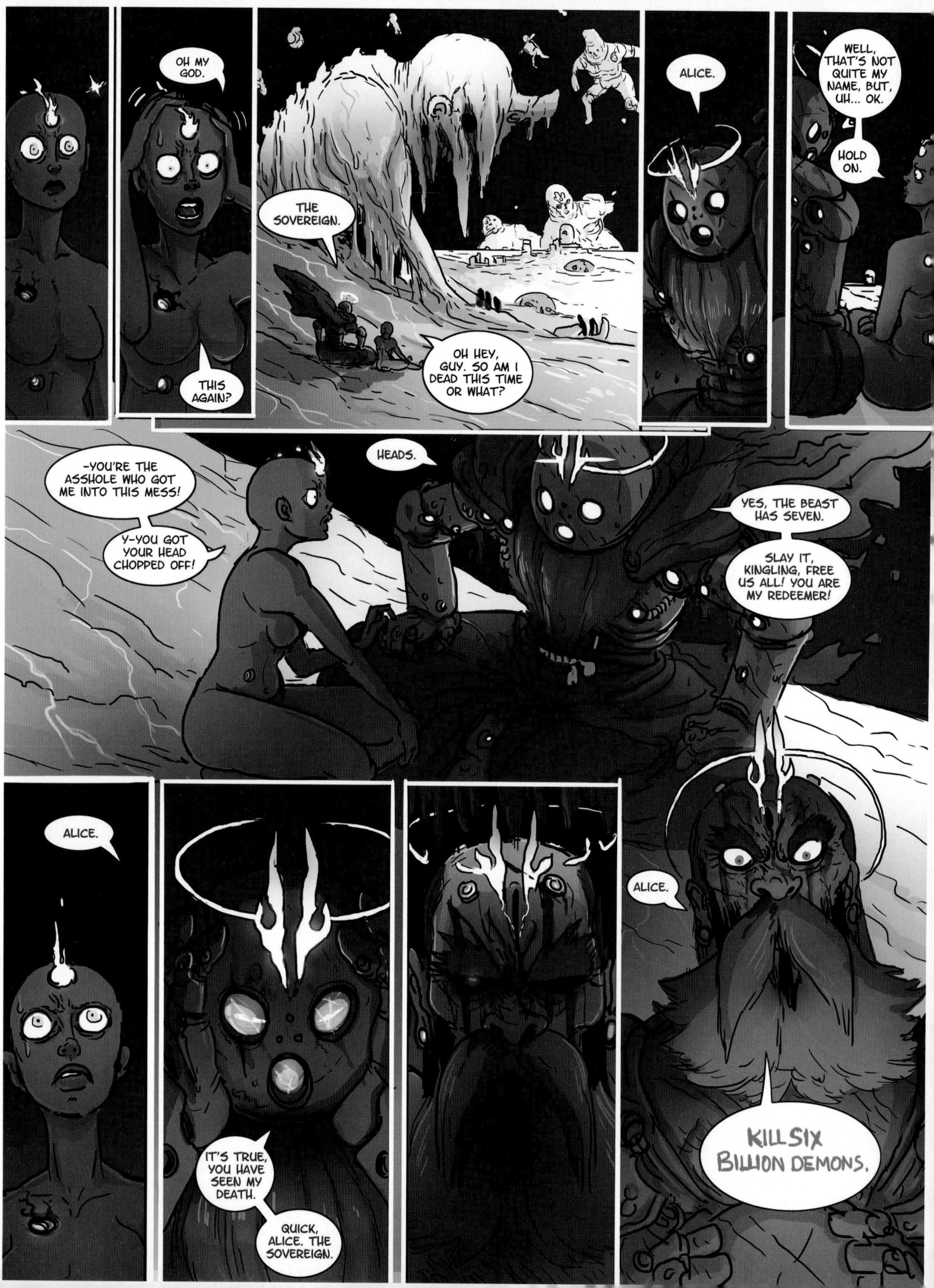
OH MY GOD.
THIS AGAIN?
THE SOVEREIGN.
OH HEY, GUY. SO AM I DEAD THIS TIME OR WHAT?
ALICE.
WELL, THAT'S NOT QUITE MY NAME, BUT, UH... OK.
HOLD ON.
-YOU'RE THE ASSHOLE WHO GOT ME INTO THIS MESS!
Y-YOU GOT YOUR HEAD CHOPPED OFF!
HEADS.
YES, THE BEAST HAS SEVEN.
SLAY IT, KINGLING, FREE US ALL! YOU ARE MY REDEEMER!
ALICE.
IT'S TRUE, YOU HAVE SEEN MY DEATH.
QUICK, ALICE. THE SOVEREIGN.
ALICE.
KILL SIX BILLION DEMONS.

1. Glory to the Divine Corpse, o breaker of infinities.

2. I am Meti, of no house but myself. In my 108th year I am surrounded by fools. My compatriots cling obsessively to their destiny, and my only apprentice is an idiot speck of a girl with more talent for eating than skill with the blade. Therefore I have decided to die drowning in the boiling gore of my enemies, of which there are many.

3. My master was the greatest lord general to the king Au Vam, Ryo-ten-Ryam, who first coaxed me into learning the ways of turning men into ghosts. As his interest quickly turned to the wholly uninteresting and most useless parts of my body, I returned the favor and relieved him of his.

4. It is my personal opinion the straight sword is best if you can obtain one, but I also favor the sabre. The spear, stave, and club are peasants' weapons of which I am wholly unfamiliar and I will not speak on them.

5. Upon meeting me, you might find that my appearance is quite dreadful and unkempt. I have been spat upon by priest, king, and merchant alike. I have no retainers, and possess nothing except a straight sword six hand spans (5 and a half kret) long (this is the proper length). This is because I am Royalty and the undisputed master of the principal art of Cutting. I will fight naked with ten thousand men.

6. From the age of thirteen I practiced every day with the straight sword. I followed a strict vegetarian regimen, and harsh training of barefoot sprints (five) between cities, squats and breathing exercises (two bells), and sword drills and resistance training (three bells).

7. By the age of sixteen, my body was a steel edifice. I was so often mistaken for a man I began to wear my hair long with no pins and unbind my breasts. I could break stone with my hands with no effort. I could sprint between the Yellow City and the Lunar dominions in a day or less and barely strain my breath. My mastery of the sword complete, I enlisted in the Middle Army's third legion, where I was widely respected as a swordswoman of incredible power.

8. When it came time to face my first real opponent, the Colossus of Pardos, in my youthful pride and immense skill, I brought all my training and mastery to bear. Scarcely half a day passed before my sword was shattered into thirty pieces, my right leg was almost torn from its socket, and my honed body was broken pathetically in a hundred and forty places. I defeated him by gouging his brains out through his breathing valves. My thumbs, in this case, proved far more useful than my training.

9. At that moment, with my thumbs in his brains, I had a revelation. I had trained far too broadly. Existence and the act of combat are absolutely no different, and the essence of both, the purity of both, is a singular action, which is Cutting Down Your Opponent. You must resolve to train this action. You must become this action. Truly, there is very little else that will serve you as well in this entire cursed world.

10. I hope that by reading this manual, you will be thoroughly encouraged to become a farmer.

Meti's Sword Manual

Mastering the Sword

1. YISUN's glory is great, and you may know this by two paths: the sanctioned words, and the sanctioned action.

2. The sanctioned words are YS ATN VARAMA PRESH. The meaning of these words is YISUN and their attainment is Royalty.

3. The sanctioned action is to Cut.

4. To Cut means division by the blade of Want, that parer of potentials that excises infinities.

5. To train with the sword, first master sweeping. When you have mastered sweeping, you must master the way of drawing water. Once you have learned how to draw water, you must split wood. Once you have split wood, you must learn the arts of finding the fine herbs in the forest, the arts of writing, the arts of paper making, and poetry writing. You must become familiar with the awl and the pen in equal measure. When you have mastered all these things, you must master building a house. Once your house is built, you have no further need for a sword, since it is an ugly piece of metal and its adherents idiots.

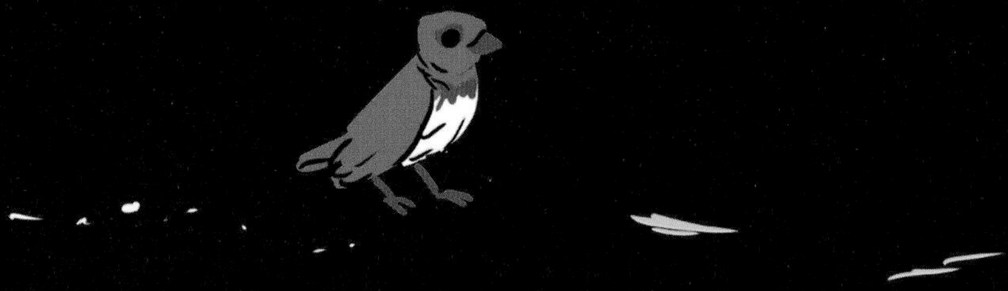

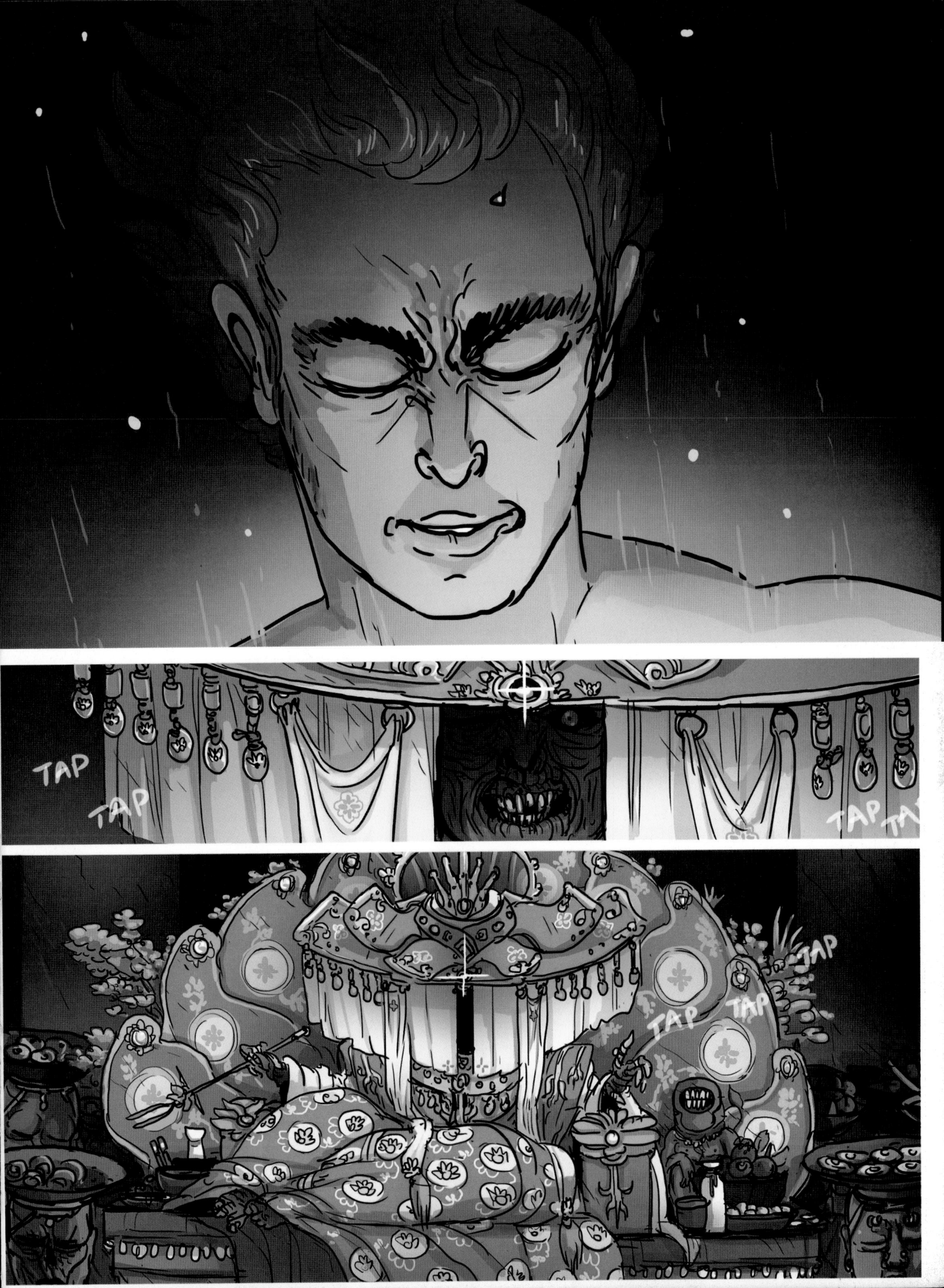
TAP
TAP
TAP
TAP
TAP
TAP
TAP

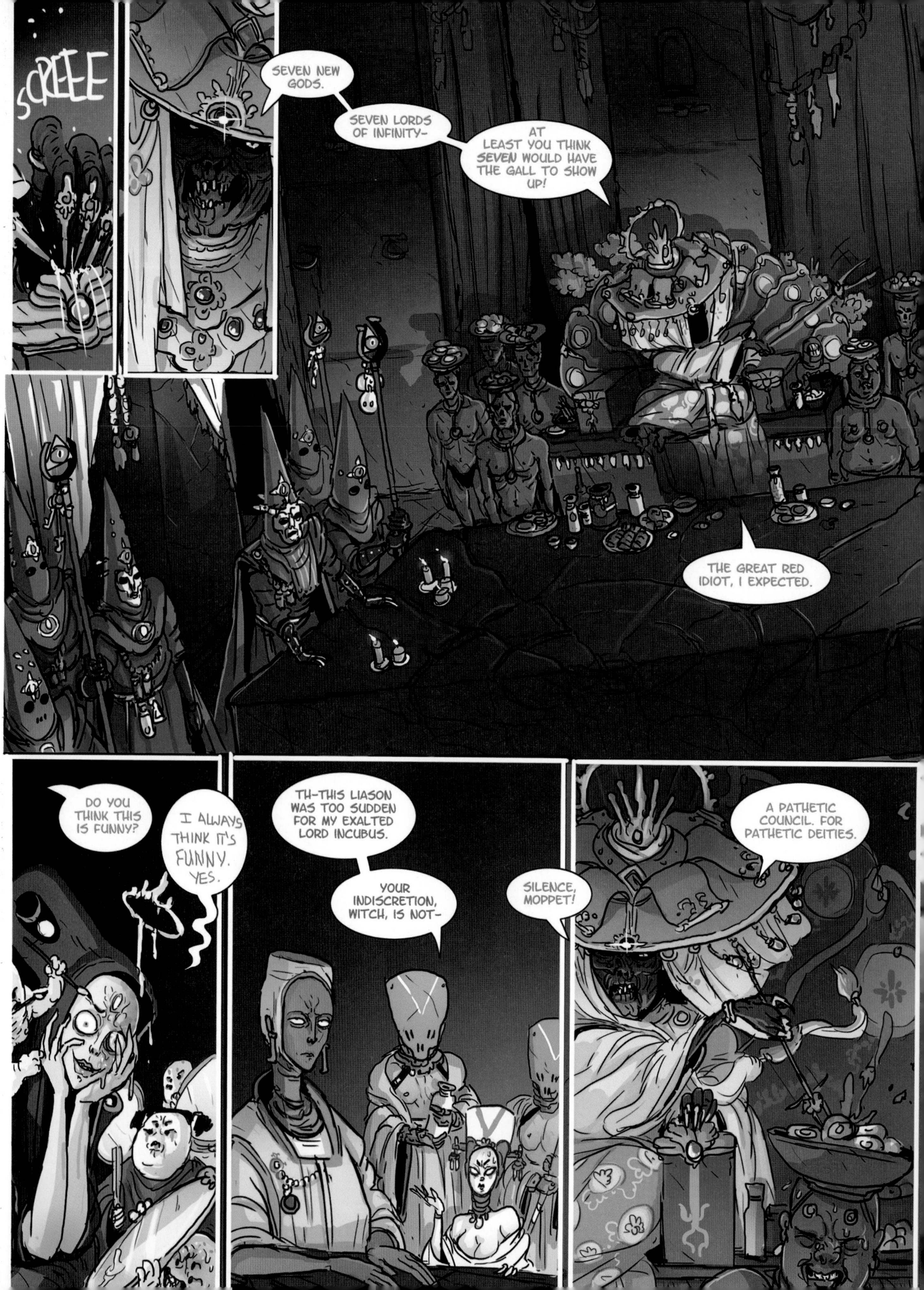
SCREEE
SEVEN NEW GODS.
SEVEN LORDS OF INFINITY-
AT LEAST YOU THINK SEVEN WOULD HAVE THE GALL TO SHOW UP!
THE GREAT RED IDIOT, I EXPECTED.
DO YOU THINK THIS IS FUNNY?
I ALWAYS THINK IT'S FUNNY. YES.
TH-THIS LIASON WAS TOO SUDDEN FOR MY EXALTED LORD INCUBUS.
YOUR INDISCRETION, WITCH, IS NOT-
SILENCE, MOPPET!
A PATHETIC COUNCIL. FOR PATHETIC DEITIES.

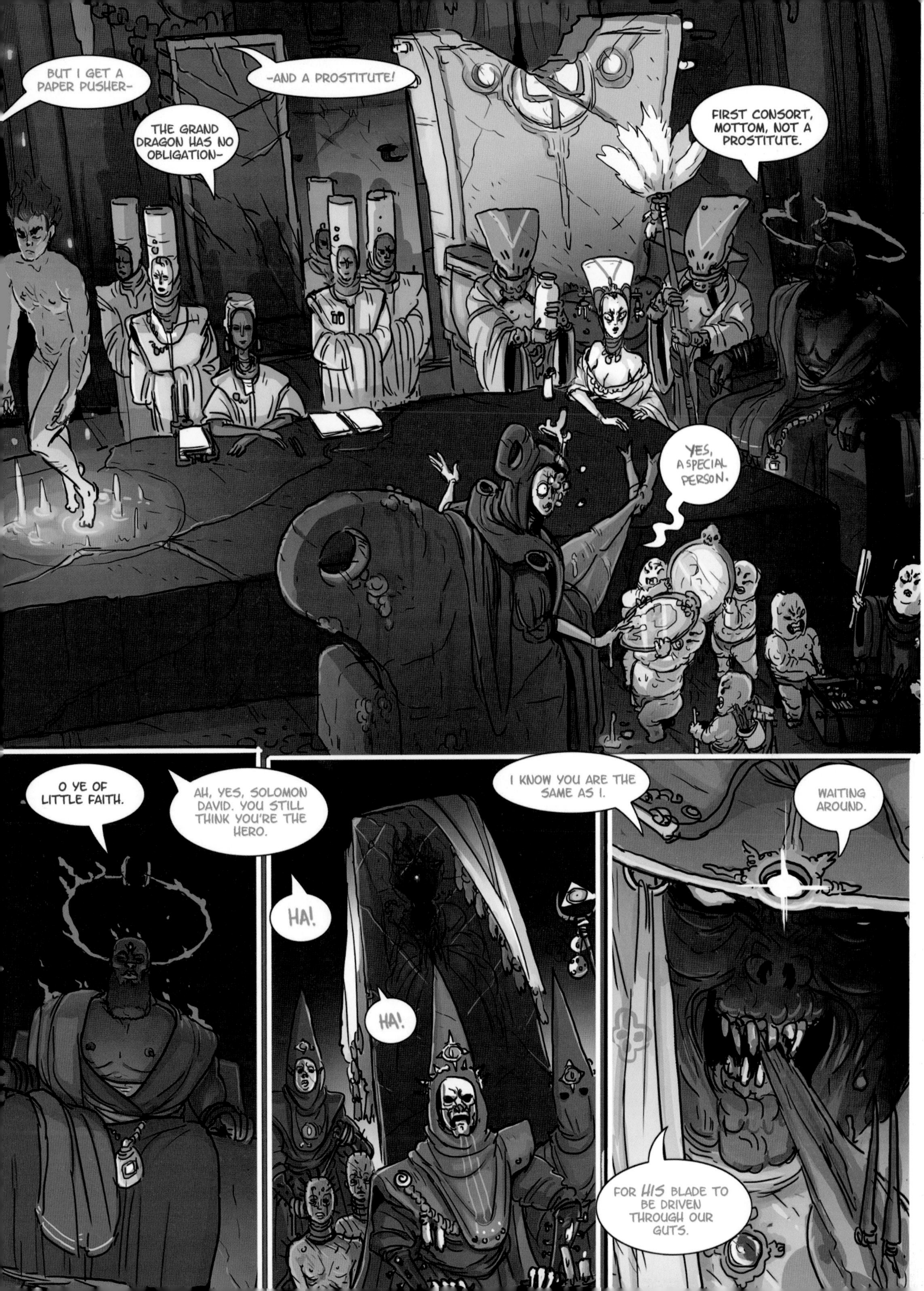
BUT I GET A PAPER PUSHER-
THE GRAND DRAGON HAS NO OBLIGATION-
-AND A PROSTITUTE!
FIRST CONSORT, MOTTOM, NOT A PROSTITUTE.
YES, A SPECIAL PERSON.
O YE OF LITTLE FAITH.
AH, YES, SOLOMON DAVID. YOU STILL THINK YOU'RE THE HERO.
HA!
HA!
I KNOW YOU ARE THE SAME AS I.
WAITING AROUND.
FOR HIS BLADE TO BE DRIVEN THROUGH OUR GUTS.

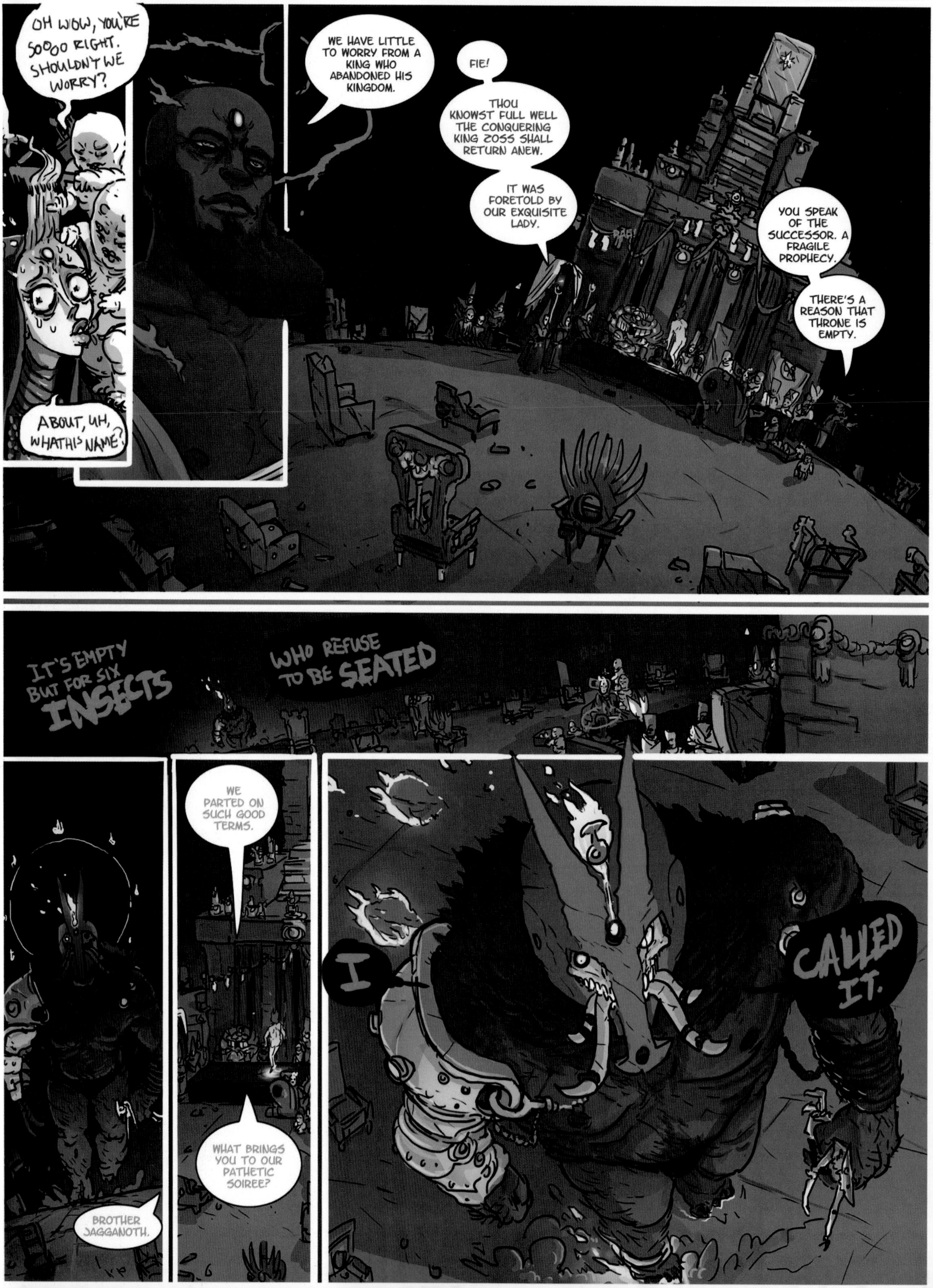
OH WOW, YOU'RE SOOOO RIGHT. SHOULDN'T WE WORRY?
ABOUT, UH, WHATHISNAME?
WE HAVE LITTLE TO WORRY FROM A KING WHO ABANDONED HIS KINGDOM.
FIE!
THOU KNOWST FULL WELL THE CONQUERING KING ZOSS SHALL RETURN ANEW.
IT WAS FORETOLD BY OUR EXQUISITE LADY.
YOU SPEAK OF THE SUCCESSOR. A FRAGILE PROPHECY.
THERE'S A REASON THAT THRONE IS EMPTY.
IT'S EMPTY BUT FOR SIX INSECTS
WHO REFUSE TO BE SEATED
BROTHER JAGGANOTH.
WE PARTED ON SUCH GOOD TERMS.
WHAT BRINGS YOU TO OUR PATHETIC SOIREE?
I
CALLED IT.

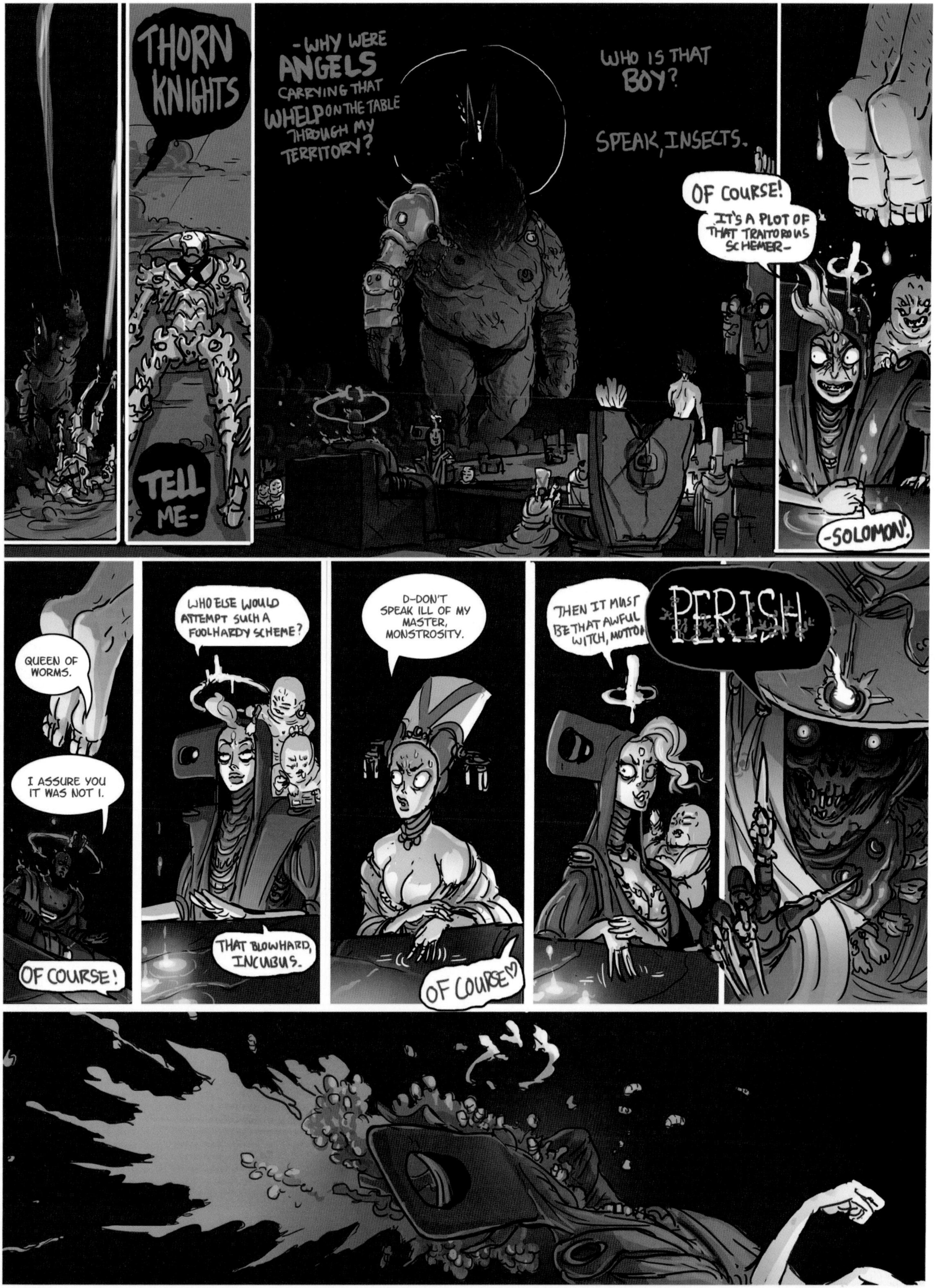
THORN KNIGHTS
TELL ME-
-WHY WERE ANGELS CARRYING THAT WHELP ON THE TABLE THROUGH MY TERRITORY?
WHO IS THAT BOY?
SPEAK, INSECTS.
OF COURSE!
IT'S A PLOT OF THAT TRAITOROUS SCHEMER-
-SOLOMON!
QUEEN OF WORMS.
I ASSURE YOU IT WAS NOT I.
OF COURSE!
WHO ELSE WOULD ATTEMPT SUCH A FOOLHARDY SCHEME?
THAT BLOWHARD, INCUBUS.
D-DON'T SPEAK ILL OF MY MASTER, MONSTROSITY.
OF COURSE♡
THEN IT MUST BE THAT AWFUL WITCH, MUTTON
PERISH

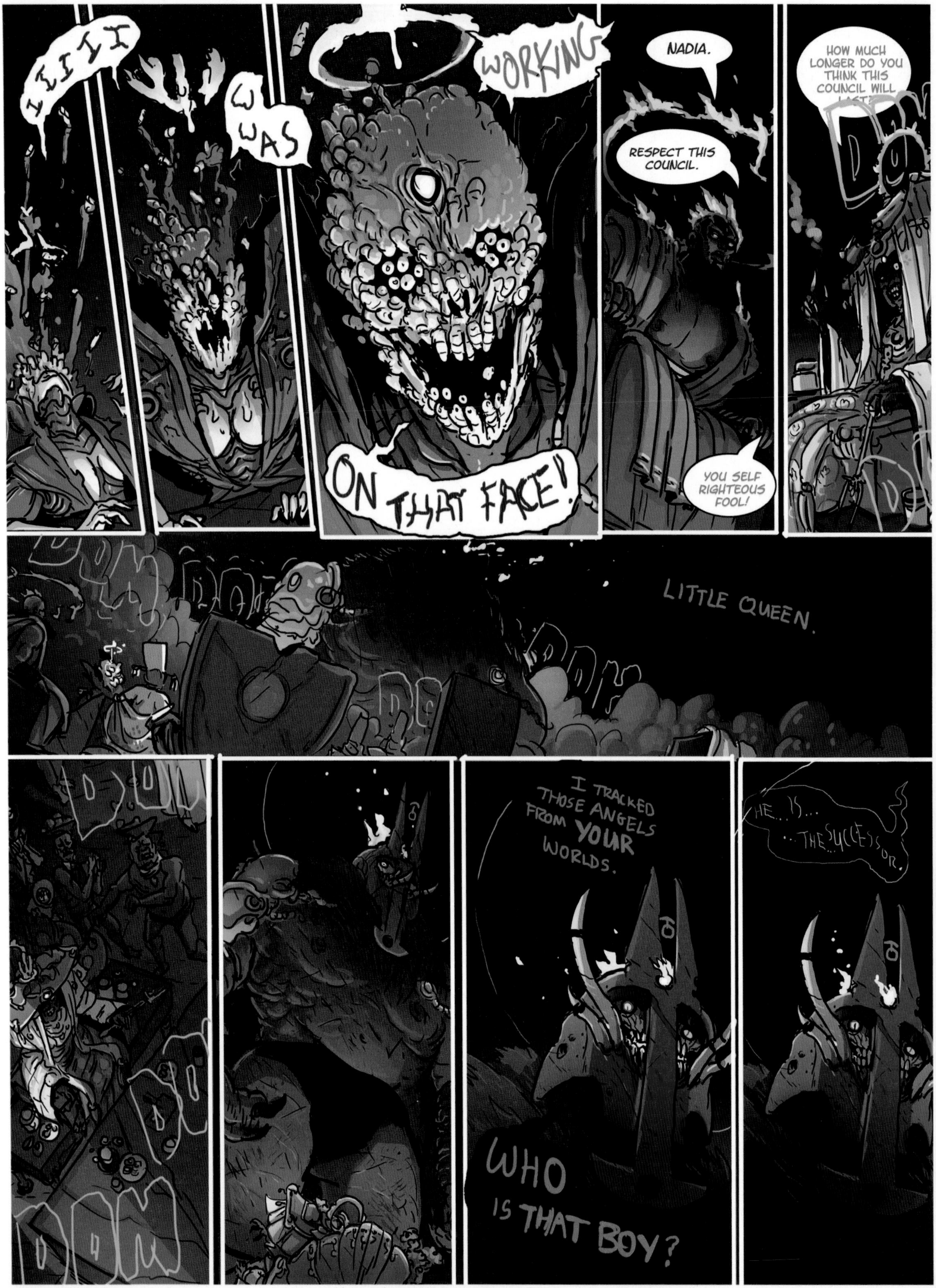
IIII
W WAS
WORKING
ON THAT FACE!
NADIA.
RESPECT THIS COUNCIL.
YOU SELF RIGHTEOUS FOOL!
HOW MUCH LONGER DO YOU THINK THIS COUNCIL WILL LAST?
DOM
LITTLE QUEEN.
DOM
I TRACKED THOSE ANGELS FROM YOUR WORLDS.
WHO IS THAT BOY?
HE... IS... ...THE... SUCCESSOR.

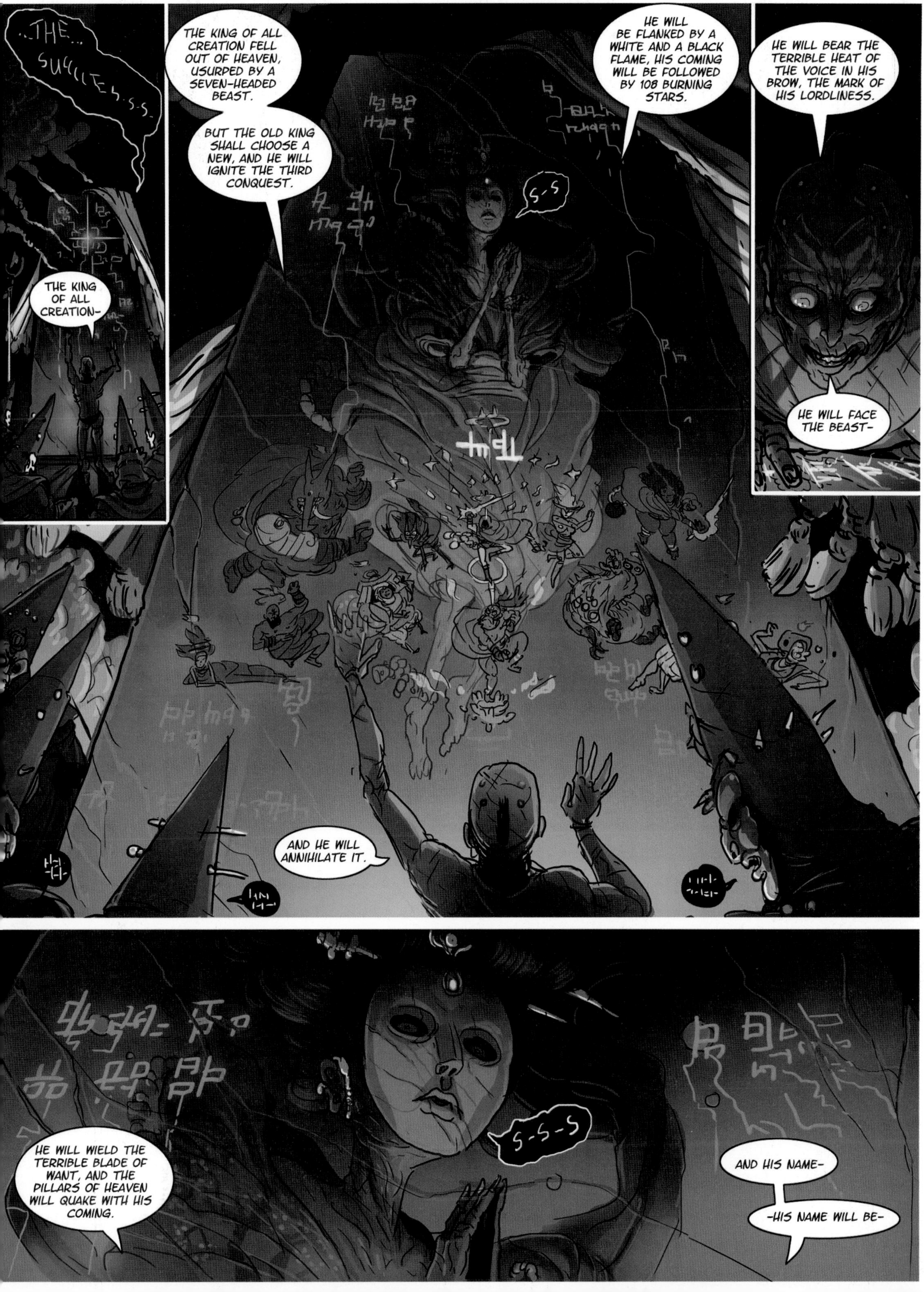

..THE... SUCCESS-S-S-
THE KING OF ALL CREATION-
THE KING OF ALL CREATION FELL OUT OF HEAVEN, USURPED BY A SEVEN-HEADED BEAST.
BUT THE OLD KING SHALL CHOOSE A NEW, AND HE WILL IGNITE THE THIRD CONQUEST.
S-S
HE WILL BE FLANKED BY A WHITE AND A BLACK FLAME, HIS COMING WILL BE FOLLOWED BY 108 BURNING STARS.
HE WILL BEAR THE TERRIBLE HEAT OF THE VOICE IN HIS BROW, THE MARK OF HIS LORDLINESS.
HE WILL FACE THE BEAST-
AND HE WILL ANNIHILATE IT.
HE WILL WIELD THE TERRIBLE BLADE OF WANT, AND THE PILLARS OF HEAVEN WILL QUAKE WITH HIS COMING.
S-S-S
AND HIS NAME-
-HIS NAME WILL BE-

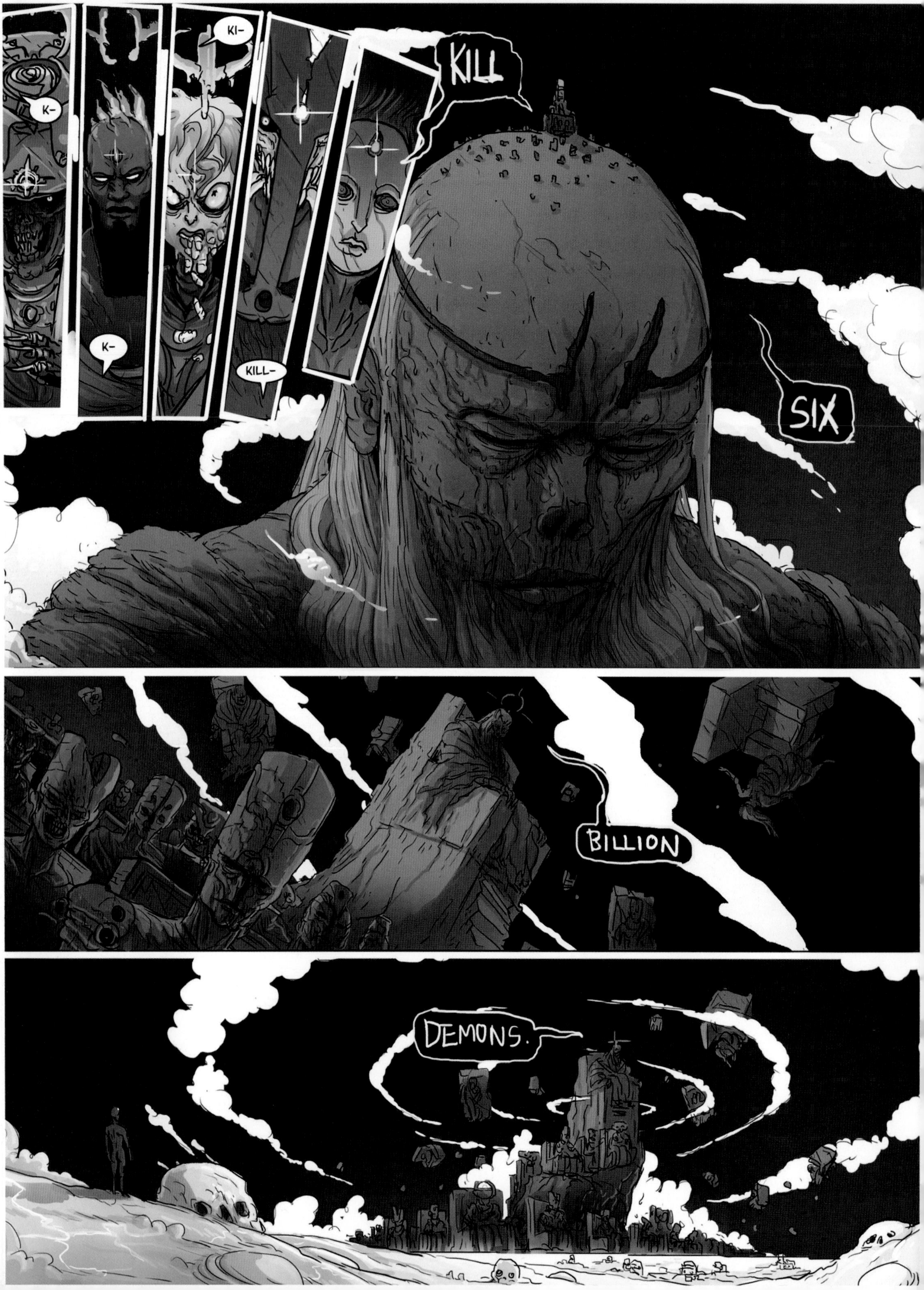
K-
K-
KI-
KILL-
KILL
SIX
BILLION
DEMONS.

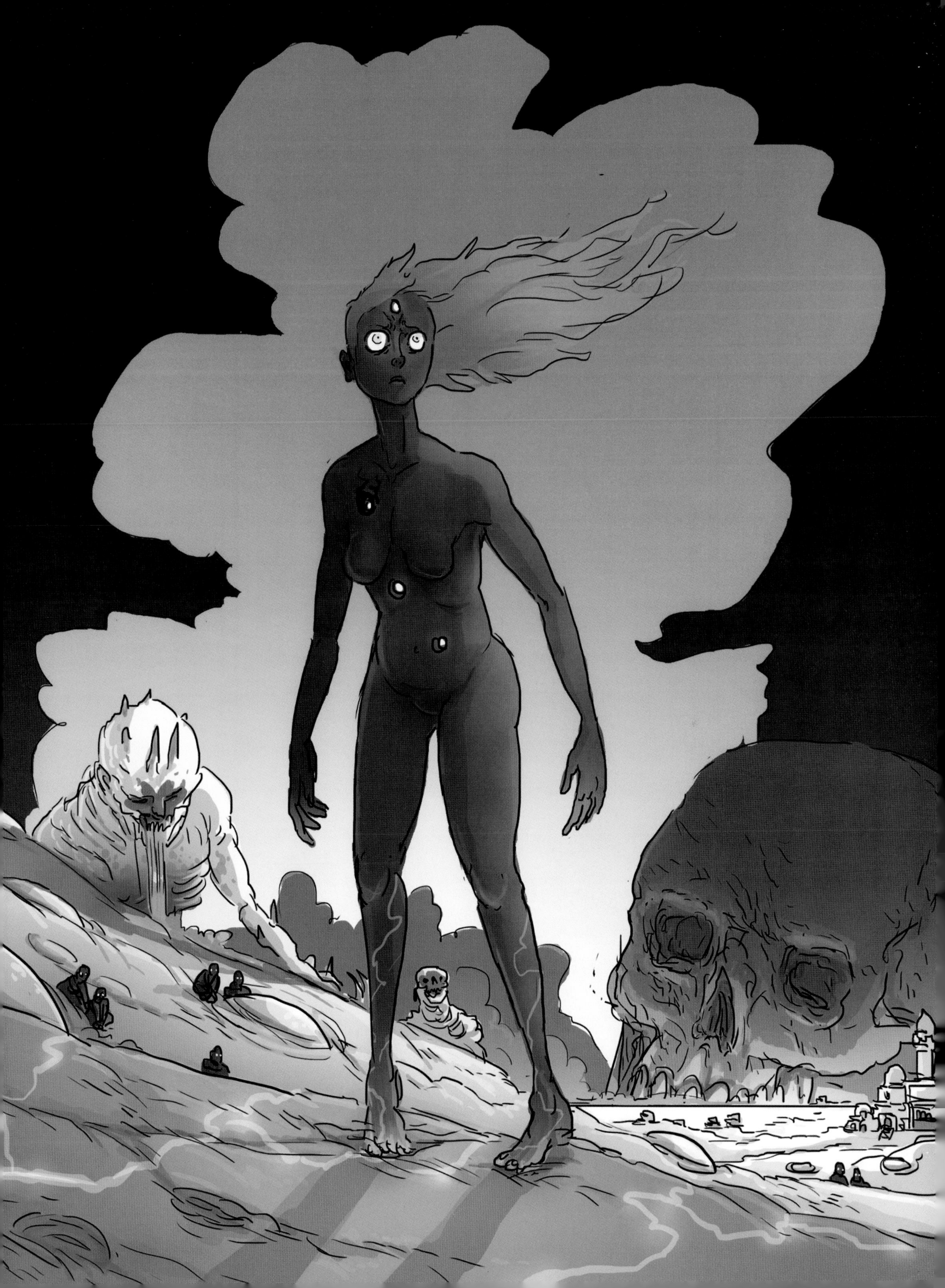

Meti's Sword Manual

The 18 Precepts

1. Consider: there is no such thing as a sword.

2. Your stance must be wide. You must not be spare with the fluidity of your wrists or shoulders. You must have a grip on the handle that is loose and unstrained. I heard it said you must be tender with your sword grip, as though with a lover. This is patently false. A sword is not your lover. It is a hideous tool for separating men from their vital fluids.

3. Going onwards, you must adjust hands as needed, do not keep the blade close to your body, keep your breathing steady. This is the life cut. You must watch your footwork. Your feet must be controlled whether planted on fire, air, water, or earth in equal measure.

4. Breathing is very important! Is the violent breath of life in you not hot? Exhale! Exult!

5. You must strive for attachment-non-attachment when cutting. Your cut must be sticky and resolute. A weak, listless cut is a despicable thing. But you must also not cling to your action, or its result. Clinging is the great error of men. A man who strikes without thought of his action can cut God.

6. To cut properly, you must continually self-annihilate when cutting. Your hand must become a hand that is cutting, your body a body that is cutting, your mind, a mind that is cutting. You must instantaneously destroy your fake pre-present self. It is a useless hanger-on.

7. A brain is useful only up until the point when you are faced with your enemy. Then it is useless. The only truly useful thing in this cursed world is will. You must suffuse your worthless body with its terrible heat. You must be so hot that even if your enemy should strike your head off, you shall continue on to decapitate ten more men. Your boiling blood must spring forth from your neck and mutilate the survivors.

8. You must never make 'multiple' cuts. Each must be singular in its beauty, no matter how many precede it. You must make your enemies weep with admiration, and likewise should your head be shorn off by such an object of beauty, you must do your best to shed tears of respect.

9. When decapitating an enemy, it is severe impoliteness to use more than one blow.

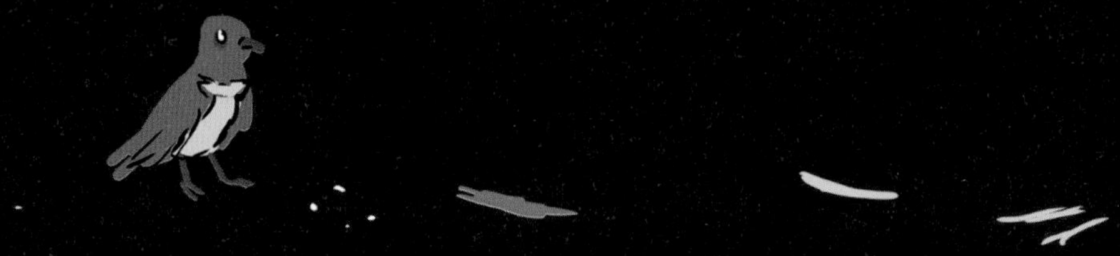

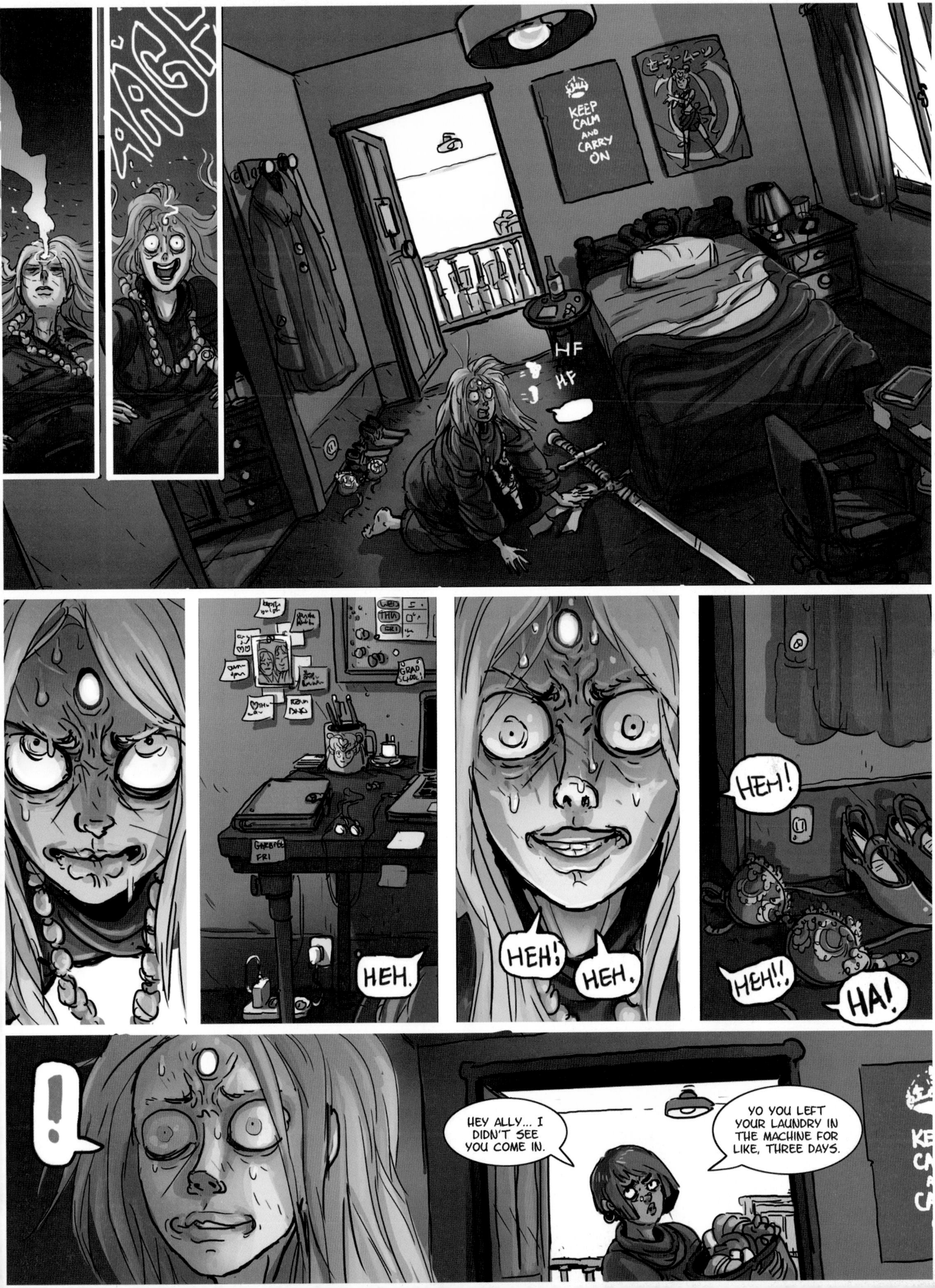

HF
HF
KEEP CALM AND CARRY ON
HEH.
HEH!
HEH.
HEH!
HEH!!
HA!
!
HEY ALLY... I DIDN'T SEE YOU COME IN.
YO YOU LEFT YOUR LAUNDRY IN THE MACHINE FOR LIKE, THREE DAYS.

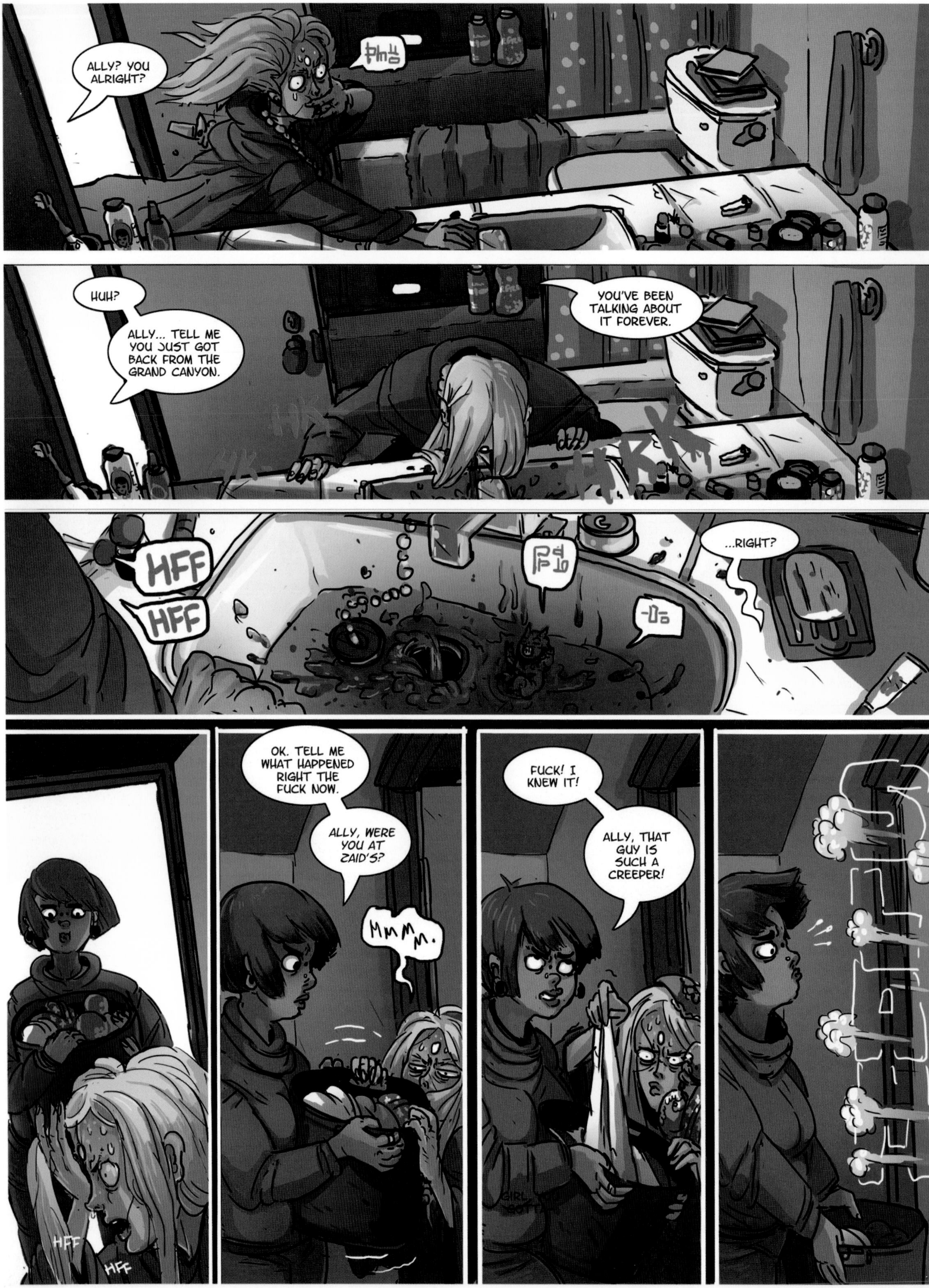
ALLY? YOU ALRIGHT?
HUH?
ALLY... TELL ME YOU JUST GOT BACK FROM THE GRAND CANYON.
YOU'VE BEEN TALKING ABOUT IT FOREVER.
HRK
HFF
HFF
...RIGHT?
HFF
HFF
OK. TELL ME WHAT HAPPENED RIGHT THE FUCK NOW.
ALLY, WERE YOU AT ZAID'S?
MMMM.
FUCK! I KNEW IT!
ALLY, THAT GUY IS SUCH A CREEPER!

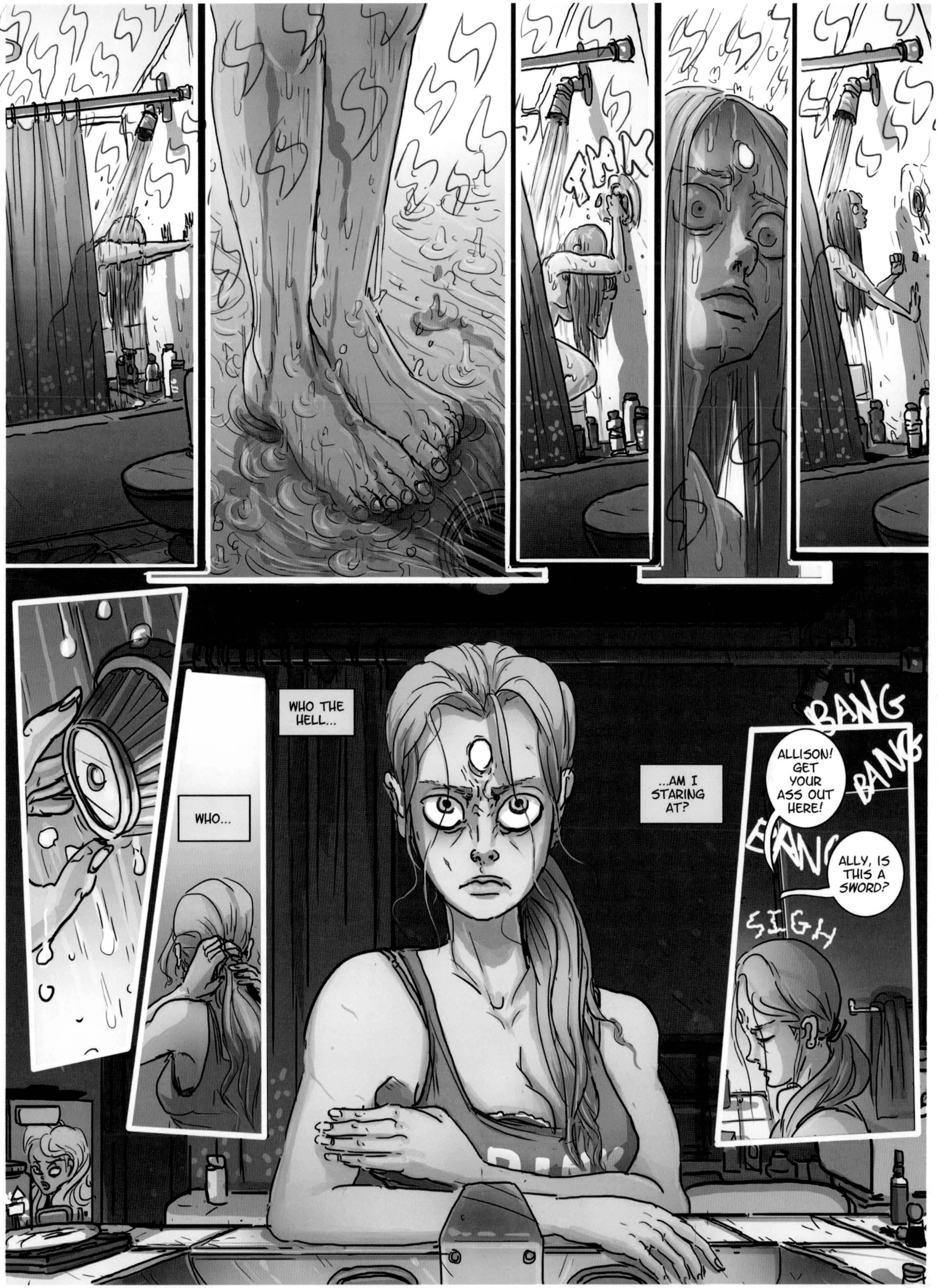
TMK
WHO...
WHO THE HELL...
...AM I STARING AT?
BANG
BANG
BANG
ALLISON! GET YOUR ASS OUT HERE!
ALLY, IS THIS A SWORD?
SIGH

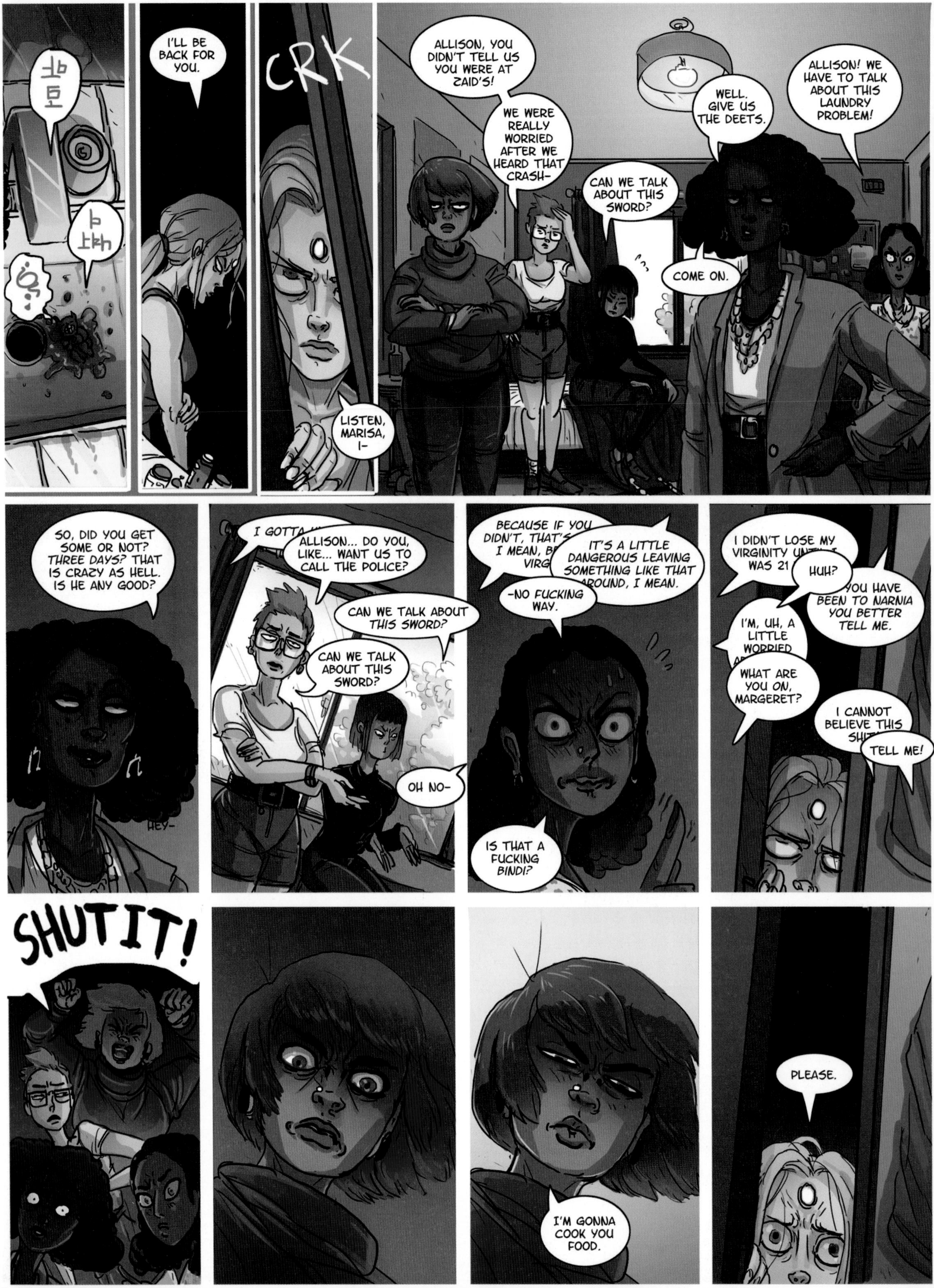
I'LL BE BACK FOR YOU.
CRK
LISTEN, MARISA, I-
ALLISON, YOU DIDN'T TELL US YOU WERE AT ZAID'S!
WE WERE REALLY WORRIED AFTER WE HEARD THAT CRASH-
CAN WE TALK ABOUT THIS SWORD?
WELL. GIVE US THE DEETS.
COME ON.
ALLISON! WE HAVE TO TALK ABOUT THIS LAUNDRY PROBLEM!
SO, DID YOU GET SOME OR NOT? THREE DAYS? THAT IS CRAZY AS HELL. IS HE ANY GOOD?
HEY-
I GOTTA
ALLISON... DO YOU, LIKE... WANT US TO CALL THE POLICE?
CAN WE TALK ABOUT THIS SWORD?
CAN WE TALK ABOUT THIS SWORD?
OH NO-
BECAUSE IF YOU DIDN'T, THAT'S I MEAN, BE VIRG
IT'S A LITTLE DANGEROUS LEAVING SOMETHING LIKE THAT AROUND, I MEAN.
-NO FUCKING WAY.
IS THAT A FUCKING BINDI?
I DIDN'T LOSE MY VIRGINITY UNT WAS 21
HUH?
YOU HAVE BEEN TO NARNIA YOU BETTER TELL ME.
I'M, UH, A LITTLE WORRIED
WHAT ARE YOU ON, MARGERET?
I CANNOT BELIEVE THIS
TELL ME!
SHUT IT!
I'M GONNA COOK YOU FOOD.
PLEASE.

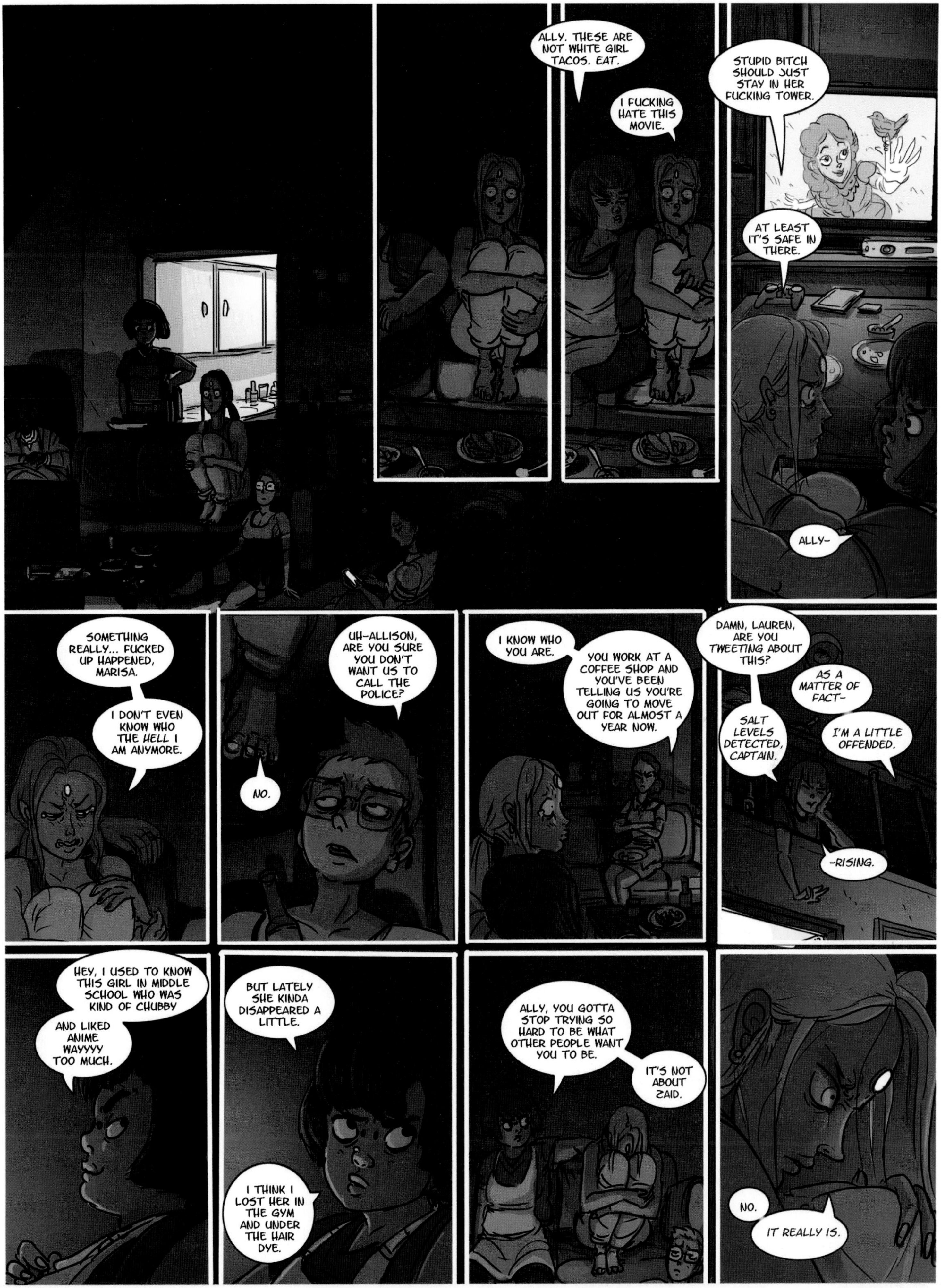
ALLY. THESE ARE NOT WHITE GIRL TACOS. EAT.
I FUCKING HATE THIS MOVIE.
STUPID BITCH SHOULD JUST STAY IN HER FUCKING TOWER.
AT LEAST IT'S SAFE IN THERE.
ALLY-
SOMETHING REALLY... FUCKED UP HAPPENED, MARISA.
I DON'T EVEN KNOW WHO THE HELL I AM ANYMORE.
UH-ALLISON, ARE YOU SURE YOU DON'T WANT US TO CALL THE POLICE?
NO.
I KNOW WHO YOU ARE.
YOU WORK AT A COFFEE SHOP AND YOU'VE BEEN TELLING US YOU'RE GOING TO MOVE OUT FOR ALMOST A YEAR NOW.
DAMN, LAUREN, ARE YOU TWEETING ABOUT THIS?
AS A MATTER OF FACT-
SALT LEVELS DETECTED, CAPTAIN.
I'M A LITTLE OFFENDED.
-RISING.
HEY, I USED TO KNOW THIS GIRL IN MIDDLE SCHOOL WHO WAS KIND OF CHUBBY
AND LIKED ANIME WAYYYY TOO MUCH.
BUT LATELY SHE KINDA DISAPPEARED A LITTLE.
I THINK I LOST HER IN THE GYM AND UNDER THE HAIR DYE.
ALLY, YOU GOTTA STOP TRYING SO HARD TO BE WHAT OTHER PEOPLE WANT YOU TO BE.
IT'S NOT ABOUT ZAID.
NO.
IT REALLY IS.

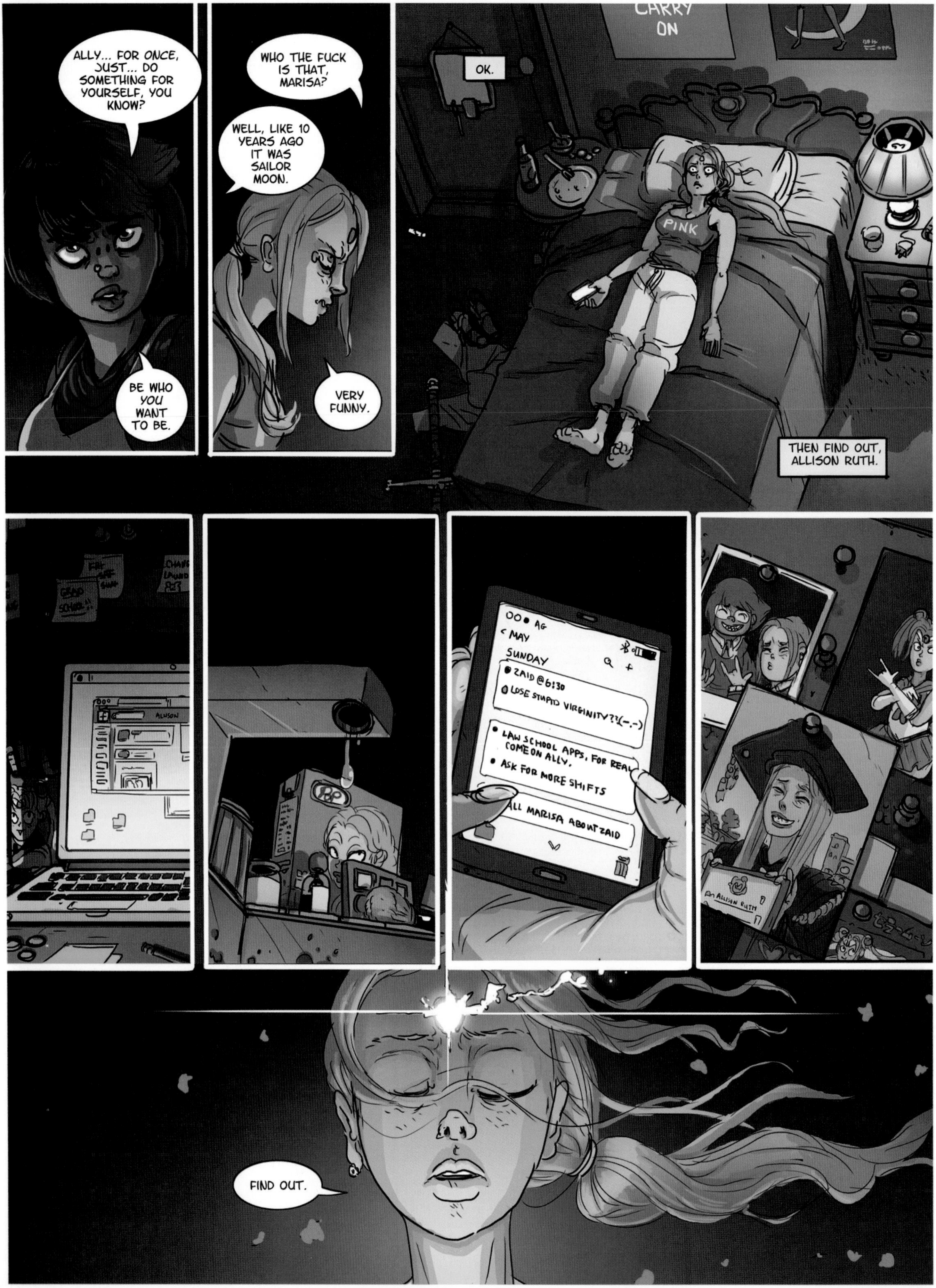
ALLY... FOR ONCE, JUST... DO SOMETHING FOR YOURSELF, YOU KNOW?
BE WHO YOU WANT TO BE.
WHO THE FUCK IS THAT, MARISA?
WELL, LIKE 10 YEARS AGO IT WAS SAILOR MOON.
VERY FUNNY.
CARRY ON
OK.
PINK
THEN FIND OUT, ALLISON RUTH.
GRAD SCHOOL
< MAY
SUNDAY
ZAID @6:30
LOSE STUPID VIRGINITY??(-.-)
LAW SCHOOL APPS, FOR REAL COME ON ALLY.
ASK FOR MORE SHIFTS
ALL MARISA ABOUT ZAID
ALLISON RUTH
FIND OUT.

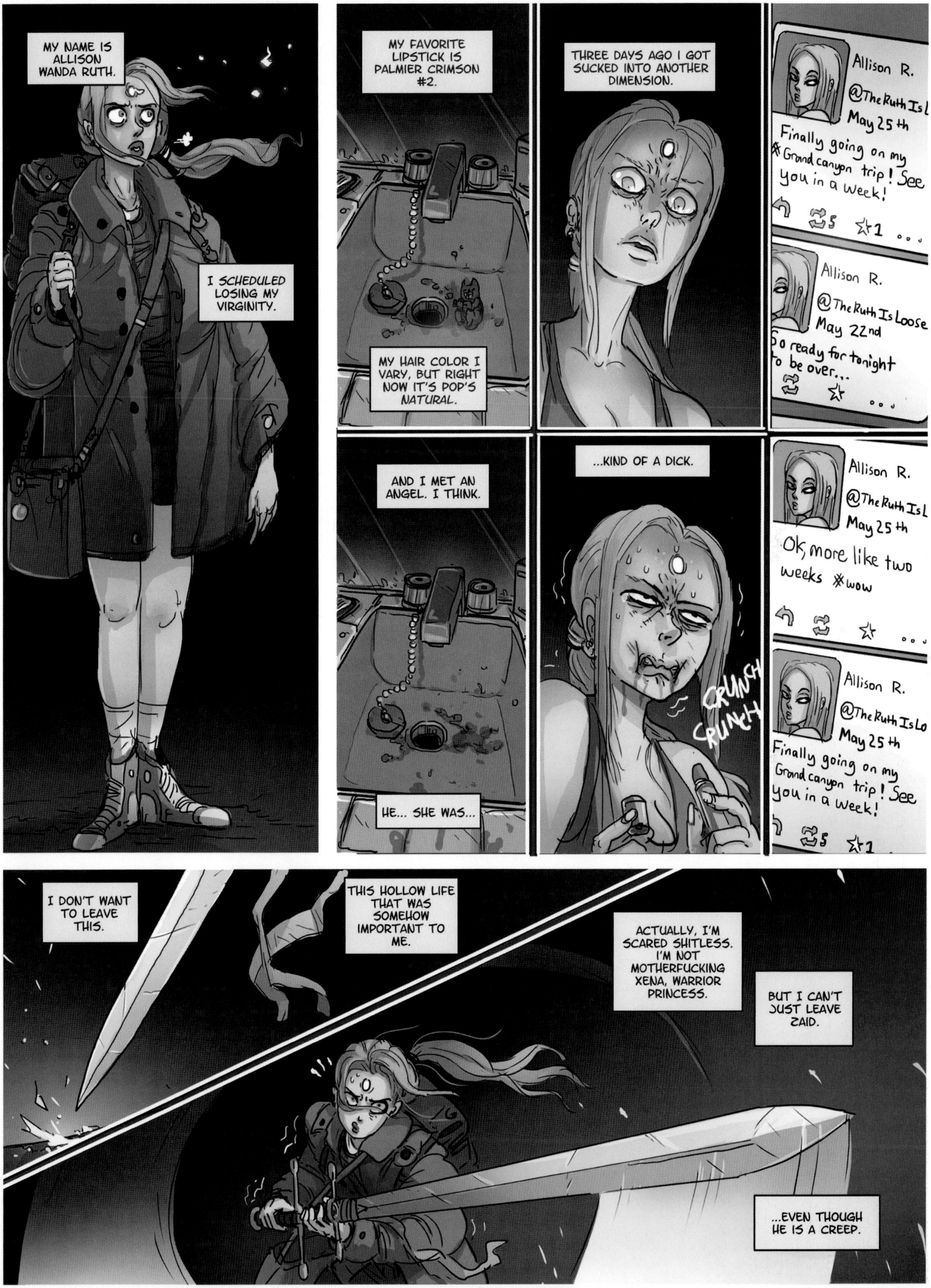
MY NAME IS ALLISON WANDA RUTH.
I SCHEDULED LOSING MY VIRGINITY.
MY FAVORITE LIPSTICK IS PALMIER CRIMSON #2.
MY HAIR COLOR I VARY, BUT RIGHT NOW IT'S POP'S NATURAL.
THREE DAYS AGO I GOT SUCKED INTO ANOTHER DIMENSION.
Allison R.
@TheRuthIsL
May 25th
Finally going on my Grand canyon trip! See you in a week!
5
1
Allison R.
@TheRuthIsLoose
May 22nd
So ready for tonight to be over...
AND I MET AN ANGEL. I THINK.
HE... SHE WAS...
...KIND OF A DICK.
CRUNCH
CRUNCH
Allison R.
@TheRuthIsL
May 25th
Ok, more like two weeks *wow
Allison R.
@TheRuthIsLo
May 25th
Finally going on my Grand canyon trip! See you in a week!
5
1
I DON'T WANT TO LEAVE THIS.
THIS HOLLOW LIFE THAT WAS SOMEHOW IMPORTANT TO ME.
ACTUALLY, I'M SCARED SHITLESS. I'M NOT MOTHERFUCKING XENA, WARRIOR PRINCESS.
BUT I CAN'T JUST LEAVE ZAID.
...EVEN THOUGH HE IS A CREEP.

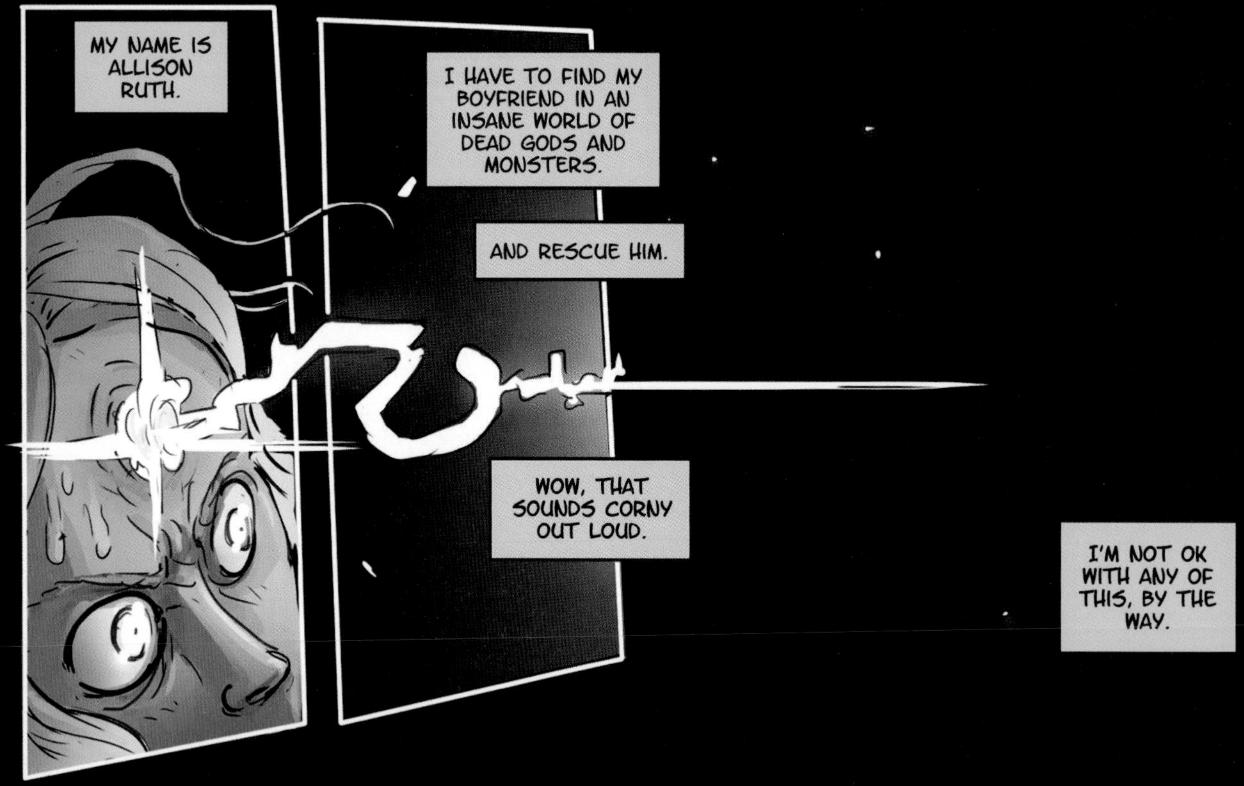
MY NAME IS ALLISON RUTH.
I HAVE TO FIND MY BOYFRIEND IN AN INSANE WORLD OF DEAD GODS AND MONSTERS.
AND RESCUE HIM.
WOW, THAT SOUNDS CORNY OUT LOUD.
I'M NOT OK WITH ANY OF THIS, BY THE WAY.

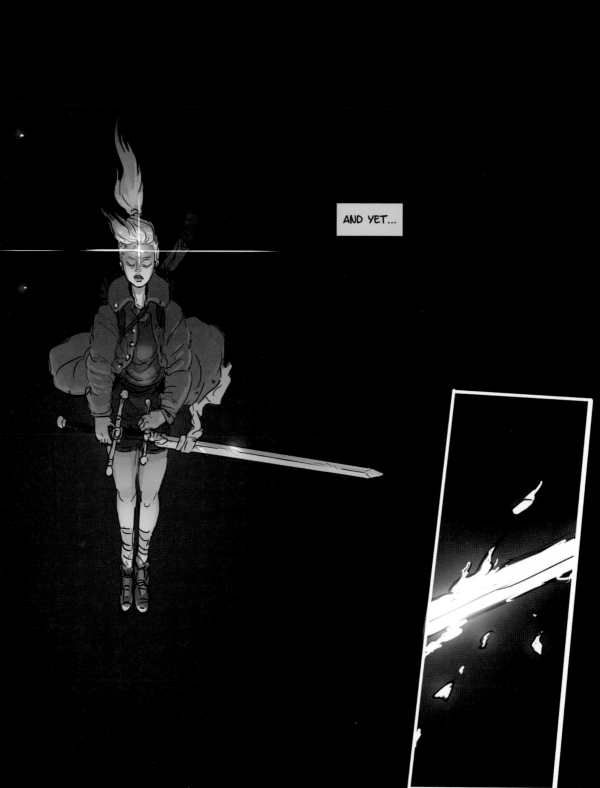

AND YET...

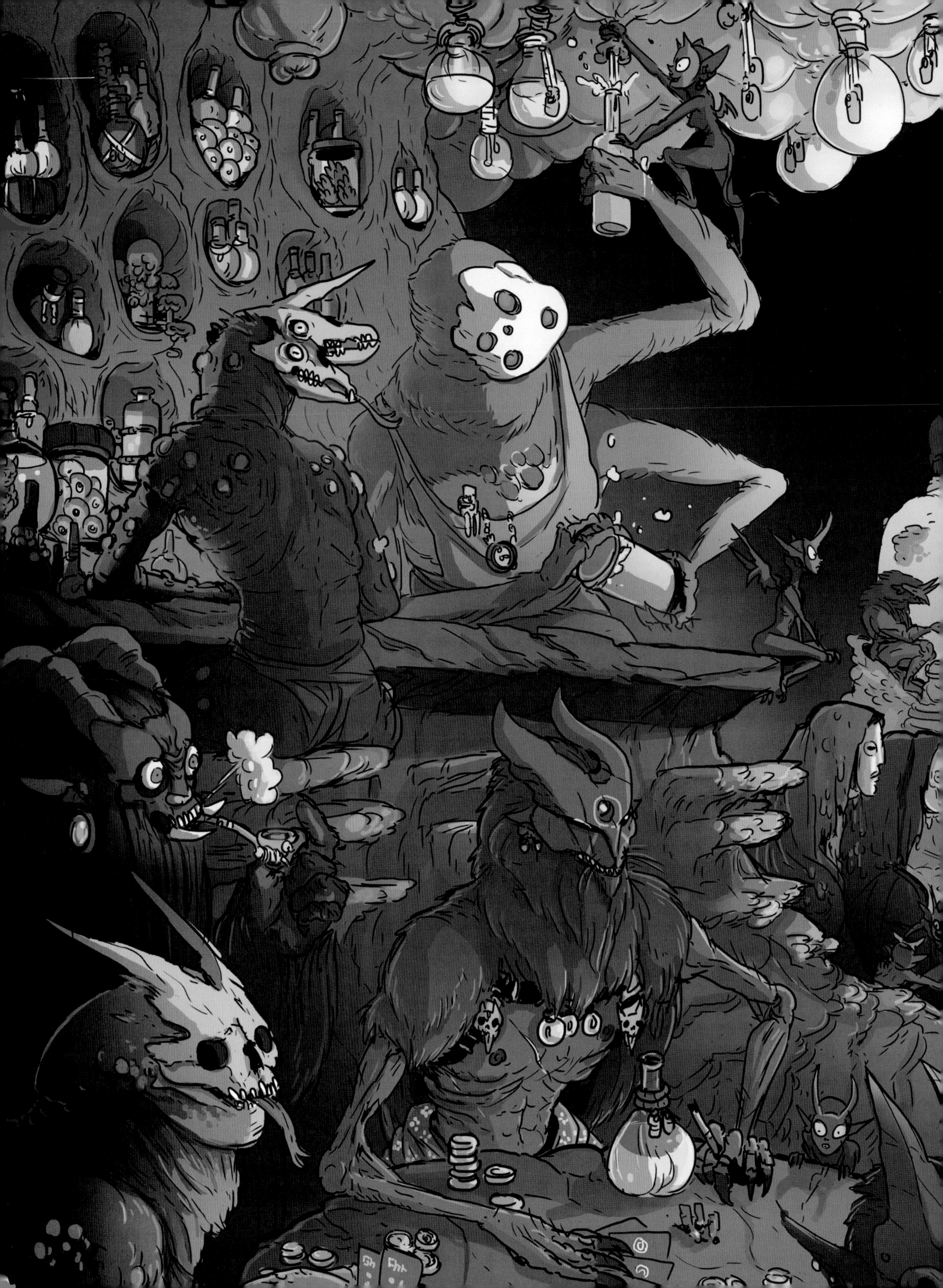

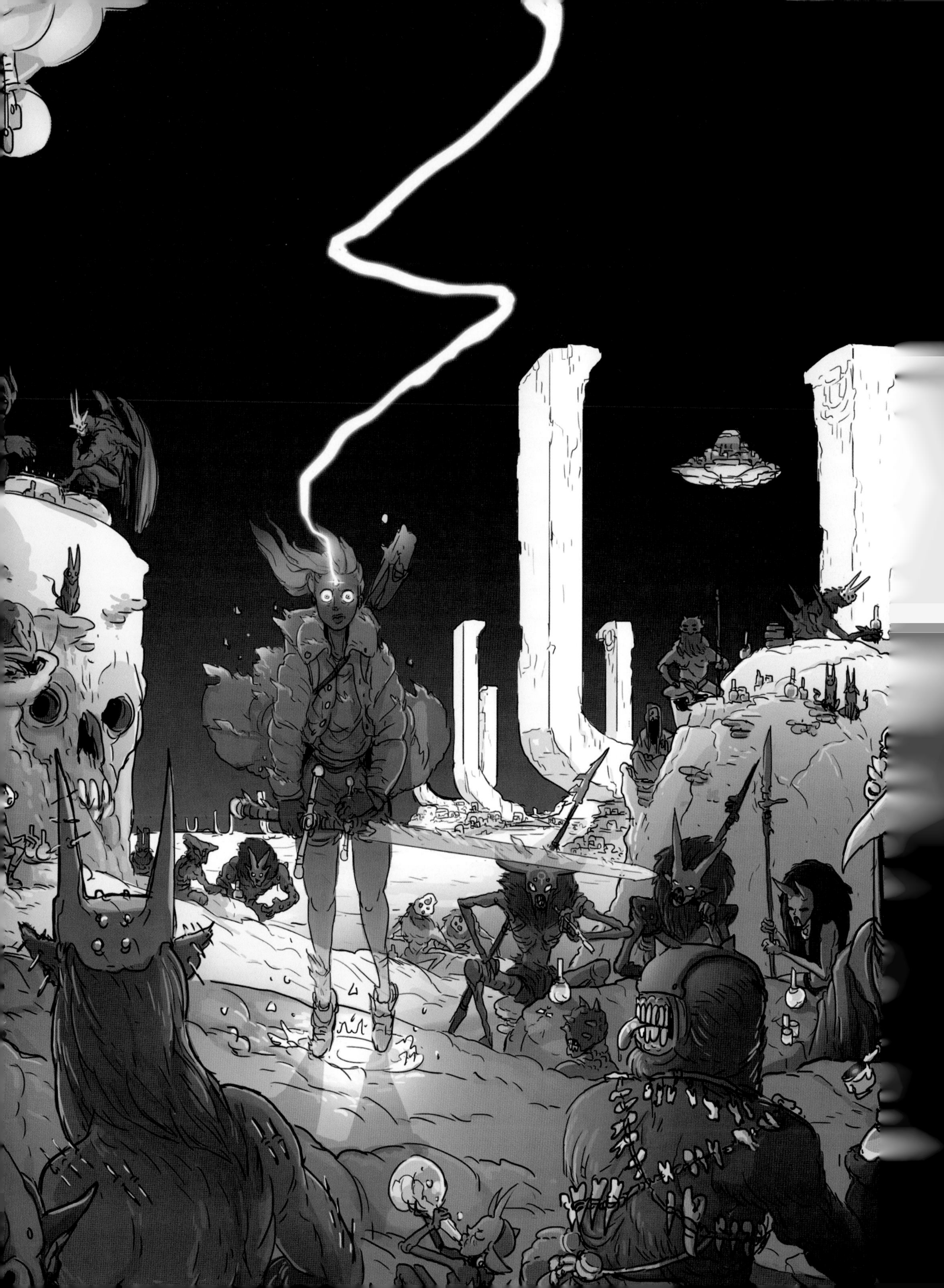

Meti's Sword Manual

The 18 Precepts

10. A man who finds pleasure in the result of cutting is the most hateful, crawling creature there is. A man who finds pleasure in the act of cutting is an artisan.

11. Man always strives to cut man. Therefore he who draws his sword the fastest is the survivor. To pre-empt this, you must live, eat, and shit as a person who has their sword drawn. It doesn't matter whether your blade, in actuality, is always out of its sheathe, though you will look like an idiot if it is.

12. Consider: the undefeated swordsman must be exceptionally poor.

13. The weak swordsman reserves his sword strokes. He clings excessively to his blade. His footwork is unsteady. His grip is too hard and he is afraid to crack the earth with his step. He has a shallow and wandering gaze, his tongue is sluggish and pale. He refuses to exhale the hot breath of the Flame Immortal.

14. The weak swordsman clings to victory. He thinks of his life, his obligations, the outcome of the battle, his hatred for his opponent, his training, his pride in his mastery. By doing so, he is an imperfect vessel for the terrible fires of Will. He will surely crack. He will not laugh uproariously if he is cleft in two by his opponent's blade. When his sword is shattered, his hands will be too reserved to tear his enemies' flesh.

15. The weak swordsman strikes his enemy down and thinks his task done. He relishes in victory. He casts away his sword and returns to his lover. Little does he know his single cut will encircle the world five times and strike him down fifty-fold.

16. The weak swordsman clings to his instrument. It is better you have a sword, but death must lie under your fingernails, if need be. Learn death with your hands and feet, death with your elbows and knees, and death with your thumbs and fingertips. It is said death with the tongue is useful, but I find words too soft an instrument to smash a man's skull.

17. In manners of terrain, you must learn to cut yourself from it. You must cut even your footprints from it, if need be. Have complete awareness of each crawling thing and each precious flower, each blade of sweet grass and each clod of bitter earth, each beating heart and each being that thrums with love, hope, and admiration. Only then are you qualified to be their annihilator.

18. Excess heat and excess coldness are undesirable. Learn to read the weather.

Closing

1. It is said the greatest warrior-kings may sublime violence and forget all they learn about the sword. This is true. But the only true path to kingship lies through regicide.

2. Moreover, only the worst kind of idiot strives to be king.

3. My extreme hope is that some measure of wisdom will penetrate the thick skull of my apprentice. If not, may reading this manual demonstrate your powerful disinterest in it, and may its true value die with me.

4. Reach heaven by violence.